I0717315

The Lies People Publish

PAUL MICHAEL GARRISON

Owl Hollow Press

Owl Hollow Press, LLC, Springville, UT 84663

The Lies People Publish

ISBN 978-1-958109-43-4 (paperback)
ISBN 978-1-958109-44-1 (e-book)

Library of Congress Cataloging-in-Publication Data

The Lies People Publish/ P.M. Garrison. — First edition.

Summary:
For Detective Kate Baxter, a family crisis, a kidnapping, literary fraud, and accidental catfishing are just another day in Fulton Springs.

For Jill and John.
Knock anytime.

Chapter One

No one welcomes a knock at the door in the middle of the night. At best it's an annoyance, a disruption to one's rest; at its worst, it's a prelude to tragedy, a fear realized, a predator to peace.

When a persistent knocking at her front door woke Kate Baxter, she rousted herself from bed with equal parts trepidation and resentment. She knew the moment her bare feet hit the frigid hardwood floor she would be yanked into full consciousness and falling back to sleep would be difficult. She wrapped herself quickly in a thick robe and grabbed her gun from its holster, which hung on an old slatted-back chair against the wall. Perhaps her imagination was tainted by her career as a detective for the Fulton Springs Police Department or by living in a less-than-upstanding neighborhood (nicknamed Crack Alley by her friends). Regardless, she was not about to answer the intrusion unprepared. True, run-of-the-mill criminals seldom knock at the door, but the psychopaths sometimes do.

The security light in the yard didn't illuminate the figure standing on the other side of the door, so Kate flipped on the porch light. She brushed back her dark blonde hair and placed an eye against the peephole, where she spied a barrel-chested man with a dark crew cut. The dark T-shirt he wore showed thick, muscular arms but could have done little to shield him from the November cold that had swept away the Indian summer previously gracing the Midwest. She fought a shiver herself despite her flannel pajamas and robe. What surprised Kate, though, was his face, a face she had known all her life, though its expression of distress was less familiar.

She turned the locks and drew back the door.

"My word, Robbie, what are you doing here?"

Lacking his usual stalwart nature, her brother chewed his bottom lip for a moment until his eyes brimmed.

"She's leaving me, Katie. Lauren wants a divorce." He enveloped her in a crushing hug.

Speechless, Kate wrapped her arms around her brother as the cold eased its bitter way into the house. She wished it had been a maniac at the door. That she could have handled.

A GENTLE KNOCK at his bedroom door, startling in the stillness, made Colin Wigley freeze. As deftly as he could, he clicked off the flashlight he was using to illuminate *Blood Portrait*, the most recent installment of the *Immortal Arts* series, and slipped his head out from under the covers onto his pillow. His mother would have an absolute cow if she caught him. Reading after lights-out would garner only a scolding if it weren't for the graphic novel. A couple of months ago, Mom had forbidden comic books on the grounds of violence, profanity, and an inordinate amount of cleavage. Dad, in his nostalgia, had backed him until Mom had shown him an issue of *Saga*. Yeah, that had clinched the ban. The vampire book hidden under his covers would surely send her over the edge.

Colin maneuvered the contraband under his slight frame, careful not to bend the pages since it belonged to his friend Brendan. He closed his eyes just as the door swung open, letting a hazy swathe of illumination from the hall night light fall across his bed.

"Colin? You awake?" his older brother's voice whispered.

Colin's eyes popped back open. "Yeah. What's up?"

Dylan closed the door behind him and crept to the wooden chair next to the bedstand, which was mostly covered by Colin's bookbag and laundry. Colin flicked the flashlight back on, careful to shine it away from the door and dampen it with his covers. It provided a campfire ambiance. He looked at his brother expectantly, but the older boy said nothing. He just perched on the edge of the chair in his boxer shorts and long-sleeved T-shirt, his arms wrapped around his bare spindly legs, his chin hovering above his knees.

"Do you want a blanket?" Colin asked, but Dylan shook his head. "What's up?"

Dylan inhaled as if he were going to say something but didn't. There seemed to be a lot going on with Dylan these days, a lot Colin didn't really understand, even though they were only a couple of years apart. But Dylan had started changing since his entrance to high school, actually the summer before. That was when he insisted on switching to boxers. Then came mood swings and talking on the phone . . . a lot . . . of both. He'd been practically spasming for a cell phone until their parents gave him one for his birthday. But then Dad had taken it away when Dylan ran the phone bill up into what Dad called "an obscene amount" one month. There'd been a lot of shouting about unlimited plans at the time. There seemed to be more shouting in general. And most curiously, Dylan had started spending huge amounts of time in the bathroom. He took longer than their mother to get ready to go anywhere.

"You know Sissy McElrath?" Dylan finally said.

To Colin, this was a pretty dumb question since Dylan had spent most of the summer with her. "Yeah."

Dylan picked a scab on his knee. "You know how we hung out all summer and everything?"

"Duh, yeah." Sissy McElrath had a pool. Colin remembered all too clearly the times Dylan had been invited over without him, turning alternately golden brown and red in the aqueous lap of middle-class luxury. He and Brendan had felt kind of ditched since Dylan usually hung out with them in summer, but Colin had felt better when Brendan's family had taken him, but not Dylan, to Florida on their summer vacation.

"We were going out, sort of."

Colin stowed the graphic novel beneath his pillow and sat up. This was getting kind of good. "Kinda figured. Did you kiss her?"

Even in the dim lighting Colin could see some color rise in Dylan's narrow face. "We'd make out sometimes."

"Like how much?" Colin's voice came out loud, and Dylan's fist shot out like lightning, making contact with his shoulder.

"Shut up! You wanna wake Mom and Dad?"

"Sorry. Ow."

"Anyway, it's over."

"Why, d'you guys have a fight?"

"Not really." Dylan shrugged pathetically. "Once school started, it was just . . . different, weird. Like sometimes, we'd hang out and it would be the same, and other times she acted like she didn't want me around."

Colin figured that this pendulous relationship accounted for at least some of the mood swings that had ravaged the Wigley household the last few months.

"Then she started saying how we should do stuff with other people, and I knew it was because this other guy asked her out." Colin almost asked who the other guy was, but Dylan's voice grew oddly thick and bubbly. Colin feared he might actually cry. Dylan hardly ever cried, even when he hurt himself. Colin thought of when the bus driver had run over their dog the previous year.

"Are you okay?"

"Yeah." Dylan wiped his nose with the back of his hand and cleared his throat. "She told me on Monday that she's only interested in doing things with *older* guys now."

Colin nodded. It was all coming together. Dylan had spent the last few days holed up in his room in antisocial-silent mode.

"That's stupid," Colin said by way of consolation. His remark had little effect, so he elaborated. "You don't want to hang out with someone stupid like that."

"Yeah," Dylan agreed, but he sounded unconvinced.

A KNOCK AT the door broke through the bombastic piano music emanating—albeit at a low decibel so as not to disturb the neighbors—from the speakers on Darshan Spence's laptop. He stopped tinkering with an article that he knew full well was finished, his handsome features twisted in annoyance. He suspected the knock came from his brother, no doubt too drunk to manage his own keys if they hadn't been confiscated by someone more responsible, if such a person were to be found at a dive bar at this hour on a Wednesday night—or rather, Thursday morning.

"Not everyone has your schedule, Darsh," he muttered in his brother's voice.

When Sanjay had simultaneously lost his job and his place to live, misgivings aside, Spence had let him move in. What else could he do? Sanjay certainly couldn't move back in with their parents; they were barely on speaking terms, which as far as Spence was concerned, was mostly Sanjay's doing regardless of how he shifted the blame. Their sisters both had families of their own. And Spence had thought he might be able to positively influence his younger brother. All that they'd accomplished, however, was pushing a strained relationship dangerously close to an embittered one: Sanjay resented being beholden to Spence, and Spence resented his brother's determination to veer headlong into dissipation.

Spence padded to the door in stocking feet. He should have been in bed hours ago, but he'd felt driven to finish this particular article. Besides, he found it difficult to sleep when he knew Sanjay was out partying. Every time he received a call to claim his little brother, Spence told himself it would be the last, but the next time around he still found himself waiting for that call. The peephole revealed an empty stoop. Spence frowned. He opened the door leaving the security chain on. The narrow view did nothing but invite the cold air in.

He closed the door, his frown deepening. It was too late on a weeknight for the neighborhood kids to be pulling pranks. Perhaps he'd misheard and the knocking had been next door. That happened occasionally, although the older couple who owned the other unit of the duplex rarely entertained past eleven, even on the weekends.

Back at his desk, he saved a copy of the article, the culmination of two months' labor off-and-on, to a USB drive on a key ring that hung from a hook. The drive, shaped like a surfboard, advertised Sammy's Surf Shop. It was a giveaway his parents had picked up on vacation last year, and since they saved everything to their desktop, they'd given it to him. It didn't have much memory and was incredibly tacky, but Spence liked that it looked like a keychain fob rather than a flash drive. It felt top secret, hidden in plain sight, and so he used it for sensitive files.

He was closing the drive's case when a second knock sounded against the door. This time, he picked up the baseball bat he left propped in the adjacent corner before he checked outside. Still no one. He looked up and down the street only to find it deserted as befitted the hour.

As he turned to go back inside, he spotted a tall brown paper bag on the hood of his car, parked on the street. Spence smiled. His friend Heidi had pulled a similar trick at the beginning of the week, texting him to look out at his car, where he had found a plate of cookies. Perhaps he had missed the text this time. He decided his heavyweight lounge pants and the fleece pullover he wore would service the short trip. He crossed the stoop, descended the few steps that led to the sidewalk, and jogged to his car to investigate.

When Spence peeked inside the bag, he drew his head back in puzzlement. It contained a bottle of wine, and Heidi, an outspoken detractor of alcohol herself, knew that he didn't drink. Anyone who knew him at all knew that. He was one of three teetotalers on the staff at the *Fulton Springs Tribune*, so it came up at pretty much every work party. Every single one.

He tucked the bat under his arm and examined the bottle as he made his way back up the twenty feet of sidewalk and steps to his door. It was still sealed and didn't look like it had been tampered with. He didn't know anything about wine, but he figured it had to be on the cheap side. He did occasionally use some in his fancier cooking endeavors, but he couldn't recall the last time. Keeping it around the house would encourage Sanjay to brand him a hypocrite, if Sanjay didn't swill it down before Spence could use it anyway. Maybe it wasn't meant for him at all. Maybe one of Sanjay's friends had left it, though Spence couldn't recall any similar generosities. In fact, he hadn't seen much of Sanjay's friends lately, apart from the teenagers he gamed with. And Sanjay was more of a beer man.

The doorknob did not turn.

"You've got to be kidding me!" It was too late and he was too tired. It figured that he'd do something stupid like lock himself out. He walked around to the back, wishing he'd put on shoes, the cold damp of the grass soaking into his socks. He reached under the fifth plank of the fence that surrounded the tiny patio and strip of grass crammed behind his house. His fingers felt along the rough wood until they found the key inserted up into the board. He tugged it free from the slot that his father, a firm believer in unconventional hide-a-keys, had cut into the board.

He hurried back to the front door, his hands and arms full with the bat, bottle, and key. Though the bottle nearly slipped from underneath his arm, he managed to juggle everything and get the door open. The sudden warmth steamed up his glasses, casting his view of the brightly lit room into a haze. He kicked back with his foot, shutting the door, and slipped the key into his pants pocket. He whipped off his glasses to wipe them clear but stopped dead. Even with his naturally poor vision, he could see the great rectangular space on the desk where his laptop was missing.

He didn't move, listening. And he heard it, an exhalation from the corner behind him. He grabbed the wine bottle by the neck and swung backhand as he spun around. He couldn't tell whether he connected with his assailant before something struck his head hard. He continued to spin as he fell, crashing against the edge of the coffee table. The wine bottle, caught between his chest and the table edge, broke and splashed its dark liquid to the floor before him. He pushed himself up only to be struck again. The wine soaked into his clothing as consciousness faded.

Chapter Two

"What am I supposed to do, Heidi?" Kate whispered into the phone.

"Oh, hon, I don't know," her friend answered. "How's he doing now?"

Kate peeked through the kitchen doorway at her brother cocooned in a blanket, asleep on the couch, then retreated to the counter where her mug of coffee steamed.

"He finally fell asleep around five. He's still out. He must be exhausted. I'm exhausted."

"He just picked up and drove all the way from Indiana after she told him?"

"Pretty much. It's totally unlike him, but then he's also pretty shaken up. It's scary, Heidi. I've never seen him like this. He cried and cried. I cried. It was awful."

"I can imagine. I know how you hate to cry."

"Yeah." Kate took a sip of coffee and found it too bitter. A trip to the store was in order. She needed sweetener, among other things. Did they sell marriage repair kits at the supermarket? "I don't think Mom and Dad know yet. Do I tell them?" She answered her own question. "No, that's not a good idea. This is what I mean: I don't know what to do. Do I get in the middle of this?"

"Correct me if I'm wrong," Heidi said, "but I thought you and Lauren didn't get along."

"We don't braid each other's hair, I can tell you that."

"Then I'm not sure she's going to respond well to you intervening, especially since she's the one who wants to flush the marriage."

"How can she be so selfish!" Kate's volume got away from her for a moment. She clenched a fist to rein in her anger. "I've never been her biggest fan, but I wouldn't have guessed in a million years she'd do this."

Heidi was silent for a moment. "The ugly fact is the divorce rate among Christians is pretty much the same as among everyone else."

Kate knew one of Heidi's older sisters was divorced so she chose her next words with care. "But we're supposed to be different."

"Yes, we are, especially in this respect. Is there someone else?"

"No—I don't know."

"There usually is."

"He never should have married her."

"That's hardly worth discussing," Heidi said. "Once you're married, it's about moving forward, not looking back. Not that I know from experience, mind you."

Kate allowed herself a small snort of mirth.

"You're right. If I'm going to be any help, I can't let my own emotions cloud my thinking."

"I'm sorry, Kate, but I've got to go. My Bible study kids are starting to trickle into the classroom."

"I'd better go too. I need to run to the store and the range, and I want to get back before Robbie wakes up."

"Maybe the range could wait."

"I really need to shoot something, and it'd be better for everyone if it wasn't something with a heartbeat."

Kate left a note on the kitchen table in case Robbie woke before she returned. At the range, she vented frustration by plugging some imaginary perps and, if truth be told, some not-so-imaginary sisters-in-law. It was easier to be angry than hurt. She'd spent the majority of the early morning listening to her big, strong cop brother blubber like a baby, which in turn had made her blubber like a baby. She hated that. *Bang. Bang.* Two more rounds center in Mr. Silhouette's chest.

Weren't there enough damaged people in the world? Did the world really need to claim Robbie too? Obviously, their marriage was damaged already, or they wouldn't be in this situation, but divorce would just add to the toll. And their girls? No doubt her nieces were a rarity in their public school, coming from a traditional, unbroken, unblended family. Not for long if Lauren had her way. Lauren would take custody, using Robbie's job against him, and he'd end up being a weekend dad. That would kill him. Whatever deficiencies Lauren might fault him for as a husband, she wouldn't dare call Robbie a bad father. Kate knew better.

She squeezed off another shot but felt the gun dip. It suddenly weighed heavy in her hands. She set it down as a tightness spread through her chest. She yanked off her eyewear and wiped her eyes before they overflowed. She had to pull it together so that she could go upstairs and try to excuse herself from work today. She wondered if Robbie had let his station know that he'd left town. A call from the road saying, "Excuse me, Captain, but I won't be in today because my life is falling apart"?

Kate left the range without checking her target. She didn't even remember to take it down.

COLIN SLID INTO Brendan's seat on the school bus. "I need your help," he quietly told his friend.

"With what?"

Colin frowned and nodded toward Dylan, who had taken an empty seat across the aisle behind them. He slouched against the window, letting his breath fog it up.

"What's up with him?"

"He's depressed."

"Depressed?

"You know Sissy McElrath?"

"Yeah, she's hot!" Brendan's freckled face split into an insipid grin revealing a mouthful of red rubberbanded braces.

"Shut up!" Colin elbowed him in the ribs, to little effect since Brendan's backpack was in the way. "She's the reason he's depressed."

"I thought they loved each other or whatever."

"They did kinda, but she dumped him."

Brendan thought on that. "That's rough, but—this may shock you—I don't really know a ton about girls or how to get them. And I'm pretty sure you don't either, so I don't see how we could help him get her back."

Colin shook the brown hair out of his eyes to give his friend a dirty look. "Don't be an idiot. I don't want to get them back together. She's a total cow."

Brendan shrugged and muttered, "She's a *hot* cow."

"She's a dumb cow for dumping Dylan," Colin corrected. "We just need to think of some way to cheer him up."

"Did you try telling him she's a dumb cow?"

"Didn't really work."

"Probably wouldn't work on me either."

The boys looked at each other. Brendan had a point; they were out of their depth.

"I'll think about it," Brendan promised. "Come over after school today, and we'll come up with something."

Colin nodded. You could always handle trouble more easily with someone at your side.

THE SENSATION of sharp and persistent cold dragged Spence back into consciousness, only to be superseded by a throbbing pain. He felt as though someone had taken a jackhammer to the back of his head and left it vibrating. He groaned, but the sound came out a hum. He couldn't move his mouth. He opened his eyes, but the blackness didn't change. A tension held his shoulders back, stretching his chest. He tried to move his arms and legs and succeeded only in sending darts of pain through his limbs, stiff from lying on cold concrete. His hands were bound behind his back and his ankles had been secured as well.

Spence lifted his head to relieve his face from the floor's iciness but decided that he preferred the cold to the explosions of pain that resulted from moving. Perhaps he could use the arctic surface to his advantage. He rolled onto his back and, as gently as he could, laid his head against the concrete. First contact was excruciating, but the cold quickly spread anesthetizing tendrils into his skull, lessening the throb. His back tensed involuntarily trying to relieve the pressure of lying on his hands, and the pressure on his elbows began to radiate through his arms in quick fashion. He wasn't sure how long he could maintain the contorted position, but it was helping with the most severe pain, the one threatening to split his skull. Now he could think beyond it. Despite the discomfort it caused, he pushed against the bonds. They didn't give or shift, and their width and lack of bulk made him conclude they were duct tape wrapped thick. Doubtless the same reason he couldn't open his mouth.

Where was he? He still couldn't see anything. He blinked repeatedly, trying to dispel the grittiness in his eyes. He'd been waiting for them to adjust, but nothing changed. He could be in a basement or garage or warehouse. He inhaled the sharp air. He couldn't smell anything beyond the pungent odor of the wine that drenched the front of his clothes, adding to his discomfort. Now that it was in his nostrils, the thick odor was inescapable and nauseous.

Who had brought the wine? Who had brought him here? Why? Panic surged through him. Was someone going to kill him? Being bound and gagged in the dark wasn't a good sign. He tried to calm himself. His breathing came in abrupt puffs, and he focused on slowing it down, smoothing it out. If ever he needed to stay calm and collected, it was now.

When the feeling in his hands began to fade, he rolled back onto his side, steeled himself, and sat up. His muscles screamed, his head reeled, and he feared he would vomit, which would be disastrous with his mouth taped shut. He began to topple but didn't fall far before he hit the springiness of chain link. He fought down the gorge rising in his throat. His head felt full of bees, buzzing and pinging off the inside of his skull; when they quieted, he scooted gingerly in one direction until his feet hit chain link. Then he moved the opposite direction until he could feel the metal strands between his almost-numb fingers. Scooting sideways proved more difficult, but it wasn't long before he hit chain link again. He was in a cage or pen and not a large one. He measured a little over six foot, and there was no way he could lie down the width of the enclosure. He thought about testing the length of it, but his movements had already worn him out.

He leaned back against the corner of the cage and rested. Though the bees had vacated, his head still resonated from the jackhammer, and his stomach still churned, barely persuaded not to revolt. His muscles jerked in uncontrollable shivers. He tried to push aside the physical distress, to focus his mind on why he was here, who could have done this to him. He was not a man of many enemies. This type of thing didn't happen to people like him. People like him lived boring lives.

Then Spence thought of Sanjay. What if his brother had crossed yet another line, had gotten mixed up in something sinister? Anyone who knew Spence knew that he didn't drink. Sanjay drank like a fish. Maybe the wine had been meant for him. If someone had been told, "Go to this house and take out the Indian guy," that could explain it. Even if they'd said "the big Indian guy," for Spence wasn't a string bean. Or they could be using him to get at Sanjay. Maybe Sanjay's money troubles were worse than Spence knew. Maybe he owed money to bad people.

Shivering in the pitch black, Spence figured the most logical conclusion was that his brother's trouble had finally enveloped him.

Chapter Three

As Kate walked down the grocery aisles, she plucked things she knew Robbie liked, or at least remembered him liking, from the shelves. As if comfort food would suffice. The bright fluorescent lighting, piped-in music, and hum of the freezer units created a hypnotic effect. Dazed, she felt not quite there, as though someone else were pushing the clattery cart past the frozen fish. She had taken the day off; maybe she could make a lasagna. Robbie loved their mom's lasagna, the same recipe Kate used. She instinctively started scouring the store for the ingredients. Somewhere between the ricotta cheese and the noodles, the idea struck her as ludicrous; but she really didn't know what else to do, so she gathered up the rest of the ingredients anyway. She needed to get back home, but she was looking for an excuse to be anywhere else.

She slipped quietly into the house in case Robbie was still sleeping, but once inside she heard the shower running. She started some coffee and put the groceries away. Robbie walked barefoot into the kitchen, dressed in a fresh pair of jeans and a flannel shirt.

"I had a change of clothes in the car," he explained. He didn't look much better for the sleep and shower.

"Is that all you've got with you?"

He nodded. Kate offered to make breakfast, but he declined. She did persuade him to take a mug of coffee, though. They sat together at the table.

"I've got a spare toothbrush, and I'm sure I've got some sweatshirts that would fit you. There's a Target just—"

"I must seem like a drama queen, showing up here in the middle of the night."

Kate reached out and gripped her brother's forearm. "No, you don't."

Robbie drew a shaky breath. "I just . . . didn't know what else to do. I couldn't be alone. I needed somebody. And I thought about you, and the next thing I knew I was on the interstate passing the Illinois border."

"It's fine, Robbie. Really, it is." She gave his arm a squeeze of assurance. "So you didn't tell Mom and Dad?"

Robbie let out an incredulous sound. "Can you imagine what Mom would say? Will say. She'll lose it. The first divorce in our family, and she didn't really care for Lauren in the first place."

With good reason, the words sprang to Kate's lips, but she swallowed them back down. "I just wanted to make sure I didn't say anything out of turn."

He ran a hand through his damp hair flicking a few droplets onto the table. "Thanks. I'll have to tell them soon enough."

"What's this really about, Robbie? Is she seeing somebody?"

"No! At least I don't think so. I mean—no, I can't believe she'd do that, not while we're still married." He fiddled with his mug. "She just doesn't love me anymore; that's what she said."

"Love is a decision."

"Well then, she's *decided* not to love me anymore."

Kate decided to say nothing more, but the look she gave Robbie over her coffee cup communicated that she expected more of a response. He sighed.

"We've been . . . distant lately. A while back she got on this kick about me quitting the force. We fought about that a lot, but I told her it was out of the question and she dropped it."

"I'm sure it's difficult on her, worrying while you're on patrol."

Robbie studied his knuckles for a while or perhaps it was his wedding ring. "That didn't really come up much."

"Then why did she want you to quit?"

"Bad hours, bad pay." He fidgeted with his lower lip. "She told me it wasn't sexy anymore, just sad." He gave a rueful smile. "She used to think it was sexy when we were first married, being with a big strong cop, the whole protect-and-serve thing. But that was before the girls were born, before the mortgage, back when she actually wanted to have sex."

"Wow, thanks for being frank."

"Sorry."

"No problem, really." The last thing she wanted him to do was shut down. "I'd have been surprised if everything was hunky-dory in the bedroom when everything else wasn't. Are you guys struggling financially?"

"We get by. I guess that's not enough anymore. We're not in debt more than anyone else with house and car payments." Robbie tossed his hands up. "Kate, I really can't say what happened. The whole drive here I tried to find the last straw, and if there was one, I missed it. She wouldn't even talk to me last night. She just said she wanted a divorce, that she didn't love me anymore and I should leave. Then she locked herself in the bedroom."

"Where were the girls during this?" Kate asked with trepidation.

"They were already asleep."

Robbie's cell phone lay on the table between them next to his wallet and keys. Kate pushed it toward him.

"Try again. I hate to admit it, but sometimes there is a large discrepancy between what a woman says and what she means."

Robbie stared at the phone. "I don't think she's playing me for a new washing machine, Kate."

"Probably not, but getting her to talk is the only next step. You don't know where to go without that. Show her that you're not giving up, that you're serious about working things out." Kate put the phone in her brother's hand. "Ask her to see a counselor with you. She owes you and the girls that much."

Robbie nodded, but he set the phone down. "I'm gonna go for a walk first, just clear my head. I need to think through what I'm gonna say."

"You might want to take your piece with you. This isn't Mr. Rogers' neighborhood."

"I noticed. Why don't you move?"

"I'm saving my pennies."

She lent him one of her oversized sweatshirts and said goodbye at the door. "I'm praying for you. You know if Mom and Dad knew, they would be too."

Robbie considered that. "Do you want to call them?"

"I can do that."

"Thanks."

Kate kept the call to her parents short, briefing them with what few details she had and asking them to pray for Robbie and Lauren. And after refilling her coffee mug, she sat down to do the same. She reminded Christ how marriage was supposed to reflect the union between himself and the church, and she asked him to preserve that picture in Robbie and Lauren. She prayed for wisdom in what she should say to Robbie and how best to help him. She hadn't prayed this earnestly in a while, and a sense of holy communion centered her. When she opened her eyes, the heartache for Robbie lingered, but she felt solid ground beneath her.

Then the phone rang. It was Parkman from the police station, asking where she was.

"I told Sergeant Polanksi I was taking a personal day. Some family stuff came up."

"Well, there's some guy in general holding who keeps asking for you. And he's making a real racket."

"What's his name?"

His answer knocked her for a loop. "Spence. Do you know him?"

"Are you sure his name is Spence?"

"Pretty sure. Indian dude—is that him?"

The thought of Spence behind bars baffled Kate, but she assured Parkman she would be down at the station as soon as possible.

ONE OF THE things that stunk about middle school was no recess. No chance to skateboard with your friends or shoot hoops. Unless you counted the short span of time after lunch before the next period began, but unless you gobbled your food down and could convince your buddies to do the same, that wasn't enough time to get in a real game of b-ball. So most everyone just stood around the Commons and talked or practiced their jump shot.

The Commons physically bridged the middle and high schools, which resided on the same property mainly because when the middle school had been built, there hadn't been room for it anywhere else. The district had said the two schools would need to share some auxiliary facilities anyway since they didn't have money for a track and pool for the middle school.

Lunchtime was one of the few times in which students from both institutions mingled in the same place, although not much mingling actually took place. The older kids mostly ignored the younger ones. Upward social interaction didn't interest Colin anyway; he just wanted to observe. Sissy McElrath sat on a bench next to a big guy in a letter jacket, and another jock stood next to them saying something so funny that it caused Sissy to throw back her pretty blonde head and laugh. She didn't really seem that different to Colin. She wore more makeup now, and she had boobs. He could tell because despite the chilly air, she wore her jacket like a shawl over her shoulders, revealing her new developments, accentuated by a tight shirt that seemed designed to tuck under them. Whether by nature or tissue manufacturing, she'd definitely gotten curvier.

Colin compared her two companions to Dylan. Yeah, Dylan really didn't stand a chance. He'd grown some the last year but only just up, and both of these guys still had a good foot on him and, even underneath their leather-sleeved jackets, they looked brawny whereas Dylan was just scrawny. They probably had cars too. Colin sighed. Yeah, even if he wanted to, getting Sissy back with Dylan was out of the question. So how could he cheer his brother up? Maybe the key was getting him to forget about Sissy.

The high school bell rang, and the older students reluctantly migrated toward their building. One of the jocks slipped his arm around Sissy's back. Just then Dylan, amid a fresh herd of students, came out of the school. Sissy didn't even look at him as she and her boyfriends passed, but Dylan stopped and watched after them, jostled by the exiting crowd, a little too obvious in his longing. Colin grimaced. Forgetting looked out of the picture too.

SPENCE BREATHED deeply through his nose. He hadn't yet gone nose blind to the strong smell of the wine, but the nausea had begun to fade. He'd been yelling through his gag for . . . who knew how long. His only gauge of time was the changes in his physical discomfort, and he could not attach much reliability to them. The pain in his head had dulled to a low steady throb. Of course, now he was tortured with a cramping bladder and a deep regret for the last two cups of coffee he had consumed to help him complete his article. Also, sitting on the cold concrete for so long made his tailbone feel as if it were being driven up into his spine.

The urge to relieve himself had overridden his fear of his captors and instigated the round of muffled bellowing, but no one came. He'd been sitting very still, focused on keeping control, but now with a modicum of regained strength, he set about freeing himself from his bonds. He had made a few feeble efforts before his bladder began threatening to explode, but now a desire to maintain his last scrap of dignity spurred him on.

With stiff, numbed fingers, he probed the bottom of the chain link for a loose end of wire. His efforts seemed futile, but he tried to distract himself from that fact by once again figuring the time. How long had he been awake? It could have been hours, but it could also have been less than sixty minutes. It felt like hours. How long had he been out? When would someone come to check on him? Would someone come? Perhaps the idea was to let him slowly die of deprivation in this cage.

He couldn't find a sharp edge. The tape wound tightly around his wrists comprised too many layers to flex loose and allow him to pull his wrists out. He could tell from the way the tape rubbed against the chain link that it was ridged and sloppy.

Not the work of a professional, and *that* Spence found reassuring. Taping the wrists in front would have worked better, but that would have allowed him to remove the tape from his mouth and perhaps ankles. So he wasn't up against a professional, but whoever it was wasn't a dummy either.

In feeling around the cage, he found the door. He rattled it. Perhaps if he could get to his feet, there would be an edge on the latch sharp enough that he could saw though the tape. He gripped the cage behind him and pushed with his feet to try to raise himself, but his stocking feet slid across the smooth concrete. He found any movement painful and arduous, but he managed to get himself into a kneeling position. He got his toes underneath him, took a deep breath, and tried to spring up into a standing position. He almost made it but for the stiffness in his ankles and legs. Instead, he pitched over against the fencing, causing it to screech in protest, and then crashed to the floor. The pain made him moan, and his bladder threatened to release. Fighting against it caused more pain.

He was not equipped for this. None of his mass comm courses had covered escaping from kidnappers. He had no military or espionage training. He didn't even watch that many action movies. He was physically strong, but his strength had failed him in the sneak attack at the house and was doing him precious little good as he lay trussed up like a Thanksgiving turkey. That was an unfortunate picture. Everybody, Spence included, knew what happened to a Thanksgiving turkey.

Chapter Four

"He's been making a racket ever since he woke up," Parkman told Kate as she walked past the front desk of the station. "If you're not getting him out, at least get him to shut up so the other guys back there can have some peace."

Kate acknowledged his comment with a backward wave of her hand, too concerned to stop. When she arrived at the holding cell, a wave of relief washed over her as she saw the hulking figure in sports shorts and a hoodie standing near the door. It was Sanjay, not her Spence. Her relief quickly faded as she thought how Sanjay's arrest would only add to Spence's grief over his brother.

"Hey, Sanj, what ya doing?"

"Oh, Katherine, thank God, you're here." Kate chafed at Sanjay's invocation of spirituality, unable to tell whether it was flippancy or a misguided appeal to her beliefs. "You gotta get me out of here."

"What happened?" she asked impassively.

"It's no big. Just a little too much to drink. Things got a little out of hand."

"We see a lot of that."

"Can you just get me out, okay? I'll pay you back if there's money involved, promise." Kate was unmoved by the earnest expression on Sanjay's round face. She didn't have a running total on how much money he hadn't paid back to Spence or his parents, but she knew it was substantial. "Darsh isn't answering his phone, and if I don't make it to the warehouse this morning, I'll lose my job."

Kate knew it would not be the first, or second, job that he would have lost this year, but she gave herself credit again for not saying what ran through her mind. She, however, couldn't resist driving a point home. "Why didn't you call your parents? Or your sisters?"

Sanjay dropped his dark brown eyes, so like Spence's, and jutted out his jaw. "We're still not really talking," he muttered. "And Tabby and Gauri, they have the kids with school and everything."

Kate regarded the man in front of her, apart from those eyes, so unlike her Spence. True, they were about the same height, but her friend maintained a trim physique while his brother looked exactly like the linebacker gone to seed that he was. The lighter skin tone influenced more strongly by their father's Irish roots was mottled from adolescent acne scars, and his black hair hung lankly over his forehead so unlike the way Spence's thick hair waved away from his smooth, oval face. And the differences didn't end with the physical.

She sighed. "Okay, but I'm not doing this for you, I'm doing it for Spence." She motioned for a guard to unlock the door. "You can't keep going on like this—"

"Yeah, yeah, listen, you can preach at me all you want after I get off work."

Kate shook her head. If Sanjay wouldn't listen to his family, why would he listen to his brother's friend? Besides, she had her own family drama with which to contend.

As she walked through the office, her partner, Potter Davis, caught her.

"I thought you were taking an unexpected day off?"

"Yeah, I have some family stuff to deal with." Kate weighed how much to share with him, and the scale came up on the light side. "But I had to come in to spring Twinkle Toes over there from a disorderly conduct."

Potter frowned at Sanjay, who was calling for a ride to take him to work. "He looks a little worse for wear. Friend of yours?"

"Not exactly. He's the Spence black sheep. Every family's got one, right?"

"I don't think mine does." Potter tilted his head. "But I'm an only child."

"Who says it isn't you?"

Potter arched an eyebrow at her. "Enjoy that day off."

As he walked away, Kate thought about returning to her house. Perhaps being an only child had more advantages than she'd previously considered.

The sizzle and smell of melting butter and cheese greeted Kate as she opened the door, and to her surprise, she found Robbie at the stove making sandwiches.

"Everything okay?" he asked over his shoulder.

Kate plopped into a kitchen chair. "So to speak. You finally get hungry?"

Robbie shrugged. "I needed something to occupy myself." He transferred a sandwich to a paper plate and handed it to her. "Your phone kept ringing. You've probably got messages."

"I'll check them in a bit. How'd the talk with Lauren go?"

"It didn't. I tried a couple of times and then remembered she's at work this morning." Lauren held a part-time clerical job a few days a week at a doctor's office.

"When she get off?"

Robbie looked at his watch. "Another hour or so."

"Well," Kate ventured. "I guess you can try again then."

"Yeah." Robbie took a big bite out of his sandwich and shoved in the hanging threads of cheddar with a thick index finger.

"Graceful," said Kate. He made a face at her, and she laughed. And for a second, things almost felt normal.

COLIN LOVED HANGING out at Brendan's house. It always looked nice, and despite that, Mr. and Mrs. Tyrell were way more relaxed than his own parents. Mrs. Tyrell made you feel like you belonged. Their house was open and full of light. It was like it was easier to breathe. Colin had tried to explain it once to

Brendan, but Brendan just looked at him like he'd grown a third eye and said, "Whatever. You should try living here."

That afternoon Mrs. Tyrell had rocked it old school with milk and chocolate chip cookies. The plate, now nearly empty, lay in the middle of Brendan's floor.

"Any ideas?" Brendan asked around a mouthful. He had a smear of chocolate on the edge of his lower lip. Colin wiped milk from his own mouth with the back of his hand and shook his head, causing his shaggy hair to fall into his eyes. Brendan gave a big sigh and rolled off his bed. "Why don't we 'start with the problem' as Mr. Martin always says?" he said imitating their science teacher. He went to his desk and turned on the computer.

"What are you doing?"

Brendan squinted over his shoulder. "Studying the enemy. If Sissy McElrath is the reason Dylan is bummed out, I say she's the key to making him feel better."

"Getting them back together isn't going to work. Trust me, I was watching her after lunch. She was all over these jocks, or they were all over her."

"Who said anything about getting them back together? Do you think she's on Social Circles?"

"Who isn't?" Colin peered over Brendan's shoulder as he brought up Sissy's social media account.

"She's wide open for viewing."

The program immediately displayed a Venn diagram indicating the overlap of Sissy's contacts with Brendan's. She was a prolific poster with a full photo gallery and detailed lists of favorites, from TV shows and bands to fashion styles.

"She puts like everything on here," Colin commented.

"Yeah, and her friends check her page all the time," Brendan said. "Look." While they viewed the page, new circles kept forming in the right margin accompanied by the viewers' names. "Hmm, I think I have a plan."

"What?"

"We trash her page. You know, post bad stuff about her. We could even do some pictures and stuff. All her friends will see it, even those jocks, I bet. She'll be totally embarrassed."

"Why is she or her friends going to care what some middle-school kids say about her?"

"We can put some details in there that make it sound like we really know some dirt on her, like I bet Dylan can tell us some stuff, like say she fooled around with all of us."

Colin thought "fooling around" was overgenerous for what had transpired between Sissy and Dylan and found it unlikely that anyone would believe Sissy would deign to do so with them.

"And we can make it look like some of the posts come from her friends," Brendan continued. "You know like hack into their accounts."

"You know how to do that?" Colin suddenly felt as if he had eaten one too many cookies.

"No, but it can't be too hard. People do it all the time on TV."

"I don't know." Colin didn't really have faith in his friend's hacking skills, but he also suspected that Brendan wouldn't let his own deficiencies stop him. "I don't see how that'll make Dylan feel better."

"Oh, trust me, if we make her feel bad, it'll make him feel better." Brendan shrugged. "It would me."

SPENCE HAD HELD his bladder well past typical endurance, to the point that he could feel the pain of it in his kidneys. If it hadn't devastated his dignity, the rushing warmth that soaked through his sweatpants might have been a small comfort in his frigid cage. As it was, it just felt like a brutal humiliation. And when the short-lived warmth passed, his discomfort only increased as his sopping wet pants turned cold and his thighs and groin began to itch. It seemed especially cruel as his wine-soaked pullover and shirt had finally dried, stiffening like cardboard. He had made no headway in freeing himself from his bonds nor was likely to make any now that he couldn't feel his fingers at all. He could feel pressure when he forced them against the cage or floor, but they retained no real tactile sense.

His mind swung like a pendulum between prayers for deliverance and raging against his brother. In truth, he didn't know what all Sanjay had gotten himself into, but Spence knew he didn't like the looks of the few guys who'd come by the house to pick up his brother after he'd moved in. He hated to make hasty judgments, but if it looked like a duck and quacked like a duck . . . He remembered a conversation they'd had after Spence had overhead Sanjay talking about meeting up with a friend to get high.

"I don't ever want to find drugs in this house, you hear me? You'll be out of here, no discussion."

"Sheesh, Darsh, calm down. We were just talking about pot."

"I don't care; I don't want it in my house."

"Bro, what year are you living in? In case you missed the headline—it ain't illegal anymore."

"I don't want it or anything like it in my house. Got me?"

"Yeah, I got you," Sanjay said, his tone both beleaguered and mocking.

Spence almost stopped himself but couldn't resist. "I know you don't have any concern about maintaining a reputation or testimony for yourself, but you can understand that I do, right?"

Sanjay rolled his eyes. "Wow, you're almost as bad as living with Mom and Dad. It's only pot; no one's going to launch an investigation against you for my smoking a joint now and then."

"You're telling me that you've never taken anything that wasn't legal?"

Sanjay didn't answer.

"That's what I thought."

"You could just mind your own business, you know."

"But what you bring into my house is my business. You don't have to live here. I'm sure Mick would let you back at his place."

They both knew that wasn't true. Sanjay had been sleeping on Mick's couch for almost a year before Mick kicked him out. When he'd caught Sanjay on that same couch with his own girlfriend, Sherry. That fling had cost Sanjay not only a friend but also the roof over his head and his job at a department store managed by Mick's brother-in-law. And losing his job had caused Sherry to lose interest. The ever-downward spiral of Sanjay Spence.

"Whatever. I get it. Your house."

Had it been a mistake, taking Sanjay in? He'd had nowhere else to go. The debacle with Mick and Sherry had alienated most of his other friends, which Spence had hoped might actually help the situation, but it seemed the replacement friends Sanjay made weren't an improvement.

Can a man take fire into his bosom and not be burned? The proverb sprang to Spence's mind. That's what he'd done with Sanjay, because he loved him, because he was his brother. Spence had brought him and all his trouble into his own house. And now he was getting burned.

Spence wondered if the abductor had contacted Sanjay yet. Did Sanjay even know he was missing? Despite his persistent nausea, Spence's stomach made an obstreperous protest at not being fed. He still had no idea of the time, but it was surely late enough that his coworkers at the *Tribune* had realized something was up. He always called in when he was sick. But would they actually think to check on him?

He leaned his head against the chain link, very close to tears. He prayed for strength. There was no reason to give up hope yet. It was early in the game, although he found calling his current situation a game ludicrously macabre.

To Spence's left a doorway opened, letting in a swath of bright light, which made Spence think it must be daytime. The silhouette of a small man clambered down the few steps to the floor. The backlighting hid his face, but Spence could see a flashlight in one hand and a half-empty liquor bottle in the other. The flashlight flicked on. Spence followed its unsteady bob as the man shuffled across the concrete to a wooden crate in front of the cage. The crate scraped against the floor as he pulled it nearer the cage.

As the man settled himself noisily on the crate, he turned the flashlight on Spence, blinding him.

"Good, you're awake." The words came leadenly. "Bet you thought I wouldn't find out till it was too late." Alcohol swished inside the bottle as the man took another gulp. He then moved the light to his own face. "See, I'm smarter than you thought."

In that instant Spence realized how wrong he had been. This wasn't Sanjay's doing; it was his.

Chapter Five

Reluctant to leave Robbie alone once again, Kate dragged him along with her to the vet. One of her voicemail messages had been the vet's receptionist asking if she had forgotten her appointment that morning, which of course with the current emotional upheaval she had. Thankfully, they could work St. Joan in that afternoon.

Besides, Kate thought, looking at her brother in the passenger seat where he held the cat on his lap, it might do him good anyway. Joan was a great comforter in Kate's experience. Joan pushed her head back against Robbie's hand as he kneaded her glossy dark coat behind the ears. He looked at Kate with a suspect expression.

"Who names their cat St. Joan?"

"People who read Twain."

"What's the other one's name? Injun Joe?"

"That's hardly politic. It's Louis."

"You weren't nearly this weird as a kid."

"Yeah, well, I'm working up to weird old cat lady, okay. And remember I didn't say a word when you named one of my nieces Prudence."

"What's wrong with Prudence?"

Kate rolled her eyes at him. "I'm assuming it was around then that the brain damage set in."

"You're a regular comedienne. Prudence is a perfectly good name."

"At least you didn't name the other one Temperance."

Robbie plucked a cigarette lighter out of the center console. "What's with all the lighters? I found three in your kitchen."

"You caught me. I'm a closet arsonist. The accelerant is in the trunk. Now if you don't be quiet, you're gonna be my next victim." Kate wasn't about to divulge her smoking history to her brother. She hadn't had a cigarette in over a month and a half, but a smoke sure sounded tempting at the moment.

As they walked up to the vet's office door, Kate's phone rang. She was less than pleased when she saw the caller. "You gotta be kidding me." She answered. "Hey, Sanjay, what's up?"

"They fired me because I was late for my shift."

The news brought Kate up short. "That's rough." She grimaced at Robbie.

"Look, you have Darsh's spare key, right? Could you bring it over? I'm at the house, but I'm locked out and he's not answering his phone."

"What about the hide-a-key?"

"It's gone. It's not there."

Kate sighed. "I'm at the vet's but I'll send my brother over with it."

Kate took the carrier from Robbie and gave him the address and her keys, singling out Spence's spare house key for him.

"Can't he wait until we're done here?" Robbie asked. "If he got fired, it's not like he has anywhere to go."

"And people ask me where I get my compassion." Kate gave him a push. "You wanted something to occupy yourself, right?"

Robbie rolled his eyes and left. Once she got Joan checked in and committed to the vet's care, Kate stepped outside to take care of her second morning message. The call had been from her friend Danny, confirming plans they'd had to go see a movie that night.

"Hey, buddy, I'm sorry to cancel on you last minute, but Robbie's in town and he's kind of in a bad way. I hope you can find someone else to go, maybe Heidi or Spence, if you can get ahold of him. We'll do something fun soon." As she ended her message, an incoming call from Robbie beeped at her. "Hey, what's up?"

"When was the last time you talked to Spence?"

"It's been a few days. Monday, I think. Why?"

"I sent Sanjay to come pick you up—"

"He's not driving my car, is he?"

"Just get over here as soon as possible."

THE COLD EDGE of the autumn air threatened to sheer a layer of skin from Colin's face as he pedaled vigorously toward the Thompsons', but he didn't mind. He found it bracing after trudging through a rather foggy day at school. He told himself that he wouldn't stay up so late tonight reading. He turned onto a street where the houses were nicer than in his neighborhood. There wasn't anything wrong with his house, but there wasn't anything great about it either. Not like the Thompsons' or the Tyrells'.

When he'd left Brendan, he'd made his friend promise that he wouldn't post anything on his own, that they'd only work on the project together (Dylan was Colin's brother after all), but his unease hadn't lessened. Brendan was his best friend, but Colin didn't have to think too hard to conjure examples of his less-than-stellar decision making. Just last year, he'd hit his neighbor's Lexus with a golf cart because he was driving it while hanging off the front. And there was the thing with that squirrel getting loose in his room. His enthusiasm often outstripped his good sense, so Colin wasn't super confident in Brendan's ability to wait for him.

Colin pulled up in front of the Thompson house. He usually came right after school, but his mom had dropped by at lunchtime to pick up a package and she'd let Beau out then. The Thompsons traveled a lot, and when they didn't take Beau with them, Colin's family took care of him. Until that summer, it had fallen chiefly to Dylan, but he'd been so wrapped up in Sissy McElrath the mantle had passed to Colin. Colin liked earning his own money, money that he didn't have to get from his parents, that he didn't have to account for, that could easily be spent on comic books or junk food.

He unlocked the door and got attacked by Beau, a bouncing yappy marshmallow, who frankly smelled.

"Calm down! Just let me put your leash on. Geez. You shouldn't be this wound up." He enjoyed the money, but he didn't really enjoy Beau all that much.

He walked Beau out and checked the mailbox in case his mom hadn't when she grabbed Mrs. Thompson's package from the porch. Beau pulled him in the opposite direction of the way they usually walked, his white fluff flattening dramatically as he pushed into the wind. Colin didn't resist, but his eyes flicked to the house they crossed in front of. The daylight was vanishing, and it made the house seem eerier to him. There wasn't anything creepy about its exterior, but he knew someone had died there not long ago, been shot, and that made it creepy. The police had even asked him about it. Guess living in a nicer neighborhood didn't always protect you from the crazies.

He'd been telling his friends about it at school, and Jimmy Smith had inserted himself into the conversation, calling him a poser and a liar. Not that Colin cared what Jimmy, who was a major jerkwad, thought. Jimmy was the type to shove you into the lockers, when he was safely flanked by his friends, and then laugh as he walked away. He'd think nothing about posting crap online about someone he didn't like.

Colin frowned. Because Jimmy was a bully. The school had made them all sit through an assembly on bullying last month. It had zero effect on the likes of Jimmy, who sat in a cluster of rude jokes the whole time, but it made Colin think. He thought about Sharice Munsinger, who went to live with her dad after sixth grade, supposedly because he lived near a better school, but everybody knew it was because Jamila Woods and her gang gave Sharice grief every day both online and off.

"C'mon, Beau." Colin gave the leash a tug and led the canine back to the Thompsons' at a quick trot, partially because the cold had seeped into him and partially because he wanted to double-check on Brendan. He kept thinking of Brendan hanging onto the front of that golf cart, and he kept seeing Sharice's face before she left school. There had to be a better plan.

EVEN WITHOUT HIS glasses, Spence could make out that the spectacled face ghoulishly illuminated by the flashlight belonged to Marion Lukas.

"You thought I wouldn't find out till it was too late, but we can see who's smarter, can't we?" Marion's words sloshed a bit as he waved the beam of light across Spence. "I'm out here, and you're in there." The beam of light stopped moving, and Marion leaned in against the cage, sniffing. "Did you piss yourself? That's disgusting!"

Anger, with a little pride, welled up in Spence, and he swiveled and kicked his legs at the other man's face. The swift action caused an explosion of pins and needles through his extremities and worse pain thundered in his head and chest, but it seemed worth it since he connected with Marion's thumb, which had been hooked in the chain link. Spence took consolation in the small victory as Marion howled and cursed. When he finally stopped rocking back and forth, Marion shone the flashlight into Spence's eyes.

"You're going tell me everything! I want to know who's seen the article, where you have copies saved. Every last one." Marion's finger in the beam of light beckoned Spence toward his side of the cage. Spence didn't move. "I can't take the tape off your mouth from over there. Don't you think we should have a conversation?"

Now he wanted to be civil. Spence vacillated a moment before scooting toward Marion. With thin fingers, his abductor reached through the fencing and clumsily peeled the tape inch by inch off Spence's mouth.

"That's better, isn't it?"

Spence tried to moisten his mouth. He licked his lips, only to take in the acrid taste of adhesive residue.

"What are you going to do with me?" he croaked.

Marion didn't answer immediately, and Spence couldn't make out the expression of his face in the gloom. "Depends on how helpful you are."

Spence started to speak again, but the sandpaper in his throat brought him up short. Finally he choked out, "I need some water."

"Here." Marion held his nearly empty bottle against the cage.

Spence shook his head and repeated, "Water."

"Take it or leave it," Marion warned. "I'd think in your condition you could use a drink."

There in the cage, at the age of thirty-one, Darshan Spence took his first drink of alcohol. The week seemed destined to be one of many firsts, none of them welcome as far as Spence could see. As Marion tilted the bottle through the chain link, the lukewarm liquid burned like acid in Spence's raw throat, causing him to gasp, choke, and sputter, sending more of the alcohol down his chin and fleece than into his mouth.

"Don't waste it." Marion pulled the bottle back and finished it off. "This is good stuff."

"You know you're not going to get away with this."

"Let's spare each other the clichés. They actually pay you to write?"

"I have friends in the police department. They'll come looking for me."

"And how are they supposed to know you're missing? So you left a broken wine bottle on the floor? Big deal. People break things all the time. I do. They'll just think you were in a hurry. 'Cuz you took your car too, see?" Marion shone the light behind him, and while Spence couldn't actually make out the details of the vehicle parked there, he could see it was the same burgundy as his.

He knew that Marion was wrong, the broken wine bottle would be a telltale sign something was amiss . . . unless it was mistaken for Sanjay's. But Sanjay would know that it wasn't his, unless he had gotten so drunk the night before that he didn't remember what happened. Spence didn't think Sanjay was much into wine, regardless. Spence forced his whirling thoughts under control. He was in a garage, probably Marion's. His car, Marion had driven his car here.

"Where's your car then?" Spence asked.

"What d'you mean?"

"You drove my car here," Spence explained to his inebriated captor. "So did you leave yours at my place?"

"I'm not stupid," Marion shot back. "It's parked down the street."

"And when they start looking around, don't you think it'll catch their attention? A strange car parked outside somebody's house all day. A car they'll trace back to you." Marion straightened up as Spence's words wormed into his mind. "See, I don't drink alcohol, so they're going to know something's up. They're going to be looking for what else is out of place."

"What? You don't drink alcohol?" Marion seemed to find the idea incomprehensible.

"Not till tonight."

"Are you Muslim?"

Spence closed his eyes and sighed. "No, I'm a Christian."

"And you don't drink?"

It was like being at one of his office parties.

"Nope, so you've already made at least two strategic errors in this endeavor."

Marion's breathing got louder. He set down the bottle and turned the flashlight off. "Be right back," he muttered. Spence watched as he ungracefully yet successfully navigated the steps. He left the door open.

Spence strained to hear what was happening. If they were indeed at Marion's house, he knew he was in a gated community on the trendy outskirts of town. He was near people who might hear him. His hopes of alerting a neighbor were stifled, however, when he heard the rock music from the other side of the wall. The volume incrementally increased until he could feel the surround sound through the floor.

As the alcohol and car flubs showed, Marion was an amateur, but Spence's kidnapper had been right in one thing. Even intoxicated, he wasn't stupid. But neither was Spence. With renewed determination and the added help of light from the doorway, Spence set himself once again to the task of freeing himself.

Chapter Six

"You going to tell me what's going on?" Kate asked as she rushed across town, Sanjay in the passenger seat. He shrugged his massive shoulders. "When we got the door open, there was a mess on the floor. Your brother asked me if I left the house that way, and I said no."

"What kind of a mess?"

"I don't know, like broken glass and stuff. I only saw it for a second, and then he pushed me back outside."

Kate hit a pothole and St. Joan yowled from her crate in the back seat.

"Sorry, sweetie." Kate's mind played over what Robbie could've seen to cause his reaction. Nothing reassuring came to mind.

"Whoa, look at that dude." Sanjay drew Kate's attention to a red Mercedes Benz speeding toward them without its lights.

"What in the world," Kate muttered as she flashed her headlights.

"He was almost off the road a second ago." As Sanjay finished speaking, the other car veered toward them, edging over the line.

"What in the world!" Kate roared as Sanjay cursed, pressing himself against the door. She jerked the wheel to the right as the other vehicle clipped them, popping the side mirror off her car and scraping the side. She braked hard, grabbed her phone, and turned the car around.

"This is Baxter. I've got a red Mercedes, probable 10-55, headed west on Bates just past the intersection of Covington.

The idiot just sideswiped me." She checked her rearview mirror. "And kept on going."

"Are you following?"

"Yes, but I'm in my POV. Can you send some lights to intercept?"

"I'll send the McNabbs. They're nearby."

The red Mercedes slowed to a roll, drifted to the shoulder, and finally stopped.

"The driver saw me following and finally pulled over." Kate followed suit several car-lengths from the other vehicle. She read out the license plate before hanging up. "Call Robbie," she said into the phone and then handed it to Sanjay. "Tell him what happened and we'll be a minute."

She took a small key and reached in front of Sanjay, not that there was much room between his huge knees and the glove box, which she unlocked to retrieve her firearm and badge. She stepped out of the car and took a few steps. A head poked out the window of the red car and then disappeared. The door opened.

"Are you okay?" called the wiry man who stepped out. He gestured at the side of his car. "Look what you did to my Benz."

Kate clenched a fist and pressed it to her mouth, thankful for the approaching lights flashing in the twilight, which would surely keep her from shooting the other driver. When the man turned and saw the approaching cruiser, he jumped back in his car.

"That didn't look suspicious at all," Kate muttered.

The two officers that exited the squad car were both named McNabb but of no relation. The captain had paired them together both for simplicity's sake and as a joke. After they'd stopped by the Mercedes, Proper McNabb, as the more senior officer was known, approached Kate, leaving the driver to Other McNabb's care.

"Detective Baxter, enjoying your day off?"

"Not so much. That guy was weaving all over the road, sideswiped us, and probably would've kept on going if I hadn't turned around and followed him."

While Proper McNabb took photos of the damage to her car, Kate watched as Other McNabb, a breathalyzer in his hand, argued with the driver of the Mercedes.

"Sir, you need to get out of the car."

"Ow! You're hurting my arm."

"Then get out of the car yourself."

"Hey, McNabb, I'm kind of in a hurry," Kate said as she studied the driver who tumbled out of the red car with Other McNabb's help. "There's some type of disturbance at a friend's house. I was on my way there when this happened."

"Yeah, you talking about the call on Delworth?"

"What—yes, he lives on Delworth. What do you mean 'call'?"

"It came through on the radio, just a second ago."

"But I—" Kate tried to process what he was saying. Why would Robbie call the police if she was already on the way? "Never mind. Can you take it from here?"

"Sure thing. It's not like we don't know where to find you."

"Yeah . . ." Even at this distance, Kate felt a familiar vibe as she heard the Mercedes driver argue with Other McNabb. She began walking with Proper McNabb toward them.

"I thought you needed to go."

"I think I know him." In the early dark, she couldn't be sure, but the voice and the build together had jogged something in her memory. As she neared, the small man with a blond goatee and receding hairline came into focus.

"If you don't take the breathalyzer, you're going to get your license suspended whether you're drunk of not," Other McNabb said. "I'm not asking you again, sir."

"I'd listen to him, Mr. Boudreau," said Kate.

Eirik Boudreau squinted at Kate from behind his glasses. "Do I know you? Are you a fan?"

"We've met. At a publishing reception a couple of months ago."

Boudreau frowned and then shrugged. "I meet a lot of people." The looseness of his head as he shrugged indicated inebriation. "And if you know who I am, then you should know

I have important friends and you should just leave me alone. I'm a very busy man."

"Seems like you've been pretty busy; it's not even six o'clock."

"Who is he?" Proper McNabb asked.

"He's a famous writer," Kate said. "Or thinks he is."

"New York Times Best Seller, cupcake," Boudreau said.

"Well, I don't care who your friends are. These guys are my friends, so I'd listen to Officer McNabb here, if I were you. Don't you have a new book coming out?" Kate turned to leave. "You don't want any bad publicity."

"There's no such thing as bad publicity!" Boudreau called after her.

Kate doubted that very much.

COLIN DIDN'T HAVE time to message Brendan until after dinner, but his friend assured him that he hadn't posted anything yet. Brendan then sent him a list of the comments and ideas he'd come up with. It was mostly run-of-the-mill vulgarities and insults, all of it mean and very little of it clever. The queasiness in Colin's stomach remained.

which one first? Brendan asked.

not tonight, Colin answered. Maybe he could distract Brendan until he came up with a better idea. *wanna play fortnite?*

can't. have to read that dumb book for english.

Their book reports on Avi's *Nothing but the Truth* were due tomorrow, so Brendan had a lot of making up to do, in one sense or the other. Colin left the computer to look for his brother. He found Dylan, shirtless and sweaty, doing push-ups in his room. He spied from the hallway as Dylan finished a set and then examined himself in the mirror, flexing his stringy muscles. For a second, Colin almost laughed, but he saw the disappointment, even anger, on Dylan's face reflected in the mirror, a mirror that still had a photo strip of him and Sissy tucked into the corner.

Colin stole closer and knocked on the doorframe.

Dylan spun away from the mirror. "What?" he demanded.

"Do you wanna play a game? Or watch something?"

"I'm busy. Leave me alone."

The door shut.

"You don't have to be a jerk about it," Colin said, but not loud enough for Dylan to hear because he didn't blame him too much.

Colin went back to the computer. He wasted a few minutes checking on other friends' pages on Social Circles before deciding to play a game on his own. He logged into *Southern Gothic* using his older cousin Tommy's account. Tommy didn't play anymore, but he said Dylan and Colin could use his account until the subscription ran out. He did give them a weirdly parental warning to be careful about interacting with other players. Colin, playing a carpetbagger, wandered through a dilapidated town swindling its inhabitants out of cash to earn points until he came across another player named LilSis27.

She was a Southern belle outfitted in a low-cut, tight-bodiced dress with lots of frills. Her blonde ponytail pulled high up on her head swung as she walked toward him. The hair was exactly the style Sissy McElrath had worn at school today. He was wondering if LilSis27 could possibly be Sissy, when she reached into her ample cleavage to pull out a disproportionately large knife and lunged at him. He managed to fight her off and make a run for his boarding house, where he'd be safe. The other character made him think of Sissy all the more now, but he knew there was no way to tell except by reaching out in the chat function. LilSis27 could be anyone.

Anyone. Colin rubbed his chin. He opened LilSis27's online profile and took a screen capture. He didn't have an idea to replace Brendan's smear campaign, but he had the seed of one.

SPENCE LAY PANTING and shivering on the concrete floor. He had edged his way around the cage trying to find a sharp edge in the chain link that he could use to saw through the tape binding his hands, but he had almost no feeling in his hands. At one point, he thought he had found a raw edge and worked the tape against it for the better part of twenty minutes before he realized that he'd fooled himself. Now he needed to rest and think, think of a better way.

Thinking was hard. Every part of him felt drained, and he couldn't stop shivering. His headache had risen again with a vengeance thanks to the music Marion had cranked up before leaving. The album with its heavy drums and wailing electric guitars played on a loop. Spence had heard it all the way through at least three times so far. Which raised the question, why wasn't Marion back yet? It shouldn't have taken him this long to drive across town and back.

Spence wondered if anyone knew he was missing yet. If Sanjay never came home and went out again straight after work . . . even if he hadn't, would he interpret whatever he saw at home as an indication of foul play? He was pretty comfortable with a mess.

It was one of the things they'd argued about since Sanjay moved in. Spence sighed. It was, in the grand scheme of things, in the light of eternity so to speak, such a minor thing, especially when Sanjay presented so many other deeper concerns. And yet that was one of the battlegrounds where Spence had chosen to sally forth. Perhaps because he knew he couldn't change his brother's heart or mind but could maybe sway his habits. Perhaps because it had just worn on him day after day, picking up, cleaning up after another adult as if he were a child.

"What is wrong with you?" Spence had just returned from a business trip to find soured and molding dishes underneath the coffee table.

"Bruh, it's just some dirty dishes."

"No, bruh, it's disgusting and a health hazard." Spence picked up an open pizza box that lay on the couch and shook it rattling the petrified crusts inside. "This stuff will draw bugs and vermin. Are you going to pay for the damage they do or pay for the exterminator to get rid of them? Given you can't even pay rent?"

"What about all your junk piled up over there?" Sanjay jabbed a finger at Spence's desk, which was littered with mail, research files, and books. Truthfully, some of the books were piled up around the desk rather than on it.

"Clutter is different than filth."

"Right."

In the end, they sorted out the living room and kitchen together, working in sullen silence punctuated by reluctant clarifications about how to handle the job. But even then, Sanjay ducked out before they finished the job. He'd taken a bag of trash out to the bin and not returned until after Spence had gone to sleep. Sometimes in those heated moments, Spence would try to recall moments when they'd been at peace. He'd think about cheering Sanjay on from the stands at his football games, the celebratory dinners afterward. The two of them playing video games late into the night on Spence's college breaks. But such memories just came across bittersweet now.

In some respects, Spence felt as if he'd been cleaning up after Sanjay his whole life, or at least trying to. He remembered as a young teen, trying to make Sanjay pick up his toys.

"Darshan, leave your brother alone."

Four-year-old Sanjay stuck out his tongue and ran outside to play.

"But, Mom, he won't pick up his stuff. His toys are everywhere."

"You worry about you, and let me worry about Sanjay."

But as far as young Spence could tell, his mother didn't worry about Sanjay, and even more alarming, his father didn't either. All through his and his sisters' upbringing, his father's strictness counterbalanced his mother's indulgence. It seemed as if by the time Sanjay came along, six years after Tabby, his parents were too tired to parent him. It seemed even clearer to Spence after he'd been away for a few years of college.

"You let him get away with everything!"

His mother clucked at him. "You're just jealous because he gets more privileges earlier."

"It's not just that. The way he talks back to you and Dad, you never would have let Gauri, Tabby, or I get away with that. He doesn't respect you."

"I don't need a parenting lesson from someone who hasn't even brought home a nice girl to meet his own parents. Maybe

we were too strict with you and your sisters; did you ever think about that?"

"Oh, trust me, I have."

"Don't get smart with me, college boy. You'll realize when you have children of your own, that you have to pick your battles."

Spence realized how he must have come off, the young know-it-all, but even a decade later, he wasn't convinced he was wrong. But perhaps his mother hadn't been either. The pick-your-battles advice had served him well in many arenas of life—work, friendships, dealing with his HOA—but maybe with his baby brother, he hadn't picked the right ones.

Chapter Seven

When Kate pulled up outside Spence's duplex, two police cars already took up the street parking directly in front of the house, their lights strobing the yard in red and blue. Robbie stood alone in the yard, his face dark, his arms crossed against his chest. He hurried to the car as Kate bolted out.

"Are you okay?" Robbie placed a strong hand on her shoulder.

"What's going on here?" Kate asked. A man with a salt-and-pepper crew cut, dressed in a dark, unimaginative suit, stepped out of the neighbors' door drawing her attention. "Detective's here already? Why'd you call it in? We were on the way. What did you call in?"

"Slow your roll a bit. I didn't know how long you'd be. I didn't think I should wait. Katie, there's blood—"

"Baxter!" Detective Kotono called from the porch, motioning her up.

Kate pushed past Robbie, her mind centered on that one word, *blood*. The trek up the sidewalk seemed long, and her legs felt leaden so that climbing the steps wore her out completely.

"What's going on?"

The older detective didn't exactly answer. Despite his toned skin and Japanese ancestry, Kotono always reminded Kate of an English bulldog. Perhaps it was his expressionless eyes or the stern, unthawing manner with which he'd treated her ever since her arrival on the Fulton Springs police force.

"Your brother says you know the occupant?"

"Yes, Darshan Spence is a good friend of mine. I've known him for years. He writes for the *Tribune*. What happened here?"

"When was the last time you spoke with him?"

"It's been a few days. Do you think he's missing?"

Kotono pointed toward Sanjay with the ink pen in his hand. "Is that his brother?"

"Yes, that's Sanjay Spence. Sam, I'm not going to ask again."

"There's clear evidence of a physical altercation."

"Robbie said there was blood."

"There is, but we don't know that it's his."

"And you don't know that it isn't. Can I see?"

Kotono motioned to the door with an open palm.

Kate nudged the door open and surveyed the room. A uniformed officer stood across the way preserving the scene. Remnants of a wine bottle lay amid dark pools that shone red-purple. Kate edged around the mess toward a smaller, less-reflective pool that appeared more viscous, less purple, and despite its smaller size much more alarming. A knot lodged in her throat, and she told herself it was a small amount of blood. She knelt down.

"Don't touch anything," Kotono said behind her.

"Not my first rodeo, Sam." Kate bit the words off. She'd never figured out what Kotono's deal was, but his partner, Kirkley, copped a similar attitude. Even the diplomatic Potter called them "too cool for school," but despite the attitude, they closed as many cases as anyone, if not more.

"It's easy to forget when you're personally involved."

He was right. She spied Spence's glasses, lying half-way beneath the coffee table, their lenses whole but the golden frames crooked, and it took everything in her not to pick them up and straighten them.

"Well, one thing you should know is that Spence doesn't drink wine."

"Ever?"

"He doesn't drink alcohol at all."

"What about the brother?"

"He does. I'm not sure about wine." Kate looked at the pattern of the pools or more accurately the negative space between them. She noted the scuffed edge of the coffee table. "Looks like he—or someone—fell against the coffee table, then lay here. The size between the puddles would match Spence. He fell hard enough to knock his glasses off."

"Mm-hmm."

She looked at Kotono, wondering if he was thinking that perhaps someone knocked the glasses off before Spence fell. Near Kotono's feet, a baseball bat lay on the floor.

"Make sure you dust that for prints."

"It's not my first rodeo either, Kate. CSU is on the way. Anything else seem out of place? You spend much time over here?"

She thought there might be an implication in that question, but Kotono's stoic tone made it difficult to judge.

"Some, not a ton. Less since Sanjay moved in."

"The brother was with you?"

"Kind of. I have a spare key. He'd lost his keys, and the hide-a-key is missing. It's very difficult to find, so I would suspect Spence or someone else in the family has it."

"You know where it was kept?"

"No, just that it was somewhere irregular. Sanjay could tell you."

"So you weren't with the brother before that?"

"No," Kate answered as she studied Spence's desk. Some papers lay on the floor around it, and though the rim of the desk was cluttered with books, sticky notes and other papers, pens and pencils, and a few odds and ends including a smart phone and a plastic surfboard key fob, a clear rectangular void existed in the middle. "He spent most of last night at the station actually, got a little rowdy while he was out on the town." Kate bent down next to Spence's computer bag, which was propped against the desk.

"You know what time?"

"No idea."

"Does he get rowdy often?"

"He's no shrinking violet," Kate said, fully aware of the direction Kotono was heading.

"Did the brothers ever tussle?"

"No. Spence is not a fighter; he wouldn't let it come to that."

Kotono motioned to the desk. "Is your friend the type to leave his phone at home?"

"Absolutely not." Kate used two fingers to peek inside the bag. "Have you seen his laptop?"

Kotono shook his head.

"Did you check his car? A burgundy Civic, older model."

"Haven't seen the car either. No sign of disturbance beyond this room. One bedroom is a wreck, but I'm guessing from the smell that whoever sleeps there is just a slob. If it was a robbery, they got what they were looking for here."

Kate had been fighting to keep panic at bay, to find an internal switch that would close down her emotions, but she was groping in the dark, and the more she saw, the less easily she could believe Spence might have left the house of his own volition. A tightness constricted around her chest and threatened to close off her throat. She sucked in a sudden, deep breath.

"You okay?" Kotono asked.

Still crouching by Spence's computer bag, Kate looked up at the other detective. She pushed everything down and back and stood slowly. "I'm fine."

"It's perfectly understandable to be worried for your friend." While the words were kind, Kotono sounded as dispassionate as if he were reading out the hours for the department gun range. Kate suspected that if she took this sympathy, wrapped herself in its meagerness, that it would cost her something, in Kotono's eyes, in Kirkley's, and possibly everyone at the department.

"I'm fine," she said, surprised herself at the strength in her voice. "What's your next step?"

"Kirkley's coming out to go over the scene with CSU while I take the brother in for questioning."

"Why don't you just talk to him here?"

One side of Kotono's mouth scrunched briefly before he answered. "Look, Baxter, you know these people, so you could probably be quite helpful as far as facts go, but you may also be a little too close to parse things objectively. It's probably good I caught this instead of you."

Kate scrutinized the other detective. "You think Sanjay's responsible."

"I think it's likely, and I'm going to find out."

"That's not—"

"Are you telling me they got along well? Because that's not what the neighbors say."

"Sanjay wouldn't do something like this."

Kotono shrugged off her protest. "You always look close to home."

He walked out the door. The autumn air that he let in cooled Kate's burning cheeks, making her realized how flushed she'd become during the exchange. She knew the penchant detectives had for finding the most likely culprit nearby, and she knew why—people are more likely to be murdered by someone they know than by a stranger. *Murdered.* She hadn't meant to think it, but now the word lodged in her brain, sickening her as she thought about Spence. She looked at the pool of blood on the floor. It was small. Spence was still alive, and he needed her to find him.

She pushed herself out the door onto the porch, where the sharp air actually made it easier to breathe. Down by the street, Kotono stood next to her brother and Spence's, but she couldn't hear their words. Sanjay flinched, his eyes wide as Kotono swept an arm toward his police car as if he were a salesman inviting Sanjay to inspect the vehicle's features. Robbie shot a questioning look to Kate, but all she could do was breathe, draw the stinging air into her lungs and push it and the panic and the dread out.

Robbie slapped a compassionate hand on Sanjay's shoulder and said something to relax him. As Kotono escorted Sanjay away, Robbie strode up the yard to the porch railing.

"What're you thinking, sis?" The porch light glinted gold in his dark eyes as he looked up at Kate, his square face open and empathetic.

Kate inhaled deeply and hid behind her hand. "I'm worried, beyond worried. And I think Sam's wasting time digging in the wrong sandbox."

"He strikes me as the territorial type."

"Oh, yeah."

"Good thing we know another detective who's not afraid of a little competition."

Kate tried to smile. That would normally describe her, but this . . . She blew, forcing her fear out in a whistling rush of breath, which hung in the porch's light for a moment before disappearing. *Life is but a vapor.* She prayed that Spence, wherever he might be, still clung to this world.

With his own meaty, callused mitt, Robbie reached up and covered her hand that lay on the railing. "Hey, where's Spence?"

"I have no idea."

He clasped his other hand around hers. "No, where's Spence?"

"In God's hands."

"Until we find him."

Kate looked at her brother and saw why he made such a good father, and her mind almost dragged her back into the sorrow of his imploding family, but she couldn't think about that now, she had to focus.

"You know technically he'll be in God's hands even after we find him."

"Then there's no point in worrying, all the way around. So what's the next move, smart mouth?"

Kate looked down the narrow, shared porch at the light glowing yellow outside the next-door unit. "We talk to the neighbors."

"We already talked to the other detective," Maribel Johnson explained with a wary expression.

"I know." Kate smiled at the older woman. "Spence is a good friend of mine, and I just want to make sure we don't leave any angle unexamined."

Calvin Johnson, who stood a good foot and a half taller than his darker, plumper wife, placed an arm around her. "I think I've seen you here before. You usually come with the little redheaded girl, right?"

"That's right!" Kate didn't point out that Heidi, the little girl, was a grown woman. After all, the Johnsons were old enough to be their parents, and Heidi's size always made her pass as younger. "Did you see or hear anything out of the ordinary last night?"

"I don't know about out of the ordinary, but I told the other detective that I heard a crash," Maribel said. "You know, a loud noise. It woke me up."

"I slept through it."

Maribel rolled her dark eyes. "He could sleep through a riot. Anyway, I just figured it was the 'big one' coming home." She cast her eyes at Calvin who took a turn in rolling his.

"Spence's brother comes in late a lot, makes a lot of noise?"

"You could say that," Calvin said. "I believe he's a bit of a good-time Charlie, and he often struggles with his keys and so forth."

"Darshan was always so quiet, but when his brother moved in, well, they can argue, and sometimes it gets loud."

Kate and Robbie exchanged a glance. Things were looking worse for Sanjay.

"Was it ever bad enough that you called the police?" Robbie asked.

"Oh, no," said Maribel. "We wouldn't do that, not to Darshan. It usually didn't last too long. I think the big one usually stormed out after a little while, either that or Darshan would cut it off. Calvin only had to go over once and ask them to quiet down, but that was because I had a hospital appointment early the next day."

"Did it ever get physical?"

"Oh, I don't think so," Calvin said. "We never heard anything like that. They mostly argued about . . ." He looked at this wife.

"Responsibility," she supplied.

"Did you hear any arguing last night?" Kate asked.

Maribel shook her head. "Just the noise, like someone fell or dropped something heavy. And a groan or two. I just figured—" She shrugged. "I didn't even get out of bed."

"Yesterday or in the last few days, did you see anyone unfamiliar poking around or any vehicles that you hadn't seen before?"

"Not that I can think of. There aren't very many people that come by their place, just some scroungy young men occasionally. Friends of the brother's, I think. I do remember hearing a car last night afterward."

It had probably been Spence's car, but had he been the one driving it, and if so, where did he go?

"I hope you find him," Maribel said. "He's a sweet, young man. Just last week he helped Calvin push our car back to the house when it stalled at the corner."

Kate wanted to agree, but her voice, just like her friend, seemed to have vanished.

THREE PEOPLE came through the Fulton Springs police station that evening who surprised Potter Davis. The first was Eirik Boudreau. Potter knew Boudreau personally, not because they'd ever met, but because he was reading his memoir, the first one at any rate. Boudreau had been a person of interest in a recent case, but Kate had handled his questioning and Potter had received her intel secondhand. Despite his partner's unflattering description of the man or maybe because of it, Potter decided to purchase a copy of Boudreau's best-selling book. In fact, it currently lay on the corner of his desk. When the McNabbs marched Boudreau into the station, Potter flipped open his copy of *Hit Me, Baby, One More Time* to look at the author photo on the back flap to verify he was seeing whom he thought he was.

Potter found the book intriguing, starting with Boudreau's oppressive upbringing in a religious family, as one expected from religious families. Although his partner, Kate, didn't seem to have minded it. Potter wasn't sure if her hang-ups should be credited to her religion or not. Everyone, after all, had their fair share. The memoir then plunged into a heady mix of drugs, minor crime, and ill-fated romance (complete with the requisite titillating descriptions). Potter knew there was some type of reformation coming (it was emblazoned all over the book jacket), but he hadn't gotten that far.

The sight of Boudreau coming through the station made him wonder if that reformation hadn't stuck or if something in Boudreau's seedier past had caught up with him despite it. But since it wasn't his case, he didn't bother to find out. Potter believed in minding his own business, and the unfinished reports on his desk provided ample reason to do so.

But that tenet of behavior was put to the test by the arrival of the second surprising individual, Sanjay Spence, accompanied not by a patrol officer but by Detective Samuel Kotono. Potter had met Sanjay's brother on a few occasions through Kate, and Spence impressed him as thoughtful and intelligent. Potter stood from his desk, but he couldn't very well march over to Kotono and ask him what was going on as the other detective ushered the larger man toward an interview room. But Kate would want to know. He picked up his phone and texted.

He looked up to see Kotono and Kirkley conferring outside the interview room. A reply buzzed in from Kate. Potter's brow furrowed as he scanned the disturbing news. She ended the message with *If you hear anything, let me know.*

Kirkley made for the door, stopping off at his desk to pick up his overcoat, a burgundy cashmere affair more fitting for a councilman than a police detective. A bit of a pretty boy, Kirkley dressed meticulously, favoring pale suits that played to his fair complexion and swept-back chestnut hair, a contrast to his partner's bronze skin still burnished from the Indian summer and salt-and-pepper crew cut. Potter intercepted him halfway to the door, still shrugging his way into the expensive coat.

"I hear you're looking for Darshan Spence."

"That's true." Kirkley popped his coat over his shoulders simultaneously flipping up the collar. He always looked ready for a photo shoot.

"Why did Sam bring in his brother?"

Kirkley had the habit of letting his head loll back, which made him quite literally look down his nose through hooded eyes at whomever he was speaking to.

"Don't you have any cases of your own, Davis?"

"The Spences are friends of Kate's."

"Then you should probably let us 'get to it,' as they say."

People liked Potter generally. It wasn't something he had to work at especially, just a natural byproduct of his ready ear and even-keeled nature, so that he tended to take it for granted. But there were always people a little too invested in the chip on their shoulder looking to scrap. They inevitably went away disappointed.

"I'm not interested in a pissing match, Trevor, just a little professional courtesy."

Kirkley worked his jaw for a second. "Couple next door says the brothers fought quite a bit, often loudly. Younger brother's got a bit of a jacket, mostly for mixing his booze with his temper. Seems like a reasonable place to start."

"But he was here last night because of just that."

Kirkley shook his head. "Not until after the neighbors heard the disturbance. Mr. Sanjay Spence may just have had a very full evening. He wouldn't be the first to hit the bar after committing a crime."

"Nobody at the bar alibis him? He's a big guy; I'd think he'd be memorable."

Potter had exhausted Kirkley's patience. "That's probably what Sam's ascertaining right now as we shoot the breeze, not getting any work done."

Potter backed out of Kirkley's way, hands raised. "Sorry to hold you up."

He watched Kirkley exit, wondering what made him and Kotono so competitive, so divisive, when they were all trying to do the same job, accomplish the same common good. Potter was the newest detective to the force, and they'd been this way since day one.

He returned to his desk and piddled with a report while he kept an eye on the interview room door. When it finally opened, Sanjay left, strain splayed plainly across his broad face. Kotono lingered in the doorway watching his suspect go.

Potter wandered over, knowing that an eager approach would win him no ground.

"How did it go?"

Kotono looked at him askance. So much for acting casual.

"You and your partner can't keep out of my case. This isn't going to be a problem, is it?"

"C'mon, Sam. Your case is barely hours old, and you know it's Kate's friend who's missing."

"All the more reason for her—and you—to steer clear."

Potter's expression barely changed (he was destined to be a man of remarkably few wrinkles), but the slight tilt of the head was one his partner would've recognized as saying "be reasonable." She saw it often enough and was thus more susceptible to it than Kotono, but the older detective eventually sighed.

"He claims he doesn't know anything. The first he heard of it was when he showed up with Baxter's brother, who to his credit wouldn't let him in the house until after we got there."

"Alibi?"

Kotono bent his head down and dug something out of the corner of his eye. "None to speak of. Says that he went to a 'couple' different places last night before he ended up here, but he doesn't seem to remember the whole evening. Or claims he doesn't."

"You think he knows where Darshan is?"

Kotono shrugged. "Maybe not. There's no doubt he was tanked up when they brought him in. But that doesn't mean he isn't responsible."

Kotono excused himself, and Potter waited until he was out of sight before grabbing his phone and texting Kate that it didn't look good for Sanjay Spence.

The last surprising person to pass through the station that night was the chief of police.

A sex-trafficking sting had brought in a crowd—perpetrators, johns, lawyers, victims, and social workers—and Potter almost didn't see him in the influx of people. It was strange that the chief, who kept bankers' hours at best, would show up in the middle of the night, and dressed in jeans and a sweater, the man didn't look as if he were there on business despite his furrowed brow. Potter, however, returned most of his attention to the paperwork he had to finish, but he couldn't keep himself from glancing occasionally at the hall the chief had gone down. And so it was he spotted the chief when he left just twenty minutes later.

When Potter finished his last report, he visited the break room for a fresh cup of coffee. He still had a couple of hours on the shift he was covering for someone else, and his energy was flagging. Other McNabb came into the room hot, followed by his partner.

"Just calm down," Proper McNabb said. "We do our jobs and don't worry about the rest."

"Everything okay?" Potter asked.

Proper McNabb gave him a sad smile. "Just the death of some youthful idealism."

Potter frowned. An idealist himself, he could empathize with the younger officer's frustration and the chafing that came from being told, "This is how the world works." He tried to think of the right encouraging words to say to the younger man who leaned against the counter, visibly fuming, but Other McNabb spoke first.

"That's BS about excessive force! If I get written up . . ."

Potter's empathy faltered, and he once again looked to Proper McNabb for a cool-headed explanation.

"The guy had bruises coming up on his arm and hand."

"Way too soon for me to have caused them! He probably fell down because he was so plastered."

"Don't worry." Proper McNabb tried to soothe the junior officer. "I'll back you up. I was there the whole time. The guy's just connected is all."

Potter guessed as to the impetus for the chief's impromptu visit.

"Your partner's gonna be pissed too."

Potter glanced around the room to ensure no one else was there even though Other McNabb was looking directly at him.

"Why?"

"Because the guy they just let walk on a DUI was the one who sideswiped her. Detective Baxter was there when we arrested him. She called it in."

"She will indeed." Potter took a sip of his coffee. "I wouldn't mention it to her right now, if I were you." Kate had enough on her mind already.

MARION LUKAS still hadn't returned. Spence could only roughly gauge how much time had elapsed by counting the plays of the looped album, but he knew the other man had been away for hours. Perhaps Lukas had stopped at a liquor store for a top-up, or perhaps he'd crashed into a telephone pole and died on site. While the thought of Lukas bleeding out behind the wheel flushed Spence with a carnal sense of justice, it didn't comfort him at all. He'd no longer have anything to fear from Lukas, but he could die just as easily from his captor's absence and in a manner much slower and grimmer.

Did he really think Lukas would kill him? Everything Spence knew about him suggested he was more swagger and strut than stone cold. Of course, that impression predated his kidnapping. But murder?

How else do you think this is going to end? Do you think he'll just let you go if you promise not to print the story?

Whether Lukas had thought his plan all the way through or not, Spence doubted the two of them could strike a reasonable compromise. The urgency of his situation plowed through his weariness, pain, and mental fog, and with much scuffling, Spence righted himself into a sitting position. Even though his hands were next to useless, he had to try. He wriggled backward until he felt and heard the spring of the chain link. He began flexing his fingers, the muscles in his hands and wrists, hoping to restore some sense of feeling. He heard a noise.

He strained to hear the noise again through the racket of the music. The loud thumping sounded again, and he realized someone was pounding on the front door. He looked toward the interior door that Lukas had left ajar. It had long been dark, but in that darkness he now saw a faint flicker of red and then blue.

His heart leapt, and he had to catch his breath. He tried to call out, but his cry for help came out a feeble croak. His throat had all but reclosed since the paltry drink Lukas had given him. The effort felt like scraping raw flesh, but he worked up as much saliva as he could, swallowed, and tried again.

"Help!"

The pounding came again.

"Help, in the garage!" His voice sounded so dry and pitiful in his own ears he couldn't believe anyone across the room would hear it, let alone outside the house. He took a deeper breath, but that brought on a sharp pain in his ribs, causing him to wince and suck air between his teeth. He used the pain.

"Help!" He didn't know whether they could hear him over the music, but this time at least he produced a respectable volume, even though his voice cracked and popped like an amateur violin solo.

He waited, but the pounding didn't come again. The faint flash of colored light disappeared.

His head fell back, and he didn't even mind the jab of pain that ensued. He was too spent, exhausted all over again. Did anyone even know he was missing yet? It was entirely possible that Sanjay had never come home, since Spence hadn't had a deadline that day, his editor and coworkers could easily assume he was doing research or home sick, and if he were very busy, his friends and other family wouldn't think anything of not hearing from him for a few days. Who would it be—his dad driving over to check on him at his mom's insistence? Danny refusing to accept silence as a "no" for a movie-night invitation? Heidi showing up with cookies or homemade bread? Katherine . . . well, with her irregular schedule, it probably wouldn't be her, but she was his best bet for someone to find him. If she knew.

As a single person who lived alone, he occasionally played the "If I Died, How Long Would It Take Them to Find Me" game. His estimate was three days. Within that window, someone from work would suspect something was wrong, and if it were over the weekend, his parents or one of his friends would check on him. One would've thought that timeframe would've shrunk after Sanjay moved in, but Spence doubted that, depending on what part of the house he died in. When Sanjay moved in, he'd thought that eventually they would reconnect somehow, that despite his baby brother's estrangement from the faith, from the family, from any semblance of adult responsibility . . . what had he been thinking? If anything, smoldering resentment had driven them further apart than ever. Sanjay was more likely to hide from him than seek him out or check on him. The admission stung, and Spence pushed it from his mind.

Now that it wasn't theoretical, three days seemed entirely too long. As he started again to flex some feeling into his hands and grab at the cage behind his back, he recited the Twenty-third Psalm in his head. If only one day had passed so far, he wasn't sure he would make three.

He worked his hands diligently and at length awakened a painful, stinging buzz in them. He gritted his teeth, telling himself to be thankful for the sensation. He probed along the bottom of the chain link, his fingers bumbling, his tactile sensitivity still dulled. But he was glad to feel anything at all. He searched again for a rough or serrated edge on a strand of wire, picking up where he had left off before. He could explore only a few inches before he ran out of reach and had to scoot over, an awkward and jarring process, one that caused pain to shoot through his head and chest. He progressed several feet in this manner before he found something. The way his finger juddered along the edge seemed promising, but most of the regained feeling had already left his hands at this point. He pressed harder and dragged his finger back over the surface. It snagged on the surface, and he convinced himself that he felt the pricking of the wire. A little heat began to grow in his fingertip. He rubbed the index finger against his thumb and could feel the slick glide caused by the blood and the angry alarm of exposed nerves fighting to be heard over his numbness. Jackpot.

Spence felt again for the wire edge and then moved down to where he hoped his wrists were aligned with it, and then he began to saw through the layers of tape while his blood dripped onto the concrete.

Chapter Eight

Kate didn't know what time it was. She didn't know where Spence was. She didn't know how to comfort her brother in the midst of his crumbling marriage, the brother who was not comforting her. Not at this moment, though he had done his best the day before; now, he lay snoring lightly on her couch while she stood on the porch surveying her run-down neighborhood, made all the sketchier by too few lampposts in the early morning darkness. Truthfully, she absorbed little of even the limited view because her mind worked over what she did know—her friend was in danger, her brother was putting aside his own hurt to help her, and she really wanted a cigarette. The period since her last one could be marked in weeks more readily than months, just shy of two, but the progress felt solid. Still the memory of that soothing inhalation, how it smoothed the ragged edge of nerves, tempted her. At the same time, even entertaining the thought disappointed her, and she knew she'd feel an even keener disappointment afterward. And Spence wouldn't want her to throw away her momentum, certainly not because of him. So instead she sucked in a huge breath of cold air, bracing rather than mollifying, hoping it would ignite her mind, help her find a way to find Spence.

With a barrage of forceful words, she'd managed to persuade Kotono into letting her accompany him late last night to talk to Spence's parents, but only just.

They know me. If you don't let me go with you, they're just going to turn around and call me. You'll make better headway with me clearing the path.

It'd gone on like that for ten minutes. She didn't know why he insisted on making any collaboration as difficult as possible, but he'd relented right as she was about to lose her temper and throw out saltier language than normally found in her mild vocabulary.

They'd rousted the Spences from their bed, and as the couple sat before her on an ancient plaid couch, Kate marked the visual similarity between them and the Johnsons, the towering man pale with silver-white hair and the woman small and dark. Had Spence ever marked the similarity, or had Mr. Johnson's beard and his mother's glasses and long gray-streaked braid obscured it?

They hadn't known anything. Hadn't heard anything. Hadn't provided any leads. Hadn't believed Sanjay could be involved. For several moments, hadn't even believed that mischief could be involved. Mrs. Spence had shaken her head, telling Kotono he must be mistaken, so different from Kate's own mother, who was always waiting for tragedy to strike, seemed almost hungry for it, that confirmation of justified fear. Mrs. Spence's denial proved crueler to the bearers of ill tidings, forcing them to convince her of her son's peril.

Spence's parents had then called his sisters with Kotono coaching them what to say and what to ask, while Kate called their friends Danny and Heidi, who she figured would more likely be tapped into Spence's day-to-day doings than Gauri or Tabby. She tried to share as little information as possible so as not to alarm them. She succeeded with Danny, but Heidi, well practiced at reading between the lines, wouldn't be distracted from the seriousness of the situation.

Kate pulled out her phone and woke the screen, its light flashing like a beacon. The hour was obscene and yet she knew her parents would be awake. Her dad rose at four every morning without reason, and her mother rose when he did, insisting it was impossible for her to sleep through his waking, why not just get up and start the day?

Kate pushed the button.

Her mother answered on the third ring. "Why, hello, sweetheart. It's early for a call. Is everything okay?"

"No, it isn't."

In the momentary silence, Kate could see her mother's mouth tightening downward, the little half-grimace she made while thinking through life's unpleasantries.

"I know. Robbie told us he was staying with you." Kate opened her mouth to redirect the conversation, but her mother moved forward with the agility of a trained auctioneer. "I can understand that he needed some space, some time to think, all that, but don't you think he should be home? Talking to Lauren instead of you? I'm sure you're giving him good advice, and Lord knows he needs a shoulder to lean on, but you know what I mean, don't you? He's not going to solve any of his problems in Fulton Springs; he certainly won't save his marriage from there. Don't you think he should be home right now?"

Kate had been holding her breath, and now she let it rush out in a cloudy gust illuminated by her security light.

"You may be right, Mom. But I think he needs to get his head straight about all of it first, and I don't think he's there yet."

"I can imagine how difficult it's been for Lauren, being married to a police officer." Unprepared for her mother's defense of her sister-in-law, Kate's ire flashed to the surface, but it faded as her mother continued. "I've always worried so much about both of you because of how dangerous your work is, and I know it must be even harder for her." Kate thought her mother was giving Lauren too much credit, but a quaver had crept into her mother's voice that tugged at the emotions Kate liked to keep safely boxed away. "And I knew it could be dangerous in other ways, but I just didn't think it would be this. It's like there are so many hazards that you can't keep your eye on all of them, and maybe I missed praying about the right ones all these years. I don't know why both of you insisted on joining the police force."

And despite her mother's final words and their inherent blame, the naked sadness in her voice seemed to distill, for the first time, all the objections to Kate's profession into something Kate couldn't brush away as outdated traditionalism but rather into something with which she could too readily empathize.

"Mom . . ." She was about to say that all professions had their pitfalls, that ill-tended marriages crumbled in every corner, but none of that offered consolation and at the moment she didn't feel up to defending her profession because she knew amongst its physical perils, it also offered its fair share of mental and emotional landmines. And it stung to think that Robbie had tread on one. "I know. I understand."

She took a breath. "But I actually called to ask you and Dad to pray about something else. My friend Spence is missing. He has been for about twenty-four hours now, and there's good reason to think he's in danger."

"Oh, honey, of course! We'll pray for him right now." And without any more ado, her mother launched into an earnest petition, reminding Kate why she had called. Her parents were never shy about their faith and never hesitant to take anything to God, regardless of how big or small. The last words her mother said before she hung up were, "You'll find him, Katie. You're a good detective. Maybe this is why. Maybe I've been too selfish with you and Robbie. You go find your friend. We'll keep praying till you do."

And in the chill of the dark morning, those words warmed her.

COLIN COULD TELL from the look on Brendan's face that he wasn't buying the new plan.

"You want to create a new Social Circle account for her instead of posting stuff on her actual account?"

"Yes, well, kind of. I don't want to create an account *for* Sissy." His voice dropped at her name in case someone on the bus was listening. "I want to create one *like* hers. We would make up a different name."

The consternation didn't leave Brendan's freckled face. "But then how will anyone see it?"

"They won't. The point is it's not for anybody but us and Dylan. We can make Dylan feel better without making Sissy feel bad. And without getting suspended for bullying."

"Who gets suspended for bullying?" Brendan shrugged and picked at the braces on his front teeth. "That'd only happen if they could prove it was us. But whatever. How's this fake account of not-Sissy going to make Dylan feel better?"

"We're gonna make it funny; that's how. Like a satire!"

"Like a what?" Brendan looked bewildered and not a little unfunny himself with his index finger still pushing his upper lip further up.

"Do you not pay attention, ever, in class?"

"You're such a dork."

"Look in a mirror, bruh." Colin shook his head. "Remember we read that story about the Lilliputians? And Miss Phillips said how the author was making fun of how people are stuck on themselves and can't see how small they are."

Brendan stopped picking at his braces and leaned sideways toward his friend, as if letting him in on a secret. "Yeah, but the story wasn't really funny."

Colin couldn't argue there. "Yeah, because she said a lot of the things the writer was making fun of happened back then." Colin thought a second. "Remember when she said Lilliput was basically like a political convention or Hollywood awards ceremony? Everybody laughed at that."

"Yeah," Brendan conceded.

"Because people got it because it was current, something they could relate to. This'll be funny to Dylan because it'll relate to him (and Sissy). Get it?"

"I guess."

Brendan went back to probing the metal casing on his teeth. Colin could tell he hadn't sold him on the idea, but maybe he'd gotten far enough. He didn't know how to explain it. Maybe if he'd paid better attention in class himself, or maybe if Brendan had. He looked down the aisle and sitting two seats in front of him was Chucky MacBride, wearing a pair of black-and-red Vans with *El Barto* graffitied on the side, and Colin remembered a popular example Miss Phillips had used in her lesson.

"Think of like when they show a real person on *The Simpsons*."

Brendan paused in his probing. "Okay, that's funny. So we're gonna *Simpsons*-ify her."

"Something like that," Colin said. Brendan still had his finger in his front teeth. "Can you take your finger out of your mouth?"

"I got my braces adjusted yesterday, and—"

A twitch of Brendan's finger sent a red rubber band pinging off Tyresha Brown's head. Her hand flew to the spot where it hit between her two thick braids. She turned around, wrath in her eyes.

"What was that?"

With his own crisis newly averted, Colin didn't feel disposed to adopt another. He pointed at Brendan.

WHEN THE MUSIC cut off, the quiet was so foreign, so large that it took Spence a moment to synthesize it, though perhaps some of that mental lethargy could be attributed to a likely concussion. He turned his eyes toward the sliver of open door, but Lukas did not appear in the seconds (which felt like minutes) that Spence instinctually held his breath, waiting. When not even a light appeared in the open space, Spence attempted once more to pull his wrists apart. He felt some give though the slack proved insufficient for him to rip through, and he sawed with a renewed vigor. Without the drowning music to mask his movements, they brought a rhythmic metallic creaking that resounded off the garage's stark walls and concrete floor. He paused, afraid the noise would give him away, but then figured he had little to lose at this point and continued. At least until the door swung open.

Lukas's descent to the garage floor sounded far steadier than before. The flashlight illuminating his path bobbed and weaved less but blinded Spence all the same when Lukas shone it in his direction. His captor sat down heavily on the crate, which squeaked in protest.

Spence tried to speak, but his throat had closed up again.

"Scoot over here," Lukas said. He moved a bottle of water into the beam of light and waggled it back and forth as if Spence needed encouragement to quench his thirst. The bottle's label bore some bright red fruit, though Spence couldn't make out what it was in the wavering light.

Spence pulled himself forward with his feet, steadying himself from behind with unfeeling fingertips when he wobbled. At the front of the cage, he swung around in tiny scoots until he just let himself fall against the chain link. Lukas put the neck of the already-opened bottle through an opening and tilted so that the water with a fake cherry taste, slightly bitter, poured too quickly. Spence gulped most of it, spilling only a little down his front, until Lukas withdrew the bottle.

"Thank you, Marion."

"Don't call me that."

Spence continued to lean on the fencing because the effort it would take to right himself seemed inordinate.

"You were gone a long time." His voice still rasped, but oiled by the water, it was coming back to life. Speaking still felt as though he were sanding his vocal cords, but his throat hurt less than the rest of him.

Lukas didn't answer. He directed the beam of light past Spence.

"Is that blood?"

Spence turned his head, his stiff neck aching with the effort. How every movement hurt! An irregular pool of blood no bigger than a quarter but bordered by additional, more-vivid smears lay at the back edge of the cage. If nothing else, he was leaving a good DNA trace for the police to find.

"I couldn't find a Band-Aid," he said, working on his gallows humor while he still could.

Lukas circled to the rear of the cage. He flicked the flashlight to Spence's back. Spence didn't bother trying to hide his hands.

Lukas swore. "What were you doing?"

"Oh, I don't know, Marion! Maybe trying to get my hands free so that I could restore the feeling in them." The agitated tone made his throat burn.

"I don't think you were accomplishing as much as you think you were. What was your plan anyway? Even with your hands free, you're still locked in."

"Then why don't you leave my hands free then?"

"I might be able to do that."

Lukas left and when he returned, he had more than the promised bandage. He sat down on the crate and flipped open a laptop. The light from the screen reflected off his glasses, making the lenses menacingly opaque.

"Band-Aid for your password." Lukas held the little strip up in the light. Spence didn't reply. "You're still bleeding."

Good, Spence thought. *The more DNA for them to find when they track you down.*

Lukas sighed. "I'll cut the tape off too, of course."

That seemed a better deal, but Spence weighed how many chips he had to bargain with.

"It's *Matt10 [hyphen] 29* with a capital *M*."

"Who's Matt?" Lukas's fingers scrambled spiderlike over the keyboard and the light reflecting on his face changed from blue to gray to white as he gained access.

"Seriously? I would have thought you'd recognize the reference. You were raised in a Presbyterian church, weren't you?"

Satisfied for the moment, Lukas set the computer down and opened a pocketknife. "Turn around." As Spence laboriously swiveled to put his hands against the fencing, Lukas responded, "I only got the church stuff in the early years and on major holidays afterward, and let's say it didn't take. Maybe you didn't dig far enough to unearth that. I hadn't pegged *you* as a Bible guy."

"How assumptive of you. You also brought me wine, so I guess we know who the better researcher is."

"I was more interested in your schedule than your worldview."

Lukas sliced through the tape and pressed the Band-Aid into Spence's hand. Spence slowly brought his hands in front of him, biting his lips together to keep from groaning at the pain that coursed through his stiff shoulders. He only partially succeeded. He had to flex his hands and fingers to reinfuse them with motor function before he could grip the bandage and wrap it around the end of his dirty index finger. He hoped it didn't get infected and then hoped he made it out of this situation to find out.

Lukas stared intently at the computer, his hand shaped like a claw as it glided over the track pad.

"You should read the article before you delete it, Marion. It'd be nice if somebody did."

"*Don't* call me that." Lukas looked at him with his eerily whited-out eyes. "Am I supposed to take that to mean no one else has seen it?"

"Just finished it tonight or however long ago you kidnapped me. I'm not real clear on when we are."

"I wondered. I had dinner with your editor a few nights ago, and he didn't give off the slightest air of caginess. Just mentioned the upcoming review of my new book."

"You actually have me to thank for that, believe it or not."

"Do I? Like I would need your help for that. Like I need a review from the paltry *Fulton Springs Tribune*."

"It couldn't hurt, right? Everybody likes the chance to love on a local boy. Even if he's only been local for a few years."

"And were they going to run this glowing review alongside your . . . character assassination?"

"You can't assassinate someone who never existed. You read that article and tell me there's anything there that isn't true."

"Truth is experiential and thus relative."

"Then why am I here?" Lukas didn't answer, just kept scrolling on the laptop. "If that were true, you wouldn't be so afraid. You've come off as pretty desperate, Marion. Lots of frauds get exposed without going on a crime spree to cover it up."

"Stop calling me Marion! That's not my name."

"It used to be. Marion Lukas."

"Well, I haven't been him for a very long time. My name is Eirik Boudreau."

Chapter Nine

"It does not look good for Spence's brother as far as I can tell," Potter said.

"They haven't been looking at any other suspects, any other leads?" Kate asked, disappointed with the news her partner relayed over the phone. She stood in the early morning gloom outside the Fulton Springs Tribune, her trench coat belted tight against the cold and damp.

"You know they're not looping me in, but it sounds like they spent the majority of last night circling the bar scene, trying to put together a timeline of Sanjay's actions, having unis review security cam footage."

"Guess it's up to me then." She shivered, either from the cold or from her burden. "Thanks for keeping an ear out."

"Anything I can do, you let me know." Potter paused. "Are you sure Sanjay has nothing to do with this?"

"I would be very surprised. He's not motivated enough for serious criminal enterprise. My brother's going over to the house for another look around, so if I'm wrong, maybe he'll find something to clue me in."

"He's a little out of jurisdiction, isn't he?"

"I told him he could be my deputy, and besides the scene's been released and we have a key." She spotted Spence's editor, Malcolm Jenner, coming down the sidewalk, a leather messenger bag slung across his chest. "Gotta go."

In front, Jenner's dark hair swept back from a face of thin features and warm brown eyes behind oval glasses, and in back, it hung down in its full length onto the collar of his overcoat, which he wore open over a tweed suit. Kate didn't want the slight man to feel ambushed, but she also had no time to spare. Not waiting for Jenner to come to her, she began her introduction, badge first, before either of them had stopped moving.

"You're kidding me?" Jenner's incredulity at the news of Spence's disappearance confirmed that Kirkley and Kotono were indeed casting a narrow net in their investigation.

"Is there anything Spence was working on for the paper that could have put him in danger?"

Jenner focused his eyes on the sidewalk. "Not that I can think of." He motioned to the Tribune's entrance. "Let's step into my office, and I can pull up his files. It's possible he was working on something I didn't know about."

As Jenner led her through a room already abuzz with clacking keyboards, coffee-pot conversations, and ringing phones, Kate asked if that was normal, for Spence to take on assignments the editor didn't know about it. Jenner shot a wry look over his shoulder and held up his index finger. He ushered her into an office full of books and framed photos but didn't speak until after he'd shut the door and turned on a desk lamp.

"Yes, it's not uncommon, and I'll tell you why. You're familiar with the concept of journalistic objectivity?"

"I've heard of it, in theory. But didn't it go out with horse-drawn buggies?"

"It's been a steady decline since then." Even in the dim lighting, Kate could clearly see the arch expression on Jenner's face as he leaned against the front of his desk. "And some argue whether the concept is even valid or helpful, but I view it, at least, as a goal, especially in these very divisive times in our nation. And while it's impossible for anyone to be fully impartial, one of the things I respect so much about Darshan Spence is that he doesn't let his politics or his beliefs—and I know he holds firmly to them—sway his reporting."

Despite the grimness of the circumstances, a smile spread across Kate's face. "That's because his beliefs place a high value on truth."

"I know you know him well. He's mentioned you multiple times." Jenner nodded toward the bullpen they'd walked through. "Some of my other reporters are much more agenda-driven, whether personal or political, and I also have to contend with bias from the top." He pushed his glasses down to scratch between his eyebrows. "To put it briefly, I trust Darshan to be as honest as possible, even if he doesn't like what he finds, and we found together that if we keep his investigative stories off the record for as long as possible, there's less likelihood of them getting killed from up above when it's something that doesn't jibe with the owners' . . . views."

"Impartial discourse in a one-party state must be hard."

"I'm not naïve enough to believe my days here aren't numbered, but your friend helps a lot. Because he helps sell papers, or online subscriptions at any rate.

Another reason I can give him carte blanche is that he's freaking good at what he does, hence the selling papers. He's a solid researcher, solid writer, and he has a way of finding stories that interest readers or maybe it's a way of making stories interesting. I fear, for myself, that his days are numbered here as well, because I'm just sure some bigger news service is going to snatch him up."

"Has he been working on something political?"

"Not that I'm aware of." Jenner circled his desk, slinging his bag onto a padded chair in the corner and then shedding his overcoat on top of it. "I mean, his last three assigned articles were all city-government pieces, but nothing that's going to ruffle feathers or at least not ones that aren't already sticking up the wrong way." He tapped into his computer. "I can look to see if he's uploaded any files since the last time I checked, maybe one of his more on-the-DL stories. Each reporter uploads their work to a drive for editing and fact-checking."

"Is it a protected drive?"

"Yeah, they have to be signed into our VPN."

Kate shifted restlessly from one sensible boot to the other as Jenner stood hunched over his computer, clicking and scrolling, until in the grayish glow of his computer screen, he winced.

"Nothing?"

"No, I'm sorry." Jenner sat down and leaned his elbows against the desk. He stared for a moment at its cluttered surface, filled with scratch paper, photos, pens, and highlighters. "I do know he was working on one article related to the publishing industry. He'd been working on it for ages, and I thought maybe it hadn't panned out, but he mentioned it again last week."

"I know he attended a launch for Chapman Books' kiddie imprint a couple of months back." In fact, Kate had gone with him to work an angle on the case she had been on. "Could it have something to do with that? Or Chapman Books?"

Jenner shook his head helplessly. "I don't know. I remember the article on the launch, even that he volunteered for the assignment, but if it had anything to do with this other piece he didn't mention it. As I said, Darshan has a nose for news and I let him follow it."

Kate pulled one of her cards from the breast pocket of her plaid button-up and handed it to Jenner. "If you do think of anything else, please call me—day or night."

As she left Jenner's office, Kate thought about that reception she and Spence had gone to. She remembered unintentionally hurting his feelings that night, and the sour memory unsettled her. She tried to push it aside and think of what else he'd said. She was positive he'd mentioned his article, but she couldn't think of the context. She'd been too caught up in her own case, snooping on Nathanael Carver, Grant Innerst, and Linley Chapman. She wrinkled her nose. And Eirik Boudreau. That's where she'd met Eirik Boudreau.

NOBODY ANSWERED Spence's door when Robbie knocked. He looked back at the battered Subaru on the street. It was the only car that hadn't been there last night, so he guessed that it belonged to Sanjay. He knocked again, then let himself in with the Kate's key.

"Hello?" he called.

He crossed the living room, now clear of wine, blood, and broken glass, though the latter had left a few scratches in the floor. He peeked into the kitchen and saw through the sliding glass door to the outside, where Sanjay, wearing a worn red hoodie, sat in a lawn chair his wide back to the door. When

Robbie slid the door open, Sanjay started and swore, his movement causing the joint he held to send a little smoke signal into the crisp air. When he saw it was Robbie, relief washed over his face. He wore the same shorts and sweatshirt as the previous night, and dark circle ringed his hooded eyes.

"Bruh, you cannot sneak up on a guy when . . . you know, the stuff that's going on."

"Sorry," Robbie said. "I knocked, but you didn't answer." He looked around the claustrophobic square of ground that was half paved with a stone slab and surrounded by high planked fencing. Sanjay struck him as a big man in a small box. Robbie wondered if there were a crank on the other side of the fence, that if turned, would send Sanjay flying out. "It's kind of cramped back here, isn't it?" His eyes trailing back to Sanjay's joint already smoked down to roachdom.

Sanjay took another hit and slowly blew out the pungent smoke. "My brother wouldn't like it if I smoked in the house."

"He's not here," Robbie pointed out.

"He wouldn't like it." Robbie wasn't sure, but he thought he heard a catch in Sanjay's voice. "Normally, I wouldn't even out here, but . . . ." The defensiveness fell away. "You know, the stuff going on." He looked up and saw Robbie eyeing his cigarette. "You're from out of state, right?"

"Indiana."

"Well, it's not illegal in Illinois, so you can relax."

"Oh, I know. I live close enough to the border that we do a brisk business in marijuana busts. But I'll take a stoner over a drunk any day." Sanjay shot him a puzzled look. "They're much more chill."

Sanjay held his hand up in a peace sign.

"I'm actually here to look through Spence's desk," Robbie said. "Kate sent me while she talks to his coworkers."

"Go for it. I'll be out here getting chill." Sanjay tossed the butt on the patio and ground it out with a once-white sneaker. He pulled another joint from the pocket of his hoodie.

"Don't overdo it." Robbie stepped back inside but paused, his hand still on the sliding door. He leaned back out. "Kate will find him. He'll be okay."

"You a detective too?"

"Nope, just an ordinary cop. Kate's the real brains in the family."

"For us, that would be Darsh." Sanjay read the confusion on Robbie's face. "My brother—Spence—his first name is Darshan."

"Oh, right." Robbie nodded toward the interior. "I should probably get to it." It felt a little heartless to abandon Sanjay looking so miserable boxed in the scrap of backyard. "Kate will find him."

"Is there anything I can do to help?"

"If I have any questions, I'll let you know." Robbie said.

Sanjay kicked the crushed roach into the dead grass and gave a sharp nod.

"You could pray," Robbie offered.

Sanjay snorted. "I'm not really a pray-er anymore."

"Now might be a good time to start again."

Sanjay didn't say anything. He put the cigarette between his lips and flexed his hands, causing the knuckles to crackle like walked-on bubble wrap. Then he lit the joint and take another hit. Robbie left him to ruminate.

Spence's desk had two tiers. Dusty photographs lined the top interspersed with small squares of paper, writing implements, and several homeless buttons. Robbie tried to remember what Kate told him to look for, but his eyes fixated on the second photo, which showed Spence grinning with his arms wrapped around two beaming little girls, nieces maybe? They were brown skinned with streaming pigtails of jet black, dressed in frilly, bow-decked frocks, nothing like Taylor and Prudence, the little blonde daughters he'd left at home, except that they were about the same ages and he recognized the exuberance on their faces. He probably had a dozen photos of himself and the girls in just that pose. That was more than enough to make his throat tighten and almost enough to send him out the door and back across the state border. But what would he say to them if he did go? He couldn't promise their family would be okay, would stay a family. Besides, Kate needed his help right now, regardless of whether he was truly up to the task.

The first photo showed a younger, somewhat trimmer Sanjay in a football uniform, his smiling face marked with eye black. Spence and other family members surrounded him, their faces excited, shining in what must have been a post-victory celebration. Robbie spotted the same little girls, a few years younger than in the other picture. In the third photo, Spence stood before a flaming grill, looking over his should with a raised eyebrow while Kate laughed in the foreground. The next picture looked like an office party, the background drab and utilitarian, everyone leaning toward the camera. Spence and an attractive, dark-haired woman stood very close together, a little apart from the others, who were all older. The last frame, a digital display, cycled through photos mostly of Spence's tribe—Kate, Danny, and Heidi. Robbie pawed through the scraps of paper, which had shopping lists, email addresses, phone numbers, and reminders scrawled on them. If one looked promising, he took a photo with his phone. He found the same type of content on the sticky notes lining the ledge. At the corner of the ledge, a surfboard keychain dangled from a delicate hook. Robbie tapped the fluorescent fob, and it clattered against the desk. The ring held no keys, so he guessed it held sentimental value. He took a picture in case "Sammy's Surf Shop" was somehow relevant.

He looked at the main surface of the desk and frowned at how much territory he had to cover there. He picked up a stack of papers and started sifting through them, dislodging a dust bunny in the process. If this stuff hadn't been moved in that long, could it really be relevant to Spence's disappearance? He pushed on, not wanting to miss anything that could help, working from left to right. A lot of it was mail—insurance statements, flyers—but there were also news clippings and printouts from the *Tribune* and other papers, more pieces of scratch paper with various notes written on them. Robbie delved into the two desk caddies that stood sentry at the back of the desk, and for his trouble found a couple of thumb drives amidst a myriad of pens, pencils, highlighters, colored tabs, and sticky notes, not to mention a letter opener shaped like a fencing foil.

He heard the pop and hiss of a can from the kitchen, and Sanjay, looking sleepy and red-eyed, stepped into the doorway, filling it completely.

"You wanna Pepsi?" He took a sip from one can and held out another with his large hand. It looked like he'd stuck two more in the pockets of his hoodie.

"You have any coffee?"

Sanjay shrugged.

"Pepsi's fine." Robbie took the can. He motioned to the first photo on the desk. "I played in high school too. What position did you play?"

"Linebacker."

"Really? Did you play in college too?"

"Nah, didn't go." Sanjay plinked the metal ring atop his can. "They offered me a scholarship though."

Robbie looked back at the photo, all those shining, smiling faces. "I bet that made your family proud."

"Something like that."

Sanjay started past him. Robbie swiveled and held up the thumb drives.

"I'm taking these with me to see if there's anything helpful on them."

Sanjay nodded without looking back. The door to his room clicked shut behind him.

Robbie picked up a book from the right side of Spence's desk, *A River Runs Through It* by Norman Maclean. The cover photo showed a picturesque river running through a forest backdropped by a clouded mountain sky at twilight. Robbie bet there was some good fishing in that river. Only a couple of books lay on the desk, but the room was full of them. Stacks on the floor stretched upward on either side of the desk. One wall was lined with bookshelves filled with hardbacks and paperbacks of all sizes.

"Time to get an e-reader, man," Robbie said. He didn't read much himself, but he cracked open a Tom Clancy every once in a while, usually when they went to the lake . . . he tried to envision those family outings without Lauren. He tamped down the pain clawing up through his chest. He flipped through the book.

Some pages were dog-eared and others had passages underlined. He made the mistake of reading one: "It is those we live with and love and should know who elude us."

It was like a cold slap.

He read it again, more slowly. In the middle of his marveling, that beast sitting on his belly tore upward at such a speed that he had no chance to stop it, and he found himself choking as it reached up through his throat to squeeze his eyes. He threw the book down and bolted through the front door onto the porch, where he hoped Sanjay would not hear him fall to pieces.

He gripped the railing and rode out the storm of emotion, occasionally swiping at an eye. He had cried so much the night before that he found it hard to believe his tear ducts held anything in reserve. The cold air helped, leeching the hot flush from his skin. He fished his phone out of the front pocket of his jeans, but he only looked at it. He wanted to believe a divorce was not inevitable, but the realization they were damaged enough to be on its precipice scared him. How did they come back from that? He didn't know if he could win Lauren back, or whether he could even overcome the betrayal he felt to try.

He pressed the phone against his forehead and tried to think. If he did call and if she did answer, what would he say? He still wasn't sure as he dialed. She didn't answer. He stuffed the phone back in his pocket.

Two young men bundled in bulky sweatshirts, jackets, and beanies zipped up the sidewalk and past the steps to cut up into the yard and then arc back around in front of Spence's stoop.

The one with red hair streaming out from under his black cap asked, "Jay in?"

"Jay? I think you've got the wrong house."

The two exchanged a look.

"Pretty sure I don't," the redhead said with a perfectly smackable face. "Sanjay Spence."

"Oh, Sanjay! Yup, he's here." Robbie looked from the redhead to the other, whose sweatshirt was emblazoned with a huge cannabis leaf. He looked at their faces and, despite the stubble on the first one and ear gauges on the other, could read their ages pretty easily. "Shouldn't you guys be in school?"

The redhead hopped off his bike. "OK, boomer."

"Whoa!" Robbie almost laughed. He held his hand up, signaling the kid to stop. "I'm serious."

"What are you, a cop?" sneered the kid.

"Yup."

The teen in the weed sweatshirt halted mid-dismount, like a dog hiking up his leg at a tree. He looked to his compatriot, who appeared skeptical but was still giving serious consideration to his next move. Unencouraged by his friend's hesitance, the second teen reseated himself on his bike and slowly backed safely out of range.

Robbie whipped his badge out, mostly for fun, and watched the redhead's skepticism vanish.

"All right!" The redhead yelled his defiant concession like a preschooler, and both boys wheeled out of the yard as quickly as they'd come into it.

Robbie glanced at the *Centerfield Police* emblazoned across the bottom of his badge and shook his head.

Back inside the house, the cacophony of artificial battle emanated from Sanjay's bedroom door, and Robbie hoped the teens had come for a gaming session and not something else. He thought about telling Sanjay the boys had stopped by but left it. He needed to finish and report back to Kate.

He shuffled over to the desk but didn't sit down, eyeing the books that lay there suspiciously, as though they might repeat their sneak attack against him. He picked up *A River Runs Through It* and set it to the other side of the desk. According to its spine, the well-worn volume underneath was entitled *Hit Me, Baby, One More Time*. A fluorescent yellow sticky note obscured most of the cover, and on the note was written a name— Marion Lukas. Robbie took a picture and set that volume with the other book.

He made short work of the papers, clippings, and files that had been underneath but not as short as he should have. He found himself constantly having to refocus. Once his phone buzzed, and five minutes after checking it, he realized he was staring at the family photo on his wallpaper. Even apart from his lax attention, Robbie didn't feel terribly productive. Nothing stood out to him as an obvious lead, nor did he pick up a common thread connecting any of the disparate items he perused. On a hunch, he dismantled the photos to see if anything was hidden in the frames. There wasn't.

He was putting the desk back to its original condition, more or less, when Sanjay emerged with several crushed cans in hand and an enormous yawn. Robbie laid the books down.

"Does Spence have a girlfriend?"

Sanjay gave a little barky laugh. "Nah, he's wound a little tight for that."

Robbie followed Sanjay into the kitchen, where he shot the crumpled cans one at a time into the wastebasket.

"He ever mention a Marion?"

"Not that I remember. The only women he talks about are Katherine and Heidi. And Lily, some girl he works with." Sanjay stopped with one can still in his hand. "I don't think they're dating. He doesn't talk about her as much as Katherine." He shrugged. "We don't really . . . gab, if you know what I mean."

"Gotcha." Robbie thumbed toward the hallway. "Is it cool if I poke around his room? Leave no turn unstoned, you know."

"Knock yourself out, but you ain't gonna find anything in Darsh's room to get you stoned. I doubt you'll find anything interesting at all."

Robbie wondered how much pot Sanjay had smoked, but what he asked was for another Pepsi.

Sanjay went to the refrigerator and pulled out a tall brown bottle. "Want something stronger?"

Even though it wasn't lunchtime yet, Robbie thought about it. Seriously thought about how nice it would be to slip into a bottle and ease the internal aching, even if just a little, not to mention the pain in his head from his tearful fit earlier.

A text from Kate buzzed in as if to remind him to stick to the job. "If I'm gonna help find your brother, I better stick with caffeine," he said as he thumbed a response to her.

Sanjay was right. Robbie found nothing of interest in Spence's bedroom—more books; a limited wardrobe that seemed expensive, meticulously cared for, and organized; some home workout equipment; a collection of movies that Robbie had never heard of, many of which were in black and white—nothing elicit, nothing revelatory, nothing that seemed remotely clue-like to him. He was used to spotting evidence at crime scenes, the obvious stuff, but this blind digging—he didn't know how Kate did it.

He stared at the top of Spence's dresser, which held a few bottles of cologne and hair products and an orderly assortment of cuff links, tie bars, and a few other pieces of gold jewelry. Maybe there wasn't anything to find. Maybe that's why Kate sent him over here, just to keep him occupied. She probably knew how dumb he was, dumb enough not to realize his marriage was disintegrating. He snapped a picture of the dresser top and left.

He didn't bother to say goodbye to Sanjay because he was pretty sure Sanjay was more than halfway through the bottle he'd originally offered Robbie and wouldn't be thrilled at the disruption. As Robbie trotted down the sidewalk, he spied a black Crown Vic, exactly like Kate's navy blue one, parked across the street down a little from the house. He didn't recognize the man behind the wheel—white with light brown hair, about his own age, wearing a tie and burgundy overcoat—but Robbie could guess well enough who he was and why he was there and thought to himself that Sanjay had better watch his step.

"WHAT ABOUT THE cloud?" Lukas asked.

"What about the cloud?" Spence repeated. He needed to work on his stall tactics, but he gave himself some leniency. He wasn't exactly in peak condition at present.

Lukas looked up from the laptop. "I'm not an idiot, and I'm giving you the courtesy of not treating you like one either. I know you have to have backed this up somewhere."

"Can we circle back to the idiot idea? Because I'm not wholly convinced you thought through this plan adequately. Why should I tell you how to destroy my article, if it just means you're going to kill me afterward?"

It suddenly occurred to Spence that he'd just given Lukas a very sound rationale for torture, and he hoped the idea didn't also occur to Lukas. Spence felt sufficiently tortured at the moment. For his part, Lukas focused back on the laptop screen and swallowed, the prominent Adam's apple bobbing in his thin neck.

"No one ever said anything about killing. I'm not a murderer."

"I would have thought the same thing." Spence gave a nod to his cage. "But here we are. Are you saying you'll let me go after all this, knowing what I know? And you expect me to believe you?"

"I'm sure we can come to an arrangement." Lukas squirmed on his crate. "One that benefits us both, but I can't think about that now. First the file, where else do you have it?"

"I haven't had anything to eat in . . . I don't know how long. I'm starving. Can I have something to eat?" He sounded as obvious as a preschooler giving reasons he couldn't comply with his bedtime. And he wasn't starving; in fact, the thought of food turned his stomach despite the hollowness he felt in his middle.

Lukas didn't seem fooled. Even in the glow of the computer screen, Spence could see his jaw muscle twitch.

"The file first. Then I'll get you some food." The tension in Lukas's voice, the way he snipped his words made Spence think now might not be the time to push further. He told him the site address and his password and then watched Lukas's face as he deleted the backup of the article, one of them anyway.

"Why did you do it?" Spence asked.

"Your article would have cost me everything."

"No, I mean why did you pass your book off as a true story in the first place? I know your previous agent submitted it to Simon & Schuster as a novel. Your writing—" The compliment stuck in his throat. "—shows you have talent. Why not keep trying with other publishers?"

"You think Simon & Schuster was our only stop? No one was interested in it as a novel." Lukas jabbed at the keyboard with his index fingers. "Editors found too many of the events implausible."

Spence would have argued that they hadn't been wrong, that those implausibilities had been the very thing that caused him to dig into the story behind the book, but he kept his tongue.

"As if implausible things don't happen in real life every day," Lukas continued. "It's ironic, isn't it? That readers will scorn a piece of fiction for something they think isn't believable but will swallow one whopper of a lie with nary a gag reflex just because it has 'true story' or 'memoir' slapped on the cover. The book always had an autobiographical slant to it, so I gave it a slight revision to punch that up, switched agents, and the next thing you know, I'm the subject of a bidding war." Lukas leaned forward, whatever he was doing on the computer forgotten. "You know, one of the editors who rejected my first book as a novel actually put in a generous bid on the second go-around. She didn't even recognize it or remember rejecting the first version. The gatekeepers are always blind."

"So you were just sticking it to the establishment?" Spence's voice started to rasp again, and Lukas held up the bottle of flavored water, letting Spence drain the rest as he answered.

"I saw an opportunity, an angle, and I took advantage of it, same as anyone else would—you included."

"I may make the news, but I don't make it up."

"I didn't do anything every other award-winning memoirist does."

"There's a big difference between embellishment and fabrication."

"Is there?"

"The whole chapter about your stint in jail? *Never happened.*" Spence sounded as if he were talking to a child. "You spent *one night* in county lock-up a few times. The scene where you were operated on by the veterinarian—complete fiction." Spence suddenly felt very tired, and though stringing words together became increasingly difficult, he kept going. "The girl your second book is about—as far as I can tell she never existed."

"It's all art. It's all true in a sense."

"If that were the case, if even a bare majority believed that, if even you believed it, I wouldn't be in this cage."

"You may have a point there."

Spence's fatigue felt palpable, like a weighted blanket, and the darkness of the garage invited him to close his eyes. His vision of Lukas illuminated by the screen light flickered in and out between the flutter of eyelashes until he succumbed. Maybe if he slept, the pain in his head would go away. He leaned his head against the cage. As he started to drift off, a question coursed through his brain.

"How did you find out?" Spence mumbled.

Lukas didn't answer. He just said, "I'll get you something to eat now."

Spence heard the scrape of the wooden crate against the floor as Lukas stood. He didn't think he could eat anything. He was entirely too tired.

"How did you . . ." But Spence was gone before he could repeat himself.

Chapter Ten

Standing outside the Tribune, Kate braced herself against the biting wind whistling its way between the downtown buildings and reread the text from her brother: *did u talk to lily?* That was how he'd responded when she told him she was leaving the paper. Though she had talked to several of Spence's colleagues, she hadn't talked to a Lily, and now her mind whirred, searching her memory banks for mentions of a Lily. The name did ring a bell, perhaps a coworker Spence mentioned in passing?

She marched back into the office and asked Marty Schultz if he knew Lily and where she might be. Curmudgeon that he was, Marty directed her without fuss to Lily's desk on the other side of the building. Kate wondered if he was being polite because he felt bad about Spence's disappearance (the whole office had to know by now) or because he felt guilty that he was glad. She knew he viewed Spence, who was young enough to be his son, as a professional rival. If he weren't so near retirement, she'd have added him to her suspect list.

A placard next to the door clearly labeled the corner office as Arts & Events. Roughly the size of Jenner's office, the space held three desks rather than one, and the desk in front held Lily Engvall's name plate. Spread across the desk was a series of photos, over which two women stood conferring. The younger woman tucked her long dark hair, impossibly straight, behind an ear and pointed at a photo of a jazz band. "Let's use this one."

"Excuse me," Kate said, as the other woman, who looked worn to the nub, moved away with the chosen photograph clutched to her chest. "Lily?"

"Yes," the young woman said brightly. When she looked up, Kate could instantly see how attractive she was. Her skin glowed with an amber undertone, hey dark eyes framed with heavy lashes behind half-moon glasses, her nose straight and slim above a full mouth spread in a dazzling, Crest-commercial smile, and she couldn't have been older than mid-twenties. Despite the temperature, she wore no tights beneath her short skirt and the sleeves of her cardigan were three-quarter. She removed her glasses (did she even need them?) and scrutinized Kate for a half-second.

"You're Katherine, right?"

"Yes, have we met?" Kate felt even more at a disadvantage because she was certain she'd never seen this woman before.

"No, no, but Spence talks about you all the time!"

"Oh."

"Not in a weird way or anything. I'm sure every reporter here wishes they had an in with the police force."

"Right." Kate tried not too bristle.

"*That* sounded awful. I'm a monster. He doesn't talk about you like you're a source. I know you guys are tight. You and Heidi and . . ."

"Danny."

"That's right, Danny. He talks about you all a lot."

Funny, thought Kate, because he's barely mentioned you at all. She wondered if there was a reason for that.

"Have you seen or talked to Spence since Wednesday night?"

Lily's face turned somber, and she hugged her arms to herself. "No. He still hasn't shown up?"

Kate shook her head.

"You know, I bet he's just chasing down leads on an investigative piece. Maybe he drove into Chicago and decided to stay for the weekend."

Kate couldn't tell if Lily was trying to convince her or herself, but her words lacked assurance.

"Speaking of," Kate said, "did he mention anything to you about the story he was currently working on? Maybe something to do with the local publishing circle?"

"Publishing?" Lily frowned into the middle distance. "I don't think so. But we do talk a lot about books and writers, so it'd be hard to say. I know he was pretty psyched about Elena Hidalgo's upcoming novel, but I don't know that there was any story there." She pursed her lips and fixed her warm brown eyes back on Kate. "He was pretty tight-lipped about the juicy pieces. He has such . . . self-restraint."

Lily looked away again, and Kate wondered if she had put Spence's self-restraint to the test. Kate spied a photo attached to the wall next to Lily's desk, an office party of some sort where everyone was leaning in toward the camera with cheesy grins. She didn't fail to notice that you couldn't have fit a ruler between Lily and Spence.

"You, um . . ." Kate started but then broke off. Get it together, Baxter. "Did he mention anything outside of work where he was having trouble? Anything he'd been upset about?"

Lily shook her head and then cocked her head at a memory. "I know he wasn't getting along with his brother, the one who moved in with him? Seemed like a lot of friction there."

He only has one brother, Kate wanted to snap. "Some other officers are looking into the family angle, but it doesn't seem likely." At least it didn't to her.

Kate wanted to ask Lily more about herself. She wanted to know more about her relationship with Spence. She wanted to know how Lily knew more about her than vice versa. And none of it really had to do with finding Spence.

She thanked Lily for her time and left her card. On the way back to her car, she tried to sort through the hodgepodge of conflicting emotions that now distracted her. Distraction that she, and Spence, could little afford.

SINCE HE'D DISSUADED Brendan from the public smear campaign, the knot in Colin's stomach had completely unclenched. But even with a new direction in place, Brendan remained impatient to plunge forward, and after they had both scarfed down their cafeteria lunches, he persuaded Colin to sneak over to the library computer lab (without a pass) rather than stay at their table or hang out in the Commons, which were the only two sanctioned after-lunch activities. All the students had school-issued tablets, but they weren't allowed in the cafeteria (too many had ended up in the trash or tray return), and Colin's and Brendan's lockers were upstairs. About sixty feet down the hall, the library was within a much more manageable sneaking distance.

"Bruh, we're going to the library," Brendan argued. "Who's going to get upset about that? It would be like yelling at us for studying."

Except they weren't going to be studying, but Colin knew there'd be little profit in arguing that point.

The lab was empty. Even if there had been a class, other students were allowed to use any open stations in the back, provided they had a pass of course. The rows of machines gave off a comforting hum underneath the constant rumble of the HVAC system. On each sleeping screen, *Keene Middle School* centered over the school crest bounced in concert like a company of dancers. Brendan chose one of the computers closest to the door, but Colin dragged him farther away.

"I don't want somebody coming in and looking over our shoulder."

"You're such a worrywart."

Colin didn't retort and instead let Brendan be the one to log onto the computer. If there was blowback, it wouldn't be coming at him. Less for Colin to worry about.

Brendan clicked on the button to create a new profile on the Social Circles website.

"Don't we need to create a fake email account first?"

"I've got like fourteen." Brendan entered an address Colin had never seen before. "I'll just use one I never check." But when he tried to progress to the next screen, a blocked message flashed up on the screen. "What gives?"

Colin pointed to the offending category in the message. "It's blocked for social media."

"Doy, but Social Circles wasn't blocked last week, just the other ones."

"I guess they figured out kids were using it on campus." Blowback, thought Colin, guessing that the system logged these blocked alerts.

Brendan growled.

"It's no big deal. We can work on it after school."

"We can find a picture now, though," Brendan countered. "We'll need a profile picture."

Colin gave up and sat down in the chair next to Brendan's. He edged closer so he could see the screen without craning his neck.

"It should look like Sissy, but not exactly like her."

Brendan had brought up the school directory. "You don't just want to use her picture?"

"No, that's not funny. Remember it should be an exaggeration." Colin brushed the fringe of brown hair out of his eyes. "Like what are the things we want to make fun of her for? Like the stuff she's proud of."

Brendan just stared at him.

"Like how she's so mature, being into older guys," Colin supplied.

"Being a cheerleader." Brendan got the picture.

"Right. What else?"

They looked at each other for a second and simultaneously said, "Boobs."

Brendan placed his fingers on the keys, but Colin's hand shot out to stop him.

"Do NOT search for 'boobs.'"

Brendan gave an exaggerated eyeroll; actually, he rolled his entire head. "Puh-lease, I'm not *that* stupid."

Colin withdrew his hand, and Brendan's fingers clattered on the keyboard as he brought up an image search of older cheerleaders. They scrolled for a few minutes, refined the query to include only blondes and exclude pro sports teams, and began scrolling again.

On page two they hit the jackpot—a busty blonde in heavy makeup and a cheerleading vest. She actually looked like Sissy, perhaps an older, more-developed, yet less-attractive sister.

"She's perfect," Brendan said, downloading the file.

"You think so?" a deep voice behind them asked. "And why is that?"

The boys turned reluctantly to see Mr. Rees, the librarian, standing behind them. He put a hand on Colin's chair and leaned over them close enough that Colin could smell the stale coffee on his breath. His ponytail fell over his shoulder to brush against Colin's neck, making his skin crawl.

"What are we looking for here, young people? 'Pictures of blonde cheerleaders.' Hmm." He hung there above them, fumigating them with caffeinated morning breath. "May I ask what school project this is for?" He finally stood up, and Colin drew in a deep breath.

Colin looked at Brendan to see if he had a good answer. He obviously did not.

"It's . . . more of a personal project," Brendan finally said.

"I bet," Mr. Rees said.

"I don't suppose you'd believe us if we said it was a social studies experiment?" Colin asked.

"No, I wouldn't." Mr. Rees then launched into a sermon on how they should all be feminists and it was important for them to respect and appreciate all women as whole individuals and not judge their physical appearance but celebrate their true beauty as women just because they were women. Somewhere in there, the bell chimed, but Mr. Rees just kept talking. Colin half expected him to pull up a PowerPoint presentation. "I think you can find a lot better use for your time than looking up pictures of cheerleaders. If you can't, I can help you find it, if you catch my drift."

He then asked for their pass, and when they couldn't produce one, he threatened them outright with detention but eventually let them go, knowing they would get a tardy in their next class. He said he'd have to think about whether their parents needed to know about "this breach of regulations and appropriateness."

As they stood to leave, Brendan quickly dragged the photo to an open email and saved it, shielding his actions from Mr. Rees with his body.

"I told you we should have waited till after school," Colin muttered as they slunk out of the library.

"Show me one place in the rules where it says you can't look up pictures of cheerleaders," Brendan said. "He's just making stuff up. That's why he didn't give us detention."

Colin hoped this scheme to cheer up Dylan worked because it was proving to be more hazardous than he first thought.

"HEY, BUDDY, how ya doing there?" Danny asked in a puppy-ish voice.

Spence pried open his eyes to see his friend, dressed in his light blue scrubs and gleaming white sneakers, squatting down beside him. Daylight shone through the garage.

"What are you doing here?"

"I came to check on you, you big dope. Nurse Danny to the rescue. You took a pretty big crack to the head, and," he continued in a mock whisper "you weren't that smart to begin with, so kinda worried about ya." Spence tried to say something, but Danny interrupted. "We all know I'm the smart one . . . and the pretty one. It's such a burden."

"But how did you know I was here?"

"You really are loopy. Where else would you be?" Danny took blue latex gloves out of his pocket and pulled them on. "You know I'll always have your back, man." He reached out toward Spence's head with both hands, and a sudden fear gripped Spence and he tried to twist away, only to topple to the concrete floor, twitching fully awake.

It was dark. The only light came from something glowing faintly down past his feet. He was alone in the garage. Danny wasn't there. Oh, how he wished Danny were there.

Of course, it was Katherine he really wanted to see breaking down the garage door, gun drawn, ponytail swinging, Potter and a bunch of other cops he didn't know at her heels. If anyone was going to rescue him, it would be her. His modern-day shield-maiden.

Shield-maiden, heh heh, get it? Because she's got the badge. He could hear what Danny would say. Danny, who took it on himself to make them all laugh with jokes either funny or bad, but who also knew when to lay off and be serious. Well, usually. As Danny had said in Spence's dream or vision or whatever it had been, you could count on Danny. All of them, Spence could count on all of them. He didn't take that for granted. He though about the situation Sanjay had gotten himself into, a place where friends were few and undependable.

Heidi tried to be as tough as Katherine, if not tougher, but she was their caretaker, making sure everyone was fed and looked after. A fellow reader, with whom he could share and discuss books. If he didn't see his friends again, Spence hoped they knew how much they meant to him. Probably not, not really. He knew Katherine wouldn't.

He struggled into a sitting position. Sharp pains still lanced through his torso. Everything else ached, his head, his shoulders, his tailbone. Not his feet or hands, he realized, because they were still numb. Tape still bound his wrists but at least his hands were in front now. Lukas had taped down far enough over his hands that he could move his thumbs only at the last joint.

The glow at the corner of the cage came from a glow stick. Why didn't Lukas just leave a light on? It was the middle of the day, wasn't it? Spence realized he didn't actually know that. He had no idea how long he'd been asleep. But in the little circle created by that glow stick he saw a sandwich on a paper plate.

Nausea or not, his stomach called an audible. *Guess, I'm hungry after all.*

He scooched over and picked up the sandwich, made with thick white bread. It was peanut butter and something sweet, not honey or any jam he recognized. The thickness of the bread and stickiness of the sandwich made it difficult for him to swallow. Each bite required several attempts. He wished Lukas had left him a bottle of water. As he made slow progress through the sandwich, it seemed not only to quiet but also to settle his stomach.

While he chewed and chewed another bite, he was struck by a craving for his mother's green chutney, a recipe handed down from his grandmother. He tried to forget about the sandwich in his mouth and taste instead that fresh tang with a sweet undercurrent and tiny kick. His mom never made it very spicey. As children, he and his siblings would eat it on just about anything, any type of chaat, slathered on roti or naan or even Wonder Bread if his mother hadn't done any baking. He chuckled, remembering when he smeared it over his mouth and chased his squealing sisters with outstretched arms and guttural noises until their mother made them go play outside.

"Why are you wasting my chutney, huh?" she said as she wiped his face vigorously with a dish towel.

"I'm not wasting it! I'm using it for zombie drool."

She was shocked or pretended to be. "My pudina chutney is not zombie drool! If that's what you think, you'll get no more."

"No!"

She made him promise not to waste any more before she relented on her threat. But when she finished the next batch, she handed him the food processor bowl still coated in grasshopper-green film.

"For the zombie," she whispered and then held a finger up to her lips with a wink.

She didn't make it as often as she used to—she didn't cook as much at all now that all the children had moved out—and he'd never made it himself. When was the last time he'd had it? When he got home, he'd ask her to make a whole quart jar just for him, to give him the recipe and he'd see if he could make it himself. When he got home. If he got home.

He tossed the rest of the sandwich back on the plate. He couldn't eat any more. It kept sticking in his throat.

Chapter Eleven

"I do not have time for this," Kate said as she stalked into the Fulton Springs police station. She'd received a 911 text, not a literal one, but the kind that meant "get your butt here or else."

Potter looked at her quizzically as she marched through the field of desks toward the lieutenant's office. Since she didn't detour past his desk, he hopped up to intercept her.

"I thought you were taking time off . . ." He lowered his voice. "To, you know."

"I am—was. LT called me down here, and it didn't sound optional. Did something big break?"

"No, I actually pulled a cold case today."

Kate growled, but by the time she reached the lieutenant's office, she'd cloaked her face in an expression she hoped read as neutral. She poked her head inside the open door.

"You wanted to see me, LT?"

Most of the detectives and officers who reported to Harvey Shin would say how easy-going he was—until he wasn't. And though he stood a couple of inches shorter than Kate and had settled into the customary thickness of middle age, he exuded a sense of control that brooked no challenge from the bigger, brawnier cops under his command, several of which Kate had seen him lay flat on a practice mat.

Shin motioned her inside. "Have a seat, Baxter."

The encounter was taking on that distinctive called-into-the-principal's-office vibe.

"Will this be quick?" she asked, thinking that maybe she could diffuse it. She sat in one of the austere padded armchairs that faced his desk. "I'm in the middle of some very serious . . . business." Shin's poker face made her falter. Principal's office indeed.

Shin looked tired, though unless he was smiling or glowering, he usually did, what with the baggage he carried under his eyes. Kate preferred tired to glowering, but she felt his expression might be leaning in that direction.

"Police business or personal business?" he asked.

Kate paused and hated herself for it. "Personal. That's why I took personal time."

"Then why am I getting complaints about you interfering in a case you're not assigned to?"

Kate bit the inside of her lip and slid forward on the navy vinyl to the edge of the chair.

"Who complained?"

Shin's expression finally changed. "You're a detective; make a deduction."

"Darshan Spence is a close friend of mine—" she said, heat rising in her voice.

"I understand that."

"I've known him since college. He's part of the reason I ended up in Fulton Springs. I can't sit by and do nothing and watch as Kirkley and Kotono do nothing—"

"Careful!" Shin said. His expression dipped from matter-of-fact to stern.

"Sir, they're focusing all their efforts on one suspect, one scenario, and it's one I can tell you is not going to pan out!" Her volume was running away from her, even as she told herself to rein it in.

"I *understand* the position you're in. I do. But Kirkley and Kotono are not amateurs, they're two of my best detectives, and they're not going to do their best work if they're looking over their shoulders for you."

"Then assign me to the case with them; I'll work with them."

Shin leaned back. "You know they do not play well with others."

Kate shifted on her chair, her jaw so tight it threatened to shatter.

"You want them to do their best work, right? For your friend."

Kate wanted to say that they weren't, that they were focusing too narrowly, that *she* had to do this. But she realized how all that would sound. Her shoulders slumped, but her voice held firm. "I can't do nothing."

"I wouldn't ask you to." Shin shifted his eyes to the desk, which was littered with papers. He picked up a coffee mug that said, *My dad can arrest your dad*, and took a sip. "Do you have any evidence they're barking up the wrong cottonwood?"

"Just an inside view, a six-year history with the family."

"Well, if you find something more substantial, you come to me, understood?"

Kate nodded, not quite sure what ground she stood on at the moment.

"I'm not saying don't look for you friend. I wouldn't if I were you. I'm saying . . ." He set his mug down on a file that already had a coffee stain on it and fixed her with a meaningful stare. "Be quiet and smart about it. Do it without flashing your badge all over town and treading on people's toes, particularly people with a lot more seniority than you. I know you think they're only focusing on the brother, but they are covering their bases, and what they're being told is 'we already talked to the cops,' meaning you. Things are slow now, so I've given them all the manpower I can spare to help search. No one is shirking here. We clear?"

"Yes, sir."

"Good, because we're not going to have this discussion again." He jerked his head toward the door. "Get back to your business."

She exited, frowning and flushed, and headed straight for Potter's desk, desperate for an unequivocally friendly face. She'd settle for Potter's impassive one.

"Are you still employed?" he asked.

"Yes, but I've been warned off being visibly attached to Spence's case."

"Meaning, don't stop, just don't get caught?"

"Pretty much."

"Could've been worse."

"Yeah," she mumbled.

"Look, I've got plenty of PTO and things are slow right now, say the word and I'll take off to help you."

"I appreciate it, but that would just draw more attention." She let out a breath. "Just keep your ears and eyes open, and if I need something, I'll let you know."

"You got it."

Kate frowned and picked up Potter's copy of *Hit Me, Baby, One More Time.*

"Why are you reading this?"

Potter shrugged. "It's interesting, current, and relevant."

"He's a jerk, and he sideswiped my car while intoxicated. I mean, yesterday. He was in here just last night."

Potter changed the subject. "What's your next move?"

"See if Robbie turned up anything helpful at Spence's place."

"Sounds like your brother came to town at just the right time."

Kate closed her eyes and pressed the fingertips of one hand to her brow. "It's not a happy visit. I can't get into it right now. I have to go."

She whirled around and crashed straight into a uniform.

"Oi, watch it, mate." The policeman wearing that uniform, no taller than Kate, hunched over a crumpled box of doughnuts showing her a ginger crewcut. He stepped back and looked up at her, revealing a young face camouflaged by a trimmed mustache. The annoyance on his face morphed into surprise. "I mean—sorry, ma'am."

"Did you—who are you?" She turned to Potter, who eyed her warily. "Who is this?"

"Taz McIver," Potter supplied. "He's a recent transfer."

"From where, Wales?"

"I'm English, not Welsh," McIver said.

"McIver, this is Detective Kate Baxter."

A smile replete with chagrin split McIver's face. "Sorry, detective."

Kate wanted to rip the mustache off his lightly freckled face. "Did you think I was a man?"

Potter hid behind his hand and went so far as to roll his chair back a few inches.

"No! I just saw your—" McIver looked back at her boots, khakis, and trench coat and then her plaid button-up but didn't let his eyes drift higher than her waist. He skipped straight to direct eye contact and tried another smile. "Can I offer you a doughnut?"

"I don't know how police roll across the Pond," Kate said, "but here, that's just cliché."

Ears aflame, she pushed past him and made her way to her car, thinking the whole way about how no one, even at a cursory glance, would mistake Lily Engvall for a man. She gripped the steering wheel and rested her forehead against it.

"I don't have time for this!"

She took a breath, said a prayer, and then opened a little box in her mind, and inside she dropped Taz McIver, Lily Engvall, Harvey Shin, Kotono and Kirkley, and her sister-in-law, Lauren. She closed the box and put Spence on top of it. She started the car.

AFTER SCHOOL, Colin got off the bus at Brendan's stop since they had decided, for secrecy's sake, that his house would be the better base of operations to continue work on the Social Circles account for Spacey Mackle-Wrath, as they had named Sissy's counterpart. At the street corner, two older boys hopped their BMXs on and off the curb, practicing various tricks.

"Did you have fun at school, little Brendan?" one of them called out.

"Yeah, did you learn valuable lessons?" the other one chimed in.

Brendan rolled his eyes at Colin and muttered, "The redhead is my dumb neighbor." He called back, "Yeah, Jayden, it was like the best day ever. I guess you missed it. They renamed the school for you. It's now called—" He ripped a loud fart. "—High School. There was an all-school assembly and everything. Smelled just like you."

Jayden fake laughed as he pedaled over. He stopped short and whipped the body of the bike all the way around, hopping over it.

"Want me to punch your face?"

"Want me to tell your mom you're a stoner?"

"Pussy."

"You need to have a chat with Mr. Rees," Colin said. Brendan snickered.

"What's that supposed to mean?" Jayden said.

"Inside joke," Brendan said. "And trust me, it's not really funny. Did you losers actually cut all day?"

"Yeah, we even got chased by a cop who tried to make us go."

"No way."

The other kid wheeled up. "For reals. He tried to grab us, but we wheeled outta there, like 'see ya.'"

The younger boys exchanged doubtful looks.

Brendan gave them a thumbs-up. "Congratulations. Keep it up, and I'm sure you'll get that job at Burger King."

"Doy, I already have a job at Burger King," Jayden said.

"Then I guess you've peaked. See ya!"

Brendan and Colin walked away as the two bikers lobbed a few heckles at their backs.

"Your neighbor's a jerk."

"He didn't use to be," Brendan said, slinging his bookbag onto the kitchen table. He went to the fridge and retrieved two cans of Mountain Dew. "We actually used to hang out and play video games."

"What happened?"

Brendan gave a Muppet-worthy shrug. "He turned fifteen, I guess?"

Colin thought about his own teenager. "Yeah, that'll do it."

"His mom's always telling my mom how worried she is about how he's 'turning out,' how he's not 'connecting' or whatever with her boyfriend. I don't blame him on the last part. Some dude rolls in after your dad's been gone six months? Plus, he's skeezy." They grabbed some chips and cookies and took their haul to Brendan's room. "Jayden may have turned into a punk, but if he ever asks if I want to skip with him, I'm gonna do it. It'd be cool, being out all day while everyone else has to be at school. Plus, he got his license last year, and his mom is totally guilt-gifting him a car for Christmas."

"Probably not as cool as you think. Especially if you were hanging out with him, car or not."

Brendan looked thoughtful as he turned his computer on. "Maybe he'll stop being a jerk someday." He crossed his fingers. "Maybe by Christmas."

Colin wondered if Brendan was right. If people changed for the worse overnight, could they suddenly change back? If not back, then at least for the better? He doubted it. Things always seemed to get more complicated, never less.

"You'd just get grounded or worse."

Brendan sighed. "With my luck, yeah."

They popped open their Mountain Dews and got to work, but as it turned out, the work ended up being a lot of fun. In one tab, they kept Sissy's profile open and in the next they had Spacey's. They would look at one part of Sissy's page and come up with a slightly twisted or exaggerated version for Spacey's. They also took inspiration from Sissy's photo galleries. Under "Likes," they listed older men, tight shirts, pompoms, and John Green novels.

"With the profile picture we picked, you better add makeup to that list," Colin said.

"We should use the same banner that Sissy has to tie the two pages together more," Brendan said.

"Yeah, yeah!"

Brendan copied some of Sissy's photos that didn't show her and reposted them on Spacey's account, changing the text to something funny or insipid. For a few, he copied the text verbatim. Sometimes Sissy could achieve comedy all by herself. Colin showed Brendan the screen capture he'd taken of

LilSis27's profile, and they added her avatar to Spacey's photo gallery.

"It sounds like a lot of fun in here," Mrs. Tyrell said from Brendan's doorway. "What are you guys laughing about so much?"

"Colin's brother is sad, so we're making a webpage to cheer him up," Brendan volunteered, a little too readily for Colin's ease, but to his relief, Mrs. Tyrell pried no further.

"That's sweet of you boys! As much as you all have been laughing, I bet it'll work. Colin, do you want to stay for dinner?"

"What? What time is it?" He looked at the computer. They'd been working on the page for nearly two hours. "I gotta go. I'm late to let Beau out." He grabbed his coat and backpack. "I'll be back after dinner," he told Brendan.

"How about, Brendan will call you when he's finished his homework instead?" Mrs. Tyrell said. She gave her son a pointed look. "Someone had two C's at midterm that need to become B's real soon."

Brendan threw his head back and made a painful death cry.

Since it was dark, Mr. Tyrell, who had just arrived home, insisted he give Colin a ride to the Thompsons' house. Thankfully, Beau hadn't made a mess, and Colin didn't mind walking him in the stiff cold breeze because he kept chuckling over the things he and Brendan had come up with. Dylan would love it.

DARSHAN SPENCE met Kate Baxter their junior year of college when they were grouped together as part of a family-unit project in a sociology class. He had no intention of depending on the group for his grade and had been pleased, if not relieved, to find Kate's work ethic and independence matched his own. Between them, they pulled the weight of the assignment. They had been cast as the children of the project and joked accordingly about their negligent parents.

Not that Spence hadn't noticed Kate previously. If the class were a chandelier, they were among the few functioning bulbs. She gave sharp and thoughtful responses in class discussion, not like the student who thought blacklisting was "a racist thing."

Well, students actually. Honestly, it'd been about a fourth of the class. Kate and Spence bonded against their classmates' ignorance as much as over their shared determination to succeed. With zero calculation, they found themselves sitting alongside each other in class on a regular basis, which quickly spread to sitting together at meals, sports games, and other social events; to introducing each other to their friends (Spence even dated Kate's roommate Polly briefly); to deep dives into their personal lives, discussions about family, their shared faith, and their professional aspirations. Then they graduated.

Spence took a job writing a newsletter and publicity materials for a nonprofit, and Kate went to the police academy. They kept in touch but less and less as time passed, until she'd texted him unexpectedly: *Looking for a fresh start. I see there are openings in Fulton Springs. Isn't that where you're from?*

In less than two months, she'd arrived in Fulton Springs with a single U-Haul. Danny, whom Spence had known for ages, latched onto her within a week of Spence's introduction, and then Kate introduced them both to Heidi, and their little tribe was complete.

When Kate moved to the area, Spence had the idea, never articulated even to himself, that they would eventually grow into a couple. The day she arrived, he'd enveloped her in a hug, and it somehow felt like coming home. Not that he thought Kate was moving there for him, but the idea of their togetherness just existed in his mind as a forgone conclusion. One that never ended up concluding. Which Spence took as evidence that intuition, however self-assured, made a lousy metric.

Now, as he shivered in the dark, he believed she would find him. He'd watched her grow from patrol officer to detective, covered her more interesting cases for the paper, not that he could explain how she'd changed because she still seemed so much the same to him, but he knew that she commanded respect from those in her profession just as he did. Still the students, proving themselves to everyone around them, to themselves. So he knew she would find him and hoped that this self-assured intuition wasn't as wrong as the other had been. Or that she didn't find him too late.

He just had to give her more time, as much time as he could.

The door swung open wide. Lukas left it yawning so that the daylight that streamed into the house's interior diffused into the garage, reducing its darkness to a dim gloom. He didn't descend the stairs, just looked down from the landing, silhouetted.

"You didn't finish your sandwich. I thought you were hungry."

"It—" Spence started, but his throat constricted, choking off the words.

Without a word, Lukas turned and left. Spence surveyed the open door, but he couldn't see much more than a partial wall with a side table against it, a glass dish resting on it filled with something dark, and a sliver of the kitchen, the refrigerator and farther back the stove, which was blocked when Lukas opened the refrigerator door. All of it blurry. As the refrigerator door swung shut, Lukas's narrow back moved out of sight.

A few minutes later, he returned with another bottle of cherry-flavored water. Spence wished he could just have tap, but it seemed like a small thing to quibble over given the circumstances. Lukas squatted down beside the pen, and once again held the bottle up, inserting the neck through the chain link to give Spence a drink.

Spence felt like an animal at an abusive petting zoo. After a long bitter draught, he reclaimed the sandwich from its paper plate and took another bite. Lukas regarded him with little expression, and though his eyes were no longer indistinguishable from a screen-reflected glare, Spence could read nothing there, whether due to the dimness or to Lukas's own blankness.

He's trying to figure it out, Spence thought. He doesn't know his next step.

He swallowed and asked the first thing that came to his mind, "What's this sandwich made of?"

"Peanut butter and date paste."

Date paste. Yes, that sounded like Eirik Boudreau, the 2.0 version, the persona Lukas was trying so hard to protect.

"Do you think this was all worth it?"

Lukas pulled the crate over and sat down. "I have more money riding on this than you'll earn in your entire lifetime."

Spence wanted to ask a question to pull more out of his captor, but instead he took another bite of the gooey sandwich. He kept his eyes on Lukas's and waited, the old trick of letting the subject fill the silence, and he knew Lukas liked the sound of his own voice.

"There's a morality clause in my contract with Roving House. Can you believe it, they still have those things? I get it's CYA in the era of cancellation, but I still find the very idea antiquated. And while my clause isn't narrow by any means, if your article ran, they could exploit that loophole to yank my book and demand back my advance. Things over there are still a tad unsteady since the . . . what euphemism shall we use, *shake-up*? Plus, *Hit Me, Baby, One More Time* is being optioned for a feature film, not some high-brow indie piece, but one that will bring in real money and of course boost sales through the roof for both books. Timothée Chalamet wants to be young me. All the cards are set up, and I can't have you knocking the house down."

Spence cleared his mouth of peanut butter. "Bull."

Lukas straightened on his seat. "What?"

"If you lost your contract with Roving House—and I'd be surprised if you did since they worked so hard to woo you from Chapman *and* they're counting on your second book being a hit probably more than you—you could still get your pick of other publishers."

"It isn't as easy as you think."

"And the controversy wouldn't chase Hollywood away. In fact, it'd probably reel them in. That's how they'd bill it, 'Based on the controversial bestseller.'"

"I'm not willing to take that risk. Don't you see? I could be set for life after this."

"And after *this*—" Spence made as much of a sweeping motion of the cage as his taped hands allowed. "—you could be doing life, so which was the greater risk?" Lukas didn't answer. "Do you really think people would care, if they found out? That readers, reviewers, and whoever else would suddenly revise their opinion of *Hit Me, Baby, One More Time* if they found out you basically made the whole thing up?"

Talking somehow was stimulating his appetite. He took a giant bite of the sandwich.

"I bet they'd revise their opinion of me," Lukas countered.

Spence shrugged with a comic eyeroll, regrettably sending lances of ache through his stiff shoulders and neck.

"You seemed to think so," Lukas said. "Otherwise, why bother to dig into my past, to write that stupid article in the first place?"

Spence laughed around a mouthful of peanut butter. "I'm not a good example of the mass populace and definitely not representative of the current zeitgeist. I believe in an objective truth, and it does matter to me. That's what drove me to investigate your story. Too many things didn't smell right. But that's counter to the current cultural narrative, isn't it?" He dropped his chin to look at Lukas over glasses he wasn't wearing. "C'mon, man. We live in a day of 'find your own truth,' 'speak your truth.' And our culture advocates for people to redefine themselves however they see fit. It doesn't matter who or what you are; what matters is how you identify yourself. And you can always change your mind. It's all fluid. So what, you wrote a bunch of things about yourself that weren't true; all you have to do is say that they *felt* true, that it better reflects how you see yourself than what literally happened. Didn't you make that argument yourself?"

Lukas leaned forward, resting his arms on his knees, the blankness in his eyes replaced with a skepticism that the dim lighting could not obscure.

"If *you* don't think people would care, why write the story in the first place?"

"Because, as I said, I believe in *a* truth, and I believed people had the right to know that you weren't honest with them." Momentarily forgetful of his pain, Spence shrugged again. "But they're the ones who get to decide what to do with that information. And even if I told them that you were a 'bad person' for misleading them, they'd still make up their own minds as to whether I was right about that."

Spence's voice had run out of oil, and the rasp returned. Unasked, Lukas held the bottle up to the cage, and Spence drained a good portion more of it.

"The book would still be the same book, so do you honestly think they would have cared that much?"

"*They* being the world at large, or *they* being the shot-callers when it comes to my fortune?"

"Aren't the latter going to make their call based on the former?" Spence pushed the last bite of sandwich into his mouth, but he felt almost too tired to chew it. He leaned his head back, mindful to not put pressure on the tender wound.

"It's possible; I suppose it's not without precedent," Lukas said, but reservation underlined his words.

"So what made kidnapping and imprisonment seem like the safer bet? Seriously, tell me."

"You're not accounting for all sides, Mr. Spence. You're ignoring other . . . facets." Lukas stood. "I think our conversation has worn you out. Perhaps you should rest."

The idea sounded at once tempting and dangerous. The interaction had left him enervated, but sleeping made him all the more vulnerable. What if he never woke?

"Yes." Spence conceded, shutting his eyes, but then for insurance, in little more than a murmur, he said, "Then I'll tell you about the book. I forgot to tell you about the book."

Lukas stopped half-way to the steps and turned abruptly back.

"What book? What are you talking about?"

But Spence was already asleep or pretending to be.

Chapter Twelve

"Do I look like a man?" When Kate returned home to find Robbie still gone, the box she had crammed all her distractions into had plenty of time to spring back open, and she pounced on him with the question as soon as he entered. He froze in the doorway, looking very much like he was considering whether it would be wise to back out and try coming in again.

"I believe it is safe to say that you, in fact, do not look like a man." He shut the door, closing off the brisk draught. "Should I ask why you're asking?"

Kate stood in the entry to the kitchen, holding a mug of coffee, which was steaming a little less than she was. "This cop at the station, new guy, mistook me for a man."

"How'd that happen?"

"He just—he just saw my outfit."

"Oh." Robbie stopped, half-pealed out of his jacket. He glanced at her clothing. "Well . . . that's a whole different question."

Even as her gaze on him turned stony, Kate didn't miss that underneath the quilted jacket he took off, he was wearing one of her sweatshirts, a gray thrift-store purchase with *Landers Wrestling* in worn block letters. Granted, it fit him trimly, whereas it wrapped her in voluminous comfort, but it seemed to prove a point all the same.

"Never mind," she mumbled and retreated into the kitchen.

Robbie followed. "I don't see how anyone would mistake you for a guy, but your clothes—like that's what I wear to Wednesday night prayer meeting. I may own that exact shirt."

"Shut up already." Kate wasn't about to admit that it was indeed a men's shirt. She liked the pattern. "Tell me what you found at Spence's."

Robbie whipped out his phone, and they sat together at the kitchen table as he walked her through his findings. He started with the most promising lead.

"The name Marion Lukas mean anything to you?"

"Absolutely nothing."

"Spence had a big note with her name on it. I thought maybe she's part of the story you said he was working on."

Kate asked for the spelling and then told Robbie to keep talking as she started a search on her personal laptop. Thankfully the name didn't have the ubiquity of a Jessica Smith or Jennifer Jones, but Kate's patience waned as she kept kept pulling up social media accounts for the same grandmother in Arkansas. The woman was on every platform possible, and though her online presence was wide-spread, Kate couldn't see any connection to anything related to the case. In fact, this woman just posted the same five photos on every site. Standing in the corner of her living room near the front door, which offered the best chance for adequate reception, Kate texted Potter, asking if he could find anything via police records.

"Maybe you should move some place with better coverage," Robbie suggested.

Kate gave her brother a tight smile as her home phone rang. "That's why I have a land line. One of the reasons."

It was Danny with none of his usual happy-go-lucky banter.

"I just saw Spence's picture on the news! *What* is going on?"

Kate closed her eyes. She'd wondered how quickly they'd go public with the search.

"I told you we were looking for him," she said, knowing full well that she'd withheld the severity of the situation.

"But you—I didn't know that he was missing-persons missing!"

"I didn't want to worry you, buddy, and you didn't seem to know anything. I was hoping he'd have turned up by now."

"What can I do?"

Nothing, she wanted to say. You can get off the phone so I can get back to looking. But she could hear the fear in his voice, how unsettled he was, had a right to be.

"Just pray. If he shows up at the hospital, let us know ASAP. If you think of anything he was working on or involved in that was out of the ordinary, call me."

Danny didn't say anything immediately. "This doesn't happen to people like Spence."

She knew he meant "people like us." She heard that a lot. In her profession, people fell rather neatly into two groups—people who lived with the imminent threat of violence, either by choice or by geography, and people accustomed to a mundane stability. For the former, danger was a latent expectancy; for the latter, a devastating surprise.

"Who was that?" Robbie asked when she hung up.

"Danny. They've released a picture and statement to the media."

On her laptop, she found the post on the *Tribune*'s website. The headline read "One of Our Own Missing," and beneath it displayed the same black-and-white headshot that could be found on the staff directory page. It had been windy the day they shot the photos, and his wavy hair had fallen forward above that serious, practically stern, face, and the photographer had insisted they leave it that way. Why didn't he smile more? He had a killer smile. He'd smiled when she asked why they shot in black and white, rather than color.

Black and white is sexy, he'd said and then grinned.

Had the photographer been a woman? Had she told him the black and white, the hair was sexy? It hadn't occurred to Kate at the time to ask. She'd just groaned and told him to get over himself.

"Do you want to look at these pictures yourself?" Robbie asked, drawing her back to the present.

"Yeah."

Robbie plugged the thumb drives he'd found into Kate's computer and started sifting through the files as she finished reviewing the photos, periodically checking her phone for an update from Potter. But the next lead arrived at the front door in the form of a diminutive high-school teacher with dark red hair.

"I couldn't sleep last night," Heidi said as she perched on the edge of Kate's couch. She let the massive leather tote bag on her shoulder slide to the hardwood floor with a clunk. Kate sat down facing her on a footstool covered in cracked leather, so close that their knees almost touched. She guessed from the lack of eye makeup and red rims that Heidi had spent a good bit of the night and perhaps day crying. "But I remembered something. Then I thought it was stupid, and then I thought, what if it *is* relevant?"

"Heidi, out with it please."

"You know how you told me not to take that proofreading job at Roving House?"

"Because those people are crazy."

"I took it anyway; it's just a few hours a week—"

Kate shook her head. Besides teaching, Heidi also coached athletics and led a Bible study at her school. "You needed something else to keep you busy?"

"I want to branch out. Anyway, a while back I told Spence I was working on *My Gal Leona*, and he asked if I could get him an ARC or if he could see the files I was working on."

"ARC?"

"Advance reader copy. He said it was related to an article he was working on." Heidi rubbed the palms of her hands against her plaid wool skirt. "I said yes at first because I was happy to help and, because Spence said it was a hush-hush thing, it felt kind of exciting, but then I started feeling guilty because it's not really my place to release those files. Then Spence had the idea that he would hand off the manuscript to the book reviewer at the *Tribune*, if I got permission to give a manuscript to the newspaper. I told my boss someone from the *Tribune* had asked for a copy, and he said it was fine as long as they held the review until close to the release date. So I gave it to Spence."

The title sounded vaguely familiar to Kate, but she didn't know why. What little she knew of the current literary scene came osmotically from Spence and Heidi. She preferred the prose of the long deceased.

"Should I know that book?"

"It's Eirik Boudreau's new memoir," Heidi answered. "It's releasing right before Thanksgiving, and by that, I mean in time for Black Friday."

Kate turned to Robbie, who loitered in the archway between the living room and kitchen. "The sticky note with the name, what book was it on?"

Robbie grimaced. "I'm not sure." He grabbed his phone from the table and scrolled through the photos until he found it, only to see that the size and placement of the note blocked out most of the text. Kate stared at him, and he scrunched his face in concentration. "I think it was something about Britney Spears."

"Spence reading a book about Britney Spears?" Kate swiveled back to Heidi, whose face mirrored her own incredulity. She looked back at Robbie as if to say, Try again.

"Here look at it." He handed the phone to his sister. "I think the cover had lines on it, like coke lines but in rainbow colors."

"*Hit Me, Baby, One More Time*?" Heidi blurted.

"That's it!"

"That's Boudreau's first book," Heidi said, which Kate already knew. She'd looked at Potter's copy just earlier that day.

"Does Boudreau talk about anyone named Marion Lukas, in either book?"

"Not in the second book." Heidi entwined her fingers in the fringe of her scarf. "I don't recall that name from the first one either, but he talks about a lot of people, and of course, like a lot of memoirists, he doesn't use the real names for all of them."

"That's all right." Kate felt an uptick in her heart rate. "It's something for us to look into." She just hoped it wasn't a false lead, that she wasn't connecting dots that weren't part of the same picture.

KATE WASN'T EXACTLY a Luddite, but she was what Potter termed "technology-resistant." He didn't know if that was why she frequently passed the online aspects of their investigating to him, but he didn't mind at all and secretly enjoyed when she would exclaim when he unearthed a well-buried lead from the miry clay of cyberspace. He also knew she currently could use all the support he could give her in finding Spence. Thus, he felt a pang of regret when her text buzzed in asking if he'd found something.

Got called out on a shooting. Just getting back into the station now. I'll have something for you soon.

The shooting had been a gang-related incident landing one shooter in the morgue and the other in the hospital, and while tragic, the damage was done and the paperwork could wait. Potter hung his heavy canvas overcoat on the back of his chair and pulled up his computer with a surreptitious look at Kirkley's and Kotono's desks. Neither detective was present. He dived into his search, but before too much time had passed, Kate called him.

"Marion Lukas—have you run across the name in Boudreau's book?"

Potter looked at the volume lying on his desk.

"No, but of course, I'm not finished yet either. Why, you think he or she is connected to Boudreau somehow?"

"He?"

"Marion can be a male name. John Wayne's birthname was Marion."

"Robbie found the name on a note attached to a copy of Boudreau's book, and a few weeks ago Spence asked Heidi for a peak at the upcoming book, so I'm hoping the connection isn't coincidental."

"I can't speak to the one that hasn't been released . . ." As he spoke, Potter's fingers rattled over the keyboard as he searched for a link between the elusive Lukas and the title of Boudreau's memoir. "But I'm not getting any hits connecting that name with the first book. Of course, that could not be the name used in the book, the whole point of writing it down."

"We thought that too."

"It's a good direction to look though," Potter said, putting as much encouragement into his voice as he could. He scanned the results of the police database. "I'm not finding any Marion Lukas in the Fulton Springs–Chicago area, definitely not one with any priors."

"Nothing?" Kate's voice carried both disbelief and disappointment.

"Don't worry. I'll keep at it. I'll find something."

After he hung up, Potter leaned back from his computer to regroup his thoughts, but the sight of Kirkley and Kotono walking Sanjay Spence back to an interview room disrupted him. If they were taking another run at Sanjay, they probably hadn't turned up anything new or at least nothing new that didn't point them in the direction they'd been heading since the investigation started. He picked up his phone to text Kate but thought better of it. This update would only distract her.

He picked up his copy of *Hit Me, Baby, One More Time*. A mountainscape in psychedelic colors stretched across the top of the back cover. The memoir chronicled the misadventures of Boudreau's late adolescence and early adulthood in Wyoming and his escape to California, long before he landed in Fulton Springs. Potter set the book down and tapped a key to bring his computer back to life.

"Go west, young man," he muttered as he redirected his search.

WHEN SPENCE SHIVERED awake, a new sandwich and a fresh bottle of water waited for him in the corner of the cage next to the defunct glow stick. Lukas also waited, seated on a dining chair with his arms crossed.

"You're finally awake."

The garage lights burned too brightly. Spence tried to blink away the bleariness in his eyes so he could discern Lukas's expression but then decided it wasn't worth the effort. Surely, his captor hadn't waited there the entire time, although perhaps he had since he'd bothered to procure a more comfortable seat. Spence coveted the chair's padding.

He inhaled heavily, trying to dispel the grogginess that sat heavily on his mind, and received a sharp pain in his ribs for his effort. The air felt colder again, so the sun must have gone down. How long ago?

Lukas interrupted his thoughts. "You mentioned a book I needed to know about." Spence didn't reply. "What were you talking about?"

"Book?" Spence stalled. His voice came out thick with sleep. "I thought we were talking about . . . we were talking about . . ." He couldn't remember. He suddenly feared the blow to his head had done more damage than he'd thought.

Lukas scooted his chair closer to the pen, scraping its back legs against the concrete in a way that pierced Spence's head. Lukas pressed his hands against the chain link, his face just a few inches from it. Spence could feel his breath, warm and sticky in the cold air.

"You said I needed to know about a book."

"I'm tired. I can't think."

Lukas curled his fingers into the fencing and shook it. "Wake up and tell me about the book!"

The rattle and vibration of the chain link did jar Spence further awake but also exacerbated the aching in his head. A full-body lethargy had blanketed him, and in spite of it, he continued to shiver.

"I need a blanket or a coat."

"Tell me about the book, and I'll get you a blanket."

Spence remembered. "We were talking about why you were so scared of the truth coming out."

"The book!"

Spence flinched. "Definitely more awake now." He found the fervor in Lukas's eyes unsettling. "I had a copy of your first book on my desk at home. Did you see it?"

"No, I didn't stay any longer than I had to."

Spence wanted to whisper a hallelujah, but he settled for closing his eyes and resting his head against the cage. "You probably want to go back and get it," he said.

"Why would I want to do that?" Lukas asked, his voice tight with skepticism. Spence wondered how long he could spin this conversation out before it resulted in bodily harm.

"It's annotated. It's full of notes, and anyone with half a brain will figure out they point straight to you. Your real name is even plastered right there on the front."

"My real name is Boudreau."

"Your old name then."

Lukas stood. "If this is some kind of a ploy . . ."

"What? You'll lock me in a cage like an animal?" Lukas didn't respond. "I think thus far, between the two of us, we've found my track record with the truth to be more reliable."

Motionless, Lukas stared down at him.

"You don't have to believe me. It's your funeral. I mean, your call."

"I'll be right back." Lukas moved toward the door.

"What about that blanket?"

Lukas put his hand on the light switch. "You'll get it when I get back with this alleged book of notes." He plunged the garage into darkness and shut the door, blocking out any sliver of illumination from the house. A few seconds later, the music started up again, the same mind-numbing album but at a lower volume. Obviously, he didn't want to risk the police coming back.

Spence leaned against the cage and reflected on how the truth and a ploy didn't have to be mutually exclusive. If the police, if Katherine, hadn't already found the book, maybe sending Lukas back for it would send him right into their path.

Chapter Thirteen

The gloom of late afternoon descended as the Baxters drove across town to Spence's house. Heidi had apprehensively suggested she come with them, but Kate sent her home with the promise to call if they needed more information. She had a feeling Heidi didn't want to see the crime scene, regardless of how well it had been scrubbed. As they sat at a red light, Kate rapidly tapped an index finger against the steering wheel while Robbie scrounged around in the center console.

"Can I help you find something?" she finally asked as the light changed.

"I'm looking for a tissue."

"Good luck with that."

Robbie gave a vigorous sniff and held up a neon green plastic lighter. "I found another lighter. This is like the fourth one." He tossed it back into the compartment and flipped the lid closed.

"Keep looking; they come in packs of seven."

"If I were a detective, I might suspect you were a smoker."

Kate could feel her brother's eyes on her. "Used to be," she said.

Robbie looked out the windshield. "When did that start?"

Kate sighed. While she didn't relish having this conversation, the confession promised a release both from the secret she'd kept from her family and from the worry over Spence's disappearance. "Not long after I joined the force."

"Seriously? This whole time?"

"Not exactly, off and on, mostly on. I quit a few months ago. You may find lighters but trust me you won't find cigarettes." She clicked her tongue. "Though I kinda regret that decision at the moment."

"That stuff'll kill you, sis. Remember Great-Uncle Linton, how he'd hack all over the place and he had to cart around that oxygen—"

"I know, yes, trust me. I got the health spiel from Danny repeatedly, a man who still eats Fruit Loops for breakfast every morning."

"So who else didn't you tell? Were you a closet smoker?"

"I didn't exactly advertise it, if that's what you mean. I don't think Heidi ever knew; otherwise, I'm sure I would have gotten a lecture from her as well."

"Mom and Dad?"

"Are you kidding? I've gotten enough grief from them about being on the force without dragging smoking into it."

"And those two things are related?"

The after-work traffic had become a parking lot, giving Kate plenty of time to consider the question. "For me at any rate, I guess. Do you remember that first shoot-out I was in, the domestic in Cloverton?"

"I remember you making me swear not to tell Mom and Dad about it."

"Afterward, I mean like right after, I could not stop shaking. My FTO pulled me aside, gave me a cigarette, and said, 'Try this.' I coughed my lungs up, but between that and the nicotine, it distracted me enough to calm me down. And so many of the cops there smoked; that's how you got to know anybody. They'd all stand in one corner of the parking lot smoking. And there you go."

"I can understand that," Robbie said. "At my station, it was the gym. A big group would always go right after our shift, and that's where I got to know them." He studied the road ahead or seemed to. "Do you drink?"

"No. One potentially addictive behavior seemed enough. Plus, I've been to enough police barbecues to know I want to steer clear of that."

"I do."

Kate gripped the wheel a little tighter. "How much?"

"Not much." He saw her the set of her lips. "*At all.* I am *not* one of those guys at your barbecues."

She'd been so immediately angry with Lauren, and for the first time, Kate considered the possibility that her sister-in-law might have some valid grievance.

"Tell me, Robbie—be honest with me—does alcohol have anything to do with Lauren kicking you out?"

"No, no it's nothing like that."

"Because, so help me, if you're—"

"Katie, do not get wound up about this. It's not related. Sheesh, I was just sharing, trying to have a moment. It wasn't a confession."

"It kinda felt like a confession."

"Well, it wasn't. It's just a couple beers every now and then, mostly social. Our church has a more balanced view on the subject than Mom and Dad's."

"Do they know?"

"No!"

"Yeah," Kate said. "I can't see that going over well, particularly with Mom."

"With her dad, you can't exactly blame her." He found something out the side window to look at. "Does it occur to you that we're both in our thirties and still keeping secrets from our parents?"

"I'm only thirty. And I think we just don't want to disappoint them—or worry them—more than necessary."

"Blessed are the peacemakers?"

"Something like that," Kate said. She pulled up outside Spence's place and shut off the car. "Does Lauren drink?"

Robbie shook his head. "Says she doesn't like the taste."

"Does she mind that you do?"

"No," Robbie said, but then a questioning look passed over his face. "I mean, we haven't talked about it in years."

Kate shrugged. "Maybe it's irrelevant, but you've got to take stock, Robbie. Little things can add up, and if you don't know why Lauren's doing this, you need to dig."

"I know, I hear you."

He let his head fall back against the headrest, a beat-up expression on his face.

"I'm sorry," Kate said. She laid her hand on his forearm and gave it a squeeze. "I'm good with the tough love but not always on when to implement it."

"Like I don't know that." Robbie leaned over and kissed the side of her head, but she thought she spied a distance in his eyes. "Let's go get that book and find your friend."

No one answered when Kate knocked. She tried again, calling out Sanjay's name. The door to the neighboring unit opened, and Calvin Johnson emerged, pulling a fisherman cardigan tight around him.

"The other detectives haven't brought him back yet."

"That's okay. I have a key." Kate held it up as proof. "I just didn't want to barge in on anyone. When did the other detectives come by?"

"Midafternoon. My wife was napping, so I heard them. It was the detective that was with you the other night and a younger white man. Is he coming back, the brother?"

"I'm sure they just had some follow-up questions for him," Robbie said as Kate opened the door. "He should be back soon."

"Will it be safe?"

Looking at the spot where Spence had fallen, where they'd found the blood, broken glass, and wine, Kate answered, "Mr. Johnson, the only safety any of us has in this life is in the hands of God." She turned toward Spence's neighbor. "You don't need to worry about Sanjay Spence; you have nothing to fear from him."

Whether it was because of her words or the weariness in her voice, Mr. Johnson nodded and moved silently back indoors.

"There goes the neighborhood," Robbie said under his breath.

He went straight to Spence's desk, flipped over a book, and then started sifting through a stack of papers.

"Where was the book?" Kate asked. She tried to ignore the office-party photo, a duplicate of the one at Lily Engvall's desk.

She had to have seen it before, right? How had she never noticed how close they stood together?

"It was here." Robbie stopped searching. "Like *right here.*"

The beat of Kate's heart quickened, but she forced herself not to jump to any conclusions.

"Maybe Sanjay picked it up. I'll check his room; you check in here, the kitchen."

"He was out back earlier today. I'll look there too."

When she pushed Sanjay's door open, a strong wave of musky staleness swept out. Kate waved a hand in front of her face.

"Crack a window, man," she muttered.

The room resembled a teenager's, clothes strewn on the floor and chairs, posters of swimsuit models on the wall, stacks of video-game and movie cases clustered around the television and gaming console that sat atop the largest dresser. The size of the TV was what implied this room didn't belong to a teen. It dominated the small room, blocking out the mirror mounted on the back of the dresser. Kate didn't see one book, or anything that could be read for that matter, amidst the clutter. She picked up an enormous hoodie crumpled on the chair to see if anything lay beneath it. Moving the sweatshirt released a sharp marijuana odor. Kate waved it away and dropped the hoodie.

Like several surfaces of the room, the bedside table held several empty beer bottles, Red Bull and Pepsi cans, and food wrappers. Kate checked the drawer but found only some loose change, a bag of weed wrappers, a vape cartridge, and an unopened package of condoms. Kate shook her head and shut the drawer.

Robbie appeared in the doorway behind her. "Wow, this and Spence's room are night and day." He cleared this throat. "It smells like dude in here."

"Baked dude. I can only imagine how high the tension was running between the two. Spence got to the point where he said he just didn't want to talk about it."

"Spence strikes me as a pretty straight-and-narrow guy."

"Yup."

"You changing your mind about Sanjay's involvement?"

"No." Kate nudged a dirty sneaker away from her with her foot. "I don't like him for this at all. Did you find the book?"

"Nada. I didn't see it in the kitchen or out back either, and everything in Spence's room is just like I left it." Robbie pursed his lips and glanced back toward Spence's bedroom.

"What?"

"As soon as I said that, I realized it's not true. I left the closet closed, but it's open now."

"Can you tell if anything is missing?"

Robbie grimaced. Kate followed as he retraced his steps to Spence's bedroom and squared himself in front of the open closet.

"Yes," he said slowly. He slid several of the hangers on the curtain rod, distributing them evenly. "I can't tell what, but it looks less full than before. Everything was spaced out last time; nothing was bunched up like this." He surveyed the dresser top. "None of the jewelry from the dresser is missing though."

Kate followed his eyes. She reached out to touch the large gold ring, which had belonged to Spence's grandfather. She seldom saw her friend without it.

"What are you thinking?" Robbie asked.

Kate ran both of her hands into her hair, pulling a good deal of it loose from her ponytail.

"I'm thinking we lost a solid clue, and I'm thinking either Spence or his abductor has been back here—" Her eyes darted back to the ring. "—most likely it was not Spence. But whoever it was, we missed him."

COLIN DEBATED whether to mention the surprise he and Brendan had to Dylan, not tell him outright of course, but to give a hint. They weren't quite finished with the page, but they were so close that he wanted to pique Dylan's interest, let him know something was coming. The secret burned in his pocket.

He still suspected that his parents, and adults in general, wouldn't receive their fake social account well. He didn't know exactly why he felt this way. It just seemed like whenever you did something fun—something "outside the box" as Mr. Martin called it—adults had a reason why you shouldn't be doing it. So he wasn't about to bring it up in front of his parents, and the table had already been set for dinner by the time he'd walked home from the Thompsons'.

Dylan wolfed down his food and dished up a second round of everything but vegetables while their parents talked about work—somebody had gotten laid off, some deadlines had been extended—and equally boring topics of conversation.

"How was your day, Colin?" Mom asked, catching him off guard.

"What?"

"Did anything interesting happen at school?"

Was this entrapment? Had Mr. Rees squealed on them after all? Would his parents care that they were looking up pictures of cheerleaders? And how could he explain it without giving away the surprise to Dylan or without getting in more trouble if they weren't supposed to be building fake social profiles anyway?

"It was fine," he said.

Mom turned her attention to Dylan, and Colin gratefully took a bite of his dinner roll.

"How about you, Dylan?"

"Fine," Dylan mumbled around a mouth of mashed potatoes.

"All I get is *fine*'s" Mom said to Dad.

"At least we don't have to pay this kind."

"That's for sure." Mom frowned at Dylan as he rolled his eyes and polished off a second helping of chicken. "The way these *fine*'s stack up, we'd be in debt before you could count to three."

When Dylan was done eating, he excused himself to rummage in the refrigerator.

"Did you pick up my protein shakes?"

"They're in the pantry," Mom answered. "They were pretty expensive." When Dylan started digging in the pantry, she called out, "You just finished eating your dinner, not that you chewed any of it. You're going to give yourself a stomachache. You don't need one of those right now."

"I'll drink it later." Dylan emerged with one in his hand, and Colin could see another stuffed in the pocket of his sweatpants. "I need them to bulk up."

Their parents exchanged a look over the decimated platter of chicken.

"They haven't even been refrigerated yet. Why don't you put them in and sit back down and have dessert with us?" Mom said. "I made brownies with chocolate chips, and your dad picked up some ice cream on the way home."

"Mint chocolate chip," Dad said.

"No, thanks. I'm good." And he was off to his room.

"Skipping dessert?" Dad said with raised eyebrows.

Mom pressed both hands against her stomach and sighed. "Maybe we should all be skipping dessert."

Dad looked at Colin. "You haven't gone crazy too, have you?"

With his mouth full, Colin shook his head. He wanted to get back to Brendan's, but he had plenty of time for brownies first.

THE GARAGE LIGHTS had been blinding, but as soon as Lukas extinguished them, Spence wished them back. The momentary reprieve now made the darkness deeper, and the longer Spence sat wrapped in its oppressive embrace, the more suffocating it became. He even longed for the paltry light of the glow stick. He cleared his sore throat repeatedly and tried to regulate his breathing, which had gradually taken on a short, spastic rhythm. Rather than wishing to prolong Lukas's absence, Spence found himself hoping the other man would hurry back.

Well, that's counterproductive, the rational part of his mind pointed out.

He thought of the sandwich at the end of the cage. Eating didn't appeal to him, but if nothing else, it might serve as a distraction. And there was the water as well. He scooted the length of the pen a few inches at a time, reaching out with his heels and, when pulling himself forward didn't work, wriggling toward his feet. He wished he'd obtained the provisions before the lights went out and hoped his filthy stockinged feet didn't land squarely on the sandwich or overturn the bottle.

He paused at the thought and adjusted his approach, keeping his feet on the floor and sliding them forward. The logistics mercifully pervaded his mind, banishing more troubling thoughts. Five more wriggles and his toes finally bumped against the plate. Then began the trickier part, pivoting and scooting in sideways so he could get his hands close enough to grab the food. After that maneuver, he needed a rest. He held the sandwich in his taped hands without taking a bite and reflected that despite the exertion, his breathing was more regular, less panicked. Although realizing that gave the panic ingress to return. Before he could completely dispel the calm, he took a giant bite of the sandwich. Best not to think about it.

It was another peanut butter and date paste sandwich, and though he hadn't thought himself hungry, as he chewed through that first mouthful of gooey sweetness, his appetite awakened with a vengeance. He gobbled the rest of the sandwich, nearly choking on its thick bread and mortar-like filling. He couldn't force the last bite down without more food to push it through. He groped for the water bottle. He removed the lid, already unscrewed, with his teeth and spat out the cap. He drained half the bottle in one gulp.

It reminded him of doing yard work, not at his house, but at Katherine's. He barely had any yard to speak off, and his neighbor, Mr. Johnson, always cut the front grass for both of them. While not big, Katherine's property held its fair share of trees, and he and Danny had offered during the summer to help clear out the fallen brush and weedwack through the overgrowth. In truth, it was a scroungy looking place on a dubious street. It had been in Spence's mind that seeing some men around the house might serve as a deterrent to unwanted attention, although he told himself such feelings were unnecessary since she was more prepared to defend herself than he was. Recent events had surely born that out. But still.

The project had stretched over three Saturdays, and even working in the mornings, the heat would drench them within an hour of starting. The three of them would break in the shade, draining bottles of water and Gatorade in a single go and making more enjoyable plans for the evening. Danny, riffing about the heat in his humorous way, would peel out of his sodden T-shirt and fling it over a low branch to dry. Spence was tempted to do the same, but self-consciousness and modesty kept him from doing so in front of Katherine. She wouldn't have minded, but she might have cracked a joke, which would've bothered him more than it should've. Somehow it seemed normal for Danny but not for him.

They would work a few hours and then collapse on the porch, too tired and flushed to eat anything, even though Katherine would offer. Danny would mop his face with his now-dry T-shirt. Katherine's clavicle shined above her tank top, and her legs, stretched out on the porch steps, glistened from the damp hem of her shorts to her hiking boots. She would say that she could even see the fire under Spence's dark complexion. In the humidity, his hair, soaked with perspiration, curled dramatically. Once, she removed her work glove and reached over to tug on a curl that had fallen over his forehead. She paraphrased the children's rhyme,

"There was a little boy,
Who had a little curl,
Right in the middle of his forehead."
Spence wrinkled his nose at her and finished the poem:
"And when he was good,
He was very, very good,
But when he was bad, he was horrid."
"Well, I think you're both horrid," Danny interjected.

But the gesture and the interplay had felt so natural, so comfortable.

Spence shivered. What he wouldn't give to feel that summer heat right now. He'd never complain about heat again. And to feel the comforting touch of a friend. He felt so cold and then suddenly drenched with sweat. His teeth chattered. A fever, no doubt. He always felt chilled when he had one, never warm. More's the pity, because he could really use some warmth right now.

He downed the other half of the water, whose bitter cherry flavor almost tasted normal now. How hoity-toity did you have to be to give your captive flavored water?

He tried to wrap his arms around his legs for warmth, but the way Lukas had taped him up made that impossible. He tried rubbing his forearms against his legs, but it didn't help and only alarmed him more as it showed how apparent his shaking was. He tried to sit very still, but that only served to amplify his shivers. As he fixated on them, the darkness began drawing close again.

He let out a lengthy exhalation, holding his mouth wide enough so that his teeth wouldn't chatter. He prayed again silently. Out of habit, he closed his eyes, and the darkness was gone. Well, not gone, but different. To be alone in the dark with God is quite different from being alone in the dark. Of course, he prayed for safety, but he asked more for calmness and clarity.

His breath came evenly now despite his trembling lips, and he felt something akin to peace wash over the panic, sweep it out in the ebb. Then another wave came, this one fatigue. In his depleted state, his little exertions, physical or otherwise, kept exhausting him. Then he realized that wasn't true, not completely.

Stupid, he told himself. The sweet sandwiches, the bitter water. All drugged.

And then he was gone again.

Chapter Fourteen

Kate knew the danger of jumping to conclusions. Sure, if you happened to jump to the right one, you saved a lot of time, but you could just as easily and far more likely jump over a key piece of evidence, over an alternative theory, over the very thing that would point you to the truth. And while she believed it was an abductor who had returned to Spence's house, she had one other possibility to rule out, and thankfully she knew right where to do it.

As she exited her car, Robbie didn't move, nor did he look at her when he said, "I'm gonna stay out here for a bit. Try calling Lauren again."

Kate wished him well and waded back into the Fulton Springs police station, unsure of what tactic she would employ to gain access to Sanjay Spence. She didn't have the energy to be creative and figured assessing the circumstances beforehand would yield a clearer strategy anyway.

To her surprise, Potter sat at his desk, peering at his computer.

"I thought you'd be gone by now."

He puffed out his cheeks with a gusty exhalation. "It was easier to stay than to go home and then have to log into everything from there."

Kate realized he was still researching on Spence's disappearance, and when she locked eyes with him, she felt the *click* that occurred between them when their very different minds synced and knew that he had caught her realization.

"You don't think I'd leave you hanging, do you?"

"Thank you," she mouthed, unable to give the words the slightest volume. She cleared her throat and pressed the heel of her hand to her forehead. "Happen to know what's going on with Sanjay?"

"They've been sweating him for a couple of hours now. They're in interview room B. I heard they executed a search of the warehouse that he was working at but didn't turn anything up."

"How'd they get a warrant for that?"

"Didn't have to. They were super cooperative apparently."

Kate told Potter what they had and hadn't found at Spence's house. She pulled a few fingerprint cards in plastic bags from the pocket of her trench coat and handed them to him.

"Can you get these over to the lab and have them run against the elimination prints?"

"Will do."

Robbie entered the office, dissatisfaction plastered across his face. He shook his head at Kate. She took his phone and showed Potter the picture of the missing book.

"Sounds as if we may be looking in the right direction then."

Kate leaned against the edge of his desk. "I need to check with Sanjay, and I am just too tired to think of a clever way to do that."

"The Kate Baxter I know is a big fan of the direct way."

"Yeah, well, that Kate Baxter doesn't want to put her job in jeopardy by further ticking off two prima donnas." Kate thought for a minute, weighing the trouble she could land in against how it would let her push forward in her own investigation. Then she recalled Shin's admonition. She growled and clenched her fists and stalked toward the lieutenant's office.

"When she was a girl, she used to do that exact thing before socking one of the neighbor kids," Robbie told Potter.

"Let's hope she doesn't sock anybody this time."

Stewing in her own frustration, Kate ignored them. She couldn't abide the hamstringing of political bureaucracy, the petty hoop-jumping. And the lieutenant's office was, of course, empty.

"Call Shin," she ordered her phone. He was the one who'd asked to have his evening disturbed.

When he answered, Kate quickly outlined what they'd found at Spence's house and what she needed to know. To his credit, Shin took as little of her time as possible before clearing her to go to Kirkley and Kotono directly.

Outside the interview room, she took a moment to tamp down her irritation. The monitor showed the two detectives seated across from Sanjay, who was almost the size of the other two men put together. He appeared crammed into the small room, like the Incredible Hulk in a Volkswagen Beetle. Kate buzzed and waited until Kirkley answered her call.

"Baxter, what do you want? We're trying to find your friend."

"I know and I appreciate that," Kate said. "I think I may have some info that could be helpful, but I—or you—would need to verify it with Sanjay in there."

Kirkley's princely features remained attentive yet reserved. His poker face could give Potter's a run for its money. "Such as?"

"I ran over to Spence's place to pick up a book, and it was gone." Before she could continue, Kirkley let his eyes fall in disregard. "*And* there are clothes missing from his bedroom as well, clothes that were there before."

"You think he came back?"

"It's possible," she said, "but I think it was more likely someone else. There's a piece of family jewelry that's still there. Spence wears it almost all the time."

"Maybe he's doing something messy and he doesn't want to lose it."

"Maybe."

"Okay." Kirkley nodded his head toward the door.

When she entered the interview room, Kotono shot a dark, questioning look to his partner but said nothing. Several empty water cups sat on the table in front of Sanjay, whose eyes lost their glassy sheen when he saw her enter. Perspiration showed through the underarms of his hooded sweatshirt, and the room, which was never particularly fresh, was taking on a locker-room funk.

Kate bypassed the pleasantries, figuring the more time she took, the more annoyed Kotono would become. She walked up to the end of the table and held out her phone so that both he and Sanjay could see the photo Robbie had taken.

"This book was on your brother's desk earlier today. Did you move it somewhere else, do anything with it?"

"No." Sanjay sounded bewildered. "I haven't messed with any of his stuff since he went missing. I mean, I wouldn't normally anyway." He leaned forward and read the note in the photo. "But your brother asked me about that one. He wanted to know if I knew who Marion was."

"Have you remembered anything about Marion?"

"No, Darsh never mentioned her to me."

"And you're sure you didn't go into his room this afternoon and move anything in his closet, take some clothes out?"

Sanjay looked to Kotono as if he might get help from him to make sense of these questions. "No," he told Kate. "We're not exactly the same size, yo."

"That's what I thought. I just needed to check."

"Does that mean—was somebody else in the house?"

Kotono held up a hand in case Kate was tempted to answer, and then he motioned her and Kirkley out of the room, leaving Sanjay further in the dark than before. After the door shut, Kotono leaned against it, hands behind his back, and waited with an insistent look to be briefed on why they had interrupted his interrogation. Kate made her pathway to the discovery sound as non-investigative as possible. Kotono didn't buy it.

"And why were you looking for this book?"

"A mutual friend came over to my place when she remembered something about an article Spence was working on, something to do with this book or its author."

"Why are you just telling us now?"

"Because I had to get LT's approval just to talk to you," Kate said. "You may recall you weren't interested in alternative theories earlier."

An awkward silence settled on the hall.

"Big little brother could be lying," Kirkley said.

Kate's fingers waggled by her side as she fought the urge to clench a fist and thump it against his head. She wished Potter were handling this; he had the patience of Job. "If he took Spence's clothes and the book, why?"

Kirkley swallowed before he answered. "To make it seem like his brother is still alive."

Kate's reserve broke, but probably not in the way Kirkley expected. She shook her head and looked at the sound-dampening ceiling tiles. "You are giving him way too much credit. It's an excellent plot, but that ain't a movie Sanjay Spence is going to star in, if you get my meaning."

"No sign of forced entry?" Kirkley asked.

Kate shook her head. "But the spare key is still missing as well as Spence's."

"Did you check for prints?" Kotono asked.

"We dusted the closet doors and the dresser, but we only got a few usable prints. Potter's sending them to the lab right now."

The other two detectives studied each other, and Kate wondered if they shared a mental shorthand similar to hers and Potter's.

"We got the lab report from the first time around," Kotono said. "The blood at the scene was a match for Darshan Spence."

Kate had expected that, assumed that, and yet hearing it stated definitively caused an aching fear to course through her.

"Look," she said. "You can double down on Sanjay if you want, or you can explore other options. It's your investigation. I've told you what I found."

As she turned away, Kotono spoke. "Have you found this Marion Lukas?"

"No, nothing so far."

"And what book was the Post-It attached to?"

"*Hit Me, Baby, One More Time* by Eirik Boudreau."

Kirkley pulled a face.

"You've met him?"

"No, but . . ." Kirkley's eyes danced to his partner.

"What?" Kate asked Kotono.

"He's a personal friend of the chief's. Apparently, Mrs. Chief is a big fan, and Boudreau runs in those circles. Have you spoken to him yet, asked him about this Marion Lukas?"

"No, not yet. We weren't sure if there even was a connection between the note and the book—still aren't. But it would make sense."

"Are your kid gloves clean?"

"Almost never. You know he was just brought in on a DUI? If he's not feeling cooperative, maybe we could leverage that."

Another exchange of looks passed between Kirkley and Kotono.

"What?" Kate demanded.

"He walked on that," Kirkley said. "The chief came down to the station himself."

Kate couldn't keep her mouth from falling open as she absorbed the blow. "It was *my* car he sideswiped."

"We heard." Kotono pushed himself away from the door. "Might be best if we ask Mr. Boudreau about this Lukas individual. Some treading lightly will be called for."

"I'm not going to argue with that." Kate simmered even as she tried to turn her own heat down. "I know how warm and cuddly you are."

"Security footage in that residential district is going to be sparse, but we can see if there is any," Kirkley said. "Compare this afternoon to the night Mr. Spence disappeared."

"You know it's possible that he's the one who came back to the house and grabbed the clothes," Kotono said, weighing Kate's reaction to his words. "Just because it was his blood on the floor doesn't mean he didn't leave the house on his own."

She shrugged. "I suppose." She moved away from the pair but turned back after a few steps. "Will you let me know what you learn?"

Kotono nodded.

As she walked back to the main CID office, McIver stepped out of the break room into her path. He opened his mouth to speak.

"Not now!" She held up a warning finger as she blew past. She had inner turmoil aplenty to deal with, and she could do without dredging up their earlier run-in.

At Potter's desk, Robbie leaned over her partner's shoulder, both of them looking at the computer screen with mirrored expressions of concentration.

"Please tell me those scowls are a good sign and that you're not looking for Waldo."

"I think I have indeed found something—someone," Potter said. "And it's most definitely not Waldo."

COLIN GOT THE all clear from Brendan earlier than expected. Apparently when motivated, Brendan could make quick work of his studies, and Spacey Mackel-Wrath oddly enough provided sufficient motivation. The two boys figured with a half-hour head start they could have the page ready to show Dylan.

Colin eased his brother's door open and poked his head in. Dylan had returned to push-ups, decline this time with his feet propped up on the bed. In quick rhythm, the elbows of his stick-like arms jutted out, sharp enough to stab someone, and then retracted. Like someone flicking an elbow switchblade open and close.

"I'm going over to Brendan's. You should come hang out later. You know, like when you're done, in a half hour or so."

"I don't want to go to Brendan's," Dylan said between pants.

"C'mon. It'll be fun."

"I don't want to have fun."

Right, because who wants to have fun? Colin thought. He debated whether he should press. If by some machination he did get Dylan over to Brendan's, cheering him up would be all the harder if he was annoyed at being there.

"You've got the whole weekend to be moody and stay in your room, but whatever, man. Your loss."

Colin didn't linger to see how Dylan took his words or if he even did. He guessed that doing so would undercut his feigned nonchalance. Besides, he could always unveil the webpage later;

it didn't have to be tonight. But he really wanted it to be tonight. He chuckled to himself.

After promising to use his bike light, promising to stay out of the road and on the sidewalk, and promising not to stop and talk to anyone, especially anyone he didn't know, Colin finally broke free from the house, though his mom had still seemed dubious about him riding over by himself.

"I ride over there *all the time*, Mom."

"I know, but it's dark out. Can't Dylan go with you?"

"He might come later." Colin hoped that was true.

"If he doesn't, call and Dad will come pick you up." One more promise.

Colin whizzed through the darkened neighborhood, the clickety spin of his wheels a steady hum. He liked the cold air and how the street lamps and traffic lights shone in the darkness like precursors to the Christmas lights that would be going up in a few short weeks, a reminder that the holiday season was just around the corner.

When he arrived at the Tyrells', Brendan flung the door open, practically beaming, the red rubber bands on his braces on full display. "We have friends!"

"Yeah, I know . . ."

"Excuse me, Spacey has friends."

"What are you talking about?"

Brendan skipped backward down the hall toward his room, waving at Colin to follow him.

"I thought the page would look realer if she had Connections." Brendan ran his finger down the side of his Social Circles account that listed his known acquaintances. "You know, comments on her posts and stuff."

"That makes sense."

"I started to create another fake account, but then I was like *that's* gonna be too much time and work, so I thought I'll just connect with her from my account—and you could do the same—and we could leave some funny comments on her posts. So I connected both of our accounts—"

"How did you do my account?"

"You check your account over here all the time. The computer saves the password."

"*That's* good to know."

Brendan threw his head back and groaned. "I'm not gonna do anything on your account, you lame-o. You're getting distracted. I only connected the two of us, but I thought more would be better, so then I did Jayden because I knew he'd probably accept anybody, and within a half hour . . . ta-da."

He toggled to Spacey's account. She already had seventy-seven Connections.

"She's more popular than you and she's not even real!" Brendan let out a peal of laughter.

Colin punched him in the side, but that did nothing to quell the laughter, and despite the verbal jab, Colin couldn't help smiling himself.

"That's crazy." An idea popped into his head. "Do you think we could make her more popular than Sissy?"

Brendan's face became all circles, and they both started laughing again.

"YOU HAVE NOTHING to worry about." Lukas's voice, though muted, dragged Spence into consciousness. Whether he was shivering when he woke or he began shortly afterward, he didn't have the presence of mind to judge; he just absorbed the state of sweaty, cold misery. He forced his eyes open to see the door to the house hanging ajar, and through that interstice he glimpsed Lukas pacing. He let his eyes slide closed again while trying to focus on the words. "I told you I'm taking care of everything. He's not going to be a problem—cause a problem. Everything's fine."

Lukas's voice carried out into the garage thanks to the absence of the dreaded looped music, but a fog had settled over Spence's mind, forcing him to concentrate in order to grasp the conversation as one-sided as it was for him. The end of the call, though nondescript, took on a vaguely tender tone.

When Spence opened his eyes again, Lukas stood before him, a narrow, rectangular bottle in one hand and in the other, a familiar book with a bright yellow sticky note on the front. The door now gaped, letting in a swathe of artificial light that mitigated the garage's darkness to a partial gloom.

"You're awake."

"Who were you talking to?" Spence croaked.

"It sounds like you could use a drink."

Lukas held the bottle up to the cage. His eyes still bleary, Spence couldn't make out the label.

"I don't want a drink."

"Take a drink," Lukas insisted.

Spence drank from the bottle, a sharp amber liquid that burned its way down into his stomach. But Lukas tilted the bottle too far and Spence aspirated and coughed, spraying the alcohol across the bottle and Lukas's hand. Lukas grimaced and switched the bottle to his other hand. He shook the liquid from his free hand, its droplets raining down on the concrete in a splatter.

"Water would be better," Spence said.

"I know you don't believe me, but it really wouldn't."

"Who was on the phone?" When Lukas didn't reply, Spence pressed forward, fighting to order his thoughts. "Someone who knows what you did? Someone who helped you?"

"You weren't lying about the book." Lukas laid the volume on the top of the cage. Through the wire, Spence could make out his abductor's name in his own writing on the sticky note. "It's… all in there all right. Just chock full."

Spence didn't like the undercurrent of Lukas's distracted tone.

"That shows you can trust me, right? I've given you all the information you asked for, more even. You wouldn't have known about the book." Spence knew better than to angle for release, but he did need to switch the tracks on Lukas's train of thought. "So how about you tell me something. Like how you found out about my article in the first place. Was it whoever was on the phone?"

Lukas nodded, but his eyes remained distant, chewing some other (and Spence feared, dangerous) idea.

"Almost no one knew I was writing it. Was it someone from out West—Wyoming? California? Or someone from New York?"

Lukas's features twisted in disdain. "Please. Like I would talk to any of those people ever again. Well, New York, yes, but out West?" He made a flatulent noise with his mouth. "I buried all that—and them—long ago."

"Then who?"

"Let's just say that one of your friends is actually more *my* friend than yours. Intimately so." Lukas winked at him, a smug smile squatting amidst his goatee. "The ladies love the fame, man. Especially the young ones."

Whether it was the drugs, the injuries, or the discomfort, Spence could not reconcile what Lukas was hinting at. He'd told no one, not that he would consider a friend, explicitly what he'd been working on. And any peripheral references would require a leap. He hadn't even told his editor; the only person at the paper he'd even discussed Boudreau with . . .

The bewilderment on Spence's face must have fallen away as the realization hit because Lukas leaned in.

"Stings, doesn't it?" He held up the plastic bottle of alcohol. "Looks like you could use another drink."

Spence turned his head away, unwilling to show Lukas any more of his hurt.

Chapter Fifteen

Before Potter could say more about his discovery, Sanjay shuffled up to the desk, his heavy hands curled up into softball-sized fists in the pockets of his blue hoodie, pulling the sweatshirt down tight against his stomach.

"Did you say something to get them to let me go?" he asked Kate.

"Not exactly, but I think I opened their eyes to some possible alternatives. Have you remembered anything more about that night that could give you an alibi?"

"Not really, but there's no way I would've gone home in the middle of a night out. That'd be a total buzz kill."

He brought one fist out from its pocket holding a vape pen, which he lifted it to his mouth.

"Nope, not in here." Kate pushed his hand back down. "Go home now, and if you think of anything that will help your case, write it down, and if you think of anything that might help us find your brother, call me. Right away."

"So those other guys still think I had something to do with Darshan disappearing?" Sanjay asked in disbelief.

"They haven't found anything to rule you out yet." Kate hated to say it, and she hated the crestfallen look her words precipitated. She lowered her voice. "You should really look into getting a lawyer."

Sanjay's eyes flicked to her face, but the blind, glassy expression she'd seen when she entered the interview room had returned.

"Go home, Sanjay."

She waited until he was out of earshot before turning to Potter. "What did you find?"

"Marion Lukas, or at least *a* Marion Lukas that might theoretically be connected to Boudreau or the events in his book. How's that for tenuous?" Robbie moved out of the way, pushing back the worn chair next to Potter's desk so that he could see the detective's screen, and Kate took his place hovering behind Potter, arms folded tight against her chest, as he explained. "I couldn't find anything promising locally or even in state, so I started digging in Wyoming."

"Why Wyoming?"

"That's where Boudreau grew up. I didn't find any hits in the counties he talks about living in, but I did find a police record for a Marion Lukas, male, in a neighboring county. The arrests were over twenty years ago, so the timeline matches up to when Boudreau would have lived in the state. They could have known each other."

"Are you sure?" Robbie asked, looking at the map on Potter's computer. "Their counties are huge."

"What were the arrests for?" Kate asked.

"There are only a few and they're pretty minor," Potter admitted. "Mostly alcohol- or drug-related. In fact, most of the charges were even dropped. There's a juvenile record. I'm still digging around a bit."

"Digging around what?" Kirkley had glided up to the desk, his gray suit somehow still unrumpled despite the evening hour. He hadn't even loosened the knot in his striped wine-colored tie.

"Potter found a record for a Marion Lukas close to where Boudreau lived out West," Kate said.

"That may be a hole you want to stop digging in. We just spoke with Mr. Boudreau on the phone, and he said the name means nothing to him."

"He could be lying," Kate said.

"Or just because he doesn't know Lukas doesn't mean Lukas doesn't know him," Potter said.

"Entirely possible. Maybe he knows Lukas is bad news and wants to distance himself. We asked if he 'remembers' anything, that he contact us, but—" Kirkley locked eyes with Kate.

"You're going to want to be very careful about pursuing this, especially without something more substantial to go on. Sam and I have some officers pulling roadway security footage near Mr. Spence's neighborhood."

Kate thanked him, though his warning rankled her.

"What's the deal with Boudreau?" Robbie asked after Kirkley left. "He a no-fly zone or something?"

"Ironically, since he has a record," Kate said. "He's the guy who sideswiped me earlier, and he was out of here in a hot minute."

"If we're not going to get information from Boudreau, then maybe our best bet is locating Lukas and leveraging one against the other," Potter said.

Kate knew that whatever Spence had unearthed, it had taken him weeks of legwork and research, time they did not have. She could only hope that the signposts he'd left behind would speed them along the path. If it wasn't too late already. She banished that thought as soon as it set its insidious foot in the doorway of her mind.

"Where's a picture of Lukas?"

"There isn't one in the file."

"Really?"

Potter shrugged.

Kate leaned over his shoulder and peered at the file, hoping something would jump off the screen, waving helpful arms in her direction. It didn't, but she did spy the number for the town jail where Lukas had spent a night here and there.

"You keep looking. I'll call the police department."

Kate punched the number into her phone and wandered into a quiet corner of the office. The hour was late enough that the station traffic had started to pick up with the it's-five-o'clock-somewhere round of weekend celebrants.

"Larsen Police Department," answered a receptionist with a pinched voice. Kate identified herself and her credentials and asked to speak with the ranking officer. "That'd be the chief, but he's just gone home for the evening. I was on the way out myself. Can I have him call you tomorrow?"

"No, I'm afraid it's urgent. I'm working a missing-person case, and we believe it might be related to someone who has a record in your county, a Marion Lukas."

"Really." The woman sounded surprised.

A surge of hope quickened Kate's heartbeat. "Yes. Are you familiar with Lukas?"

"Oh, no, nothing like that. It's just we got another request for information about him not too long ago. A reporter from . . ." Kate heard shuffling on the other end of the line. "The *Fulton Springs Tribune*. I'm guessing this is connected?"

"I am certainly hoping so. What did you send him?"

"Pretty much everything that's under public record. I remember there were some sealed files."

Kate obtained a promise that the chief would return her call as soon as possible and hung up. She tilted her head back, eyes closed, and took a long deep breath and held it in. The air nearly whistled as she blew it out in an even longer exhalation. She swung around to see Potter relentlessly ploughing through cyberspace, but her brother was gone.

"Where's Robbie?"

"He stepped outside for some fresh air." Potter nudged his mouse with his middle fingers, the smallest of frowns marking his chin. "Does your brother know Spence well?"

"Not really. I mean, they've met several times, but Robbie wasn't in school with us or anything like that. Why?"

"I don't mean to pry, but is there something else wrong? He seems to be having a pretty difficult time of it."

A pang of guilt resounded in Kate's chest. For a minute she'd forgotten, caught in the current of possible leads and the newfound détente with Kirkley and Kotono.

"Yeah, there is. My sister-in-law wants a divorce, or at least she says she does."

Potter pursed his lips. "That's always tough."

"Always tough," Kate echoed. She wanted to explain but wasn't sure she could. "I know you don't believe in God—"

"Well . . . technically, I'm *agnostic*."

"Imagine if you did," Kate said.

Potter nodded.

"As Christians, when we marry, we make our vows, not only to each other, but also to God. It's a covenant, something sacred. It symbolizes the relationship between Christ and the church. Or at least it's supposed to. So breaking those vows, breaking that covenant . . ."

"Has greater import than simply ending a relationship. I can respect that. I'm sorry." Kate could see the wheels turnings and knew he wasn't done. "But surely, given what you've seen on the job if nothing else, you recognize that sometimes divorce is the better option, even necessary."

Kate sighed. "Yes, I recognize that, and that's what happens when one person puts themselves first, before their spouse."

"I can't really argue with that," Potter said, "but sometimes people just change—"

"Listen, we can discuss this as fully as you'd like—once we find Spence. I can't really afford a lengthy theological discussion right now."

"Gotcha." Potter pressed his lips together. He glanced at his computer but looked back to her with his trademark earnestness. "I am sorry, for your brother. Even when it's mutual or amicable, divorce can be, for lack of a better word, traumatic."

"Thanks. You found anything?"

"Not anything that connects this Lukas to Boudreau, outside of the general geography. In fact, I'm not finding anything on Boudreau in this area, but according to his memoire, he should have a record."

"Have you checked neighboring counties?"

"I'm combing through the whole state to be safe."

"Do you think Boudreau is a pen name?"

Potter stopped tapping on the keyboard of his laptop. "It could be . . . I suppose."

Kate knew what he was thinking. "It doesn't really fit him though. He's not one to hide his light under a bushel."

The two detectives locked eyes, and Kate felt the *click*, that moment when their thoughts synced.

Potter was the one who voiced it. "Unless he was hiding from something or someone."

His fingers flew across the keyboard, and in an instant the focused expression on his face fell to a frown.

"Driver's license is issued in his name. It was a good thought though."

"Yeah," Kate murmured. "Just the wrong one."

IT TOOK COLIN and Brendan less time than estimated to put the finishing touches on Spacey's Social Circles account, but even after the full half hour elapsed, Dylan still hadn't shown. Not that the boys minded, because they had embarked on the new quest of making Spacey more popular (or at least more "connected") than her real-world counterpart. The more Connection requests they sent, the more they got in return. Colin insisted, however, that they be strategic about whom they connected with.

"We don't want Dylan to find it—her—until we've had a chance to show him ourselves, you know?"

"Yeah, I get it," Brendan said as he rejected a request from someone on Dylan's soccer team. Avoiding direct or even secondary links to Dylan's account proved difficult, and at times, Brendan balked at Colin's safeguards. "We're gonna show him like anytime now, right? We don't have to be *that* careful." He jabbed a key with his index finger.

Colin didn't respond, but he also did not relent. They'd put in too much work to ruin the surprise. Besides, each new Connection they did make brought a cascade of multiple invites from unwitting members of that user's social circle so it wasn't as if their Connection well was running dry. They were still fifty shy of their goal when Brendan started snickering.

"What's so funny?"

Brendan clamped his tongue between his smiling lips before answering. "I got an idea."

With a short flurry of typing, he brought up Mr. Rees's account on the screen.

"No!" A laugh lurked behind Colin's objection.

"C'mon! Five bucks says he doesn't even remember the picture." When Colin didn't answer, Brendan pressed. "Remember, he doesn't even see women physically, whatever that means."

Colin couldn't hold back his laughter anymore. "Do it."

Brendan hit the invite key.

"What are you losers laughing about?"

The boys turned to see Dylan standing in the doorway, his lanky torso buried in a bulky jacket over a hooded sweatshirt, his cheeks and nose flushed grapefruit red from the November night.

"I thought you weren't going to come," Colin challenged.

Dylan shrugged with one shoulder. "Better than listening to Mom and Dad complain about the governor again."

Brendan nudged Colin with his forearm. "Do you think he's ready?"

Colin cloaked his excitement and good humor with a stoic expression. "He might be."

"Ready for what?"

"We want to introduce you to someone."

Brendan quickly maximized Spacey's account on the screen and hopped up from the chair. The younger boys stepped back from the computer at the same time. Colin fought the urge to make a flourish toward the monitor because that would probably be dorky. Dylan's eyes flicked back and forth between the two of them, distrust furrowing his brow, but he eventually made his way to the desk and sat down. He glanced at the screen and then back at Colin.

"What's going on?"

Colin gave a clownish shrug. "We found this girl. Thought she'd be perfect for you."

Dylan stared at him in consternation and then looked back at the screen.

"Who is this?" he asked almost immediately.

Colin caught the intake of breath as Brendan opened his mouth, and he gave his friend a surreptitious shake of the head. Against his nature, Brendan acquiesced, and the two waited for Dylan to piece things together himself. Once he actually gave the screen more than a fleeting look, it didn't take terribly long, but it was still a process.

He scrolled with a frown.

"Wait a minute . . ."

Colin swayed side to side, his hands balling up the ends of his T-shirt sleeves.

"This isn't . . . is this . . . ?"

Dylan clicked to another section of Spacey's account. Brendan practically vibrated.

"Did you guys—"

Dylan snorted. Colin couldn't tell whether the snort was amused or derisive, but Dylan scrolled again. Colin slowly angled himself for a better view and could see, even from the side, that a half smile had wedged itself onto that dour face. Then came a barely suppressed chuckle.

"Ha!" The smile turned full fledge as Dylan gave himself over to a hearty laugh, his head tilted back. The other two boys, fairly bursting by now, joined in, which made Dylan laugh again, a joyous contagion.

Dylan leaned forward and the three huddled around the computer, delving into the wealth of inside jokes afforded by Spacey Mackle-Wrath's social media account. After exhausting the humorous landscape, Dylan leaned back in the chair and swiveled toward his brother.

"You guys did all this?"

Colin nodded vigorously. A swelling had filled his chest, and he thought that if it didn't dissipate soon, he might explode.

"Wow, that's some funny stuff. Pretty cool." Dylan scratched at the peach fuzz on his upper lip thoughtfully. He kept his eyes on the screen. "Thanks."

Colin had thought his chest couldn't hurt anymore. He was wrong. He looked over Dylan's head at Brendan, whose goofy grin mirrored his own.

A notification chimed on the computer.

"Somebody wants to talk to us," Brendan said in a funny voice, his eyebrows raised. He reached over and tapped a key.

Hey, girl. How you doing?

All three boys stared at the screen, speechless.

DISAPPOINTMENT IS LIKE a tidal wave, strange in its wake. It rushes in, ravaging, and its residual ache makes a person believe that sleep is now an impossibility, but as the force of its impact diminishes, it dulls the soul, dissipating energy and leading to that very thing—sleep, not rest, but sleep. Spence didn't recall drifting off, and coming to confused him all the more.

The first sensation was heat, so foreign after the garage's perpetual cold. He perspired heavily but not from fever or at least not from fever alone. Next, he registered simultaneously a tinny hum and a growing stink. He grimaced at the fetid mélange of old urine, sour wine, and a body and clothing in want of washing, all awakened and amplified in the new warmth, overpowering the nose blindness he had arrived at earlier. Turning his head brought the all-too-familiar sensations of stiffness and pain, but it also allowed him to see the source of the heat and hum: a small electric heater that squatted between the cage and his car. It bathed the area in a lurid orange light.

Spence closed his eyes and tried to breathe through his mouth. A stitch between his shoulder blades that had plagued him between his bouts of sleep flared up. When he flexed his back to ease it, he felt his hands move, move away from each other. He stared down at them, resting in his lap. The duct tape that circled his wrists and came up over his thumbs still clung to his sleeves and hands, but it had been sliced through. He figured he must be dreaming. A fever dream, that's why it was so warm. His ankles, like his hands, had been hastily freed.

Still not quite believing what he saw, Spence slowly moved his limbs, unfolding himself in gloriously painful movements from where he huddled in the corner of the pen. Each new expansion of his range elicited either a grunt or hissing intake of breath, and yet the aching felt perversely delicious as he stretched, relieving the tension on the muscles that had borne the brunt of being bound. When he'd extended his legs in a wide V, he pushed against the floor, which felt merely cool now against his palms, and arched his back, but instead of the same conflicting sensations, a sharp pain coursed through his torso. He gasped, put a protective arm around his ribs, and sat as straight as he could.

In the far corner of the cage sat a large dark cylinder. Before he could puzzle out what lay piled next to it, the overhead bulbs blazed on, overtaking the shadowy orange light. Lukas stood at the top of the steps, his hand still pressed against the switch. The two regarded each other from across the garage, but Spence couldn't discern what lay behind Lukas's stare. His captor broke off, casting his eyes down, as he descended to the garage floor. Grimacing, he drew back before he reached the cage.

"You stink worse now."

"It's hot," Spence said. "I appreciate the heat, but could you turn it down a bit?"

"Well, you're about to get naked, so you may want me to hold off on that request." Lukas pointed to the corner of the cage. The cylinder was a large bucket, and next to it sat a pile of clothing and towels topped with a fresh bar of soap. "As I said, you stink. When I went back to your house for the book, I grabbed some fresh clothes for you."

Spence didn't know how to interpret this gesture. He studied Lukas, who kept his eyes on the cage's new furnishings.

"There's something to eat after you've cleaned up."

In the corner across from the bucket, a paper plate held a new sandwich and several minibar-sized plastic bottles of alcohol. He wondered what Danny would say about mixing alcohol and concussions. He couldn't imagine it was advisable.

"Can I get some water instead?"

"Drink those first. They'll help with any pain you still have." Lukas shuffled back a step. "I'll give you some privacy."

"Thanks."

"I'm not an animal." Lukas met Spence's gaze momentarily, a fierceness in his eyes challenging Spence to disagree.

Chapter Sixteen

While Kate waited for the police chief in Wyoming to return her call, she went in search of her brother. Some fresh air sounded like a good idea at any rate, not quite as good as a Marlboro perhaps but with less guilt afterward. But she didn't make it outside because she found Robbie standing in the lobby, staring at a bulletin board. He didn't turn toward her when she approached. The paper he was studying so diligently listed the current job openings at the station.

"It's quite the drive to Centerfield," she said.

Robbie didn't answer. She slipped her hand into his arm and rested her cheek on his shoulder. She let her eyes rest on the green ridged background of the bulletin board exposed between the open positions and a coat-drive flyer. She didn't need to read the list to know that he could easily slip into several of those roles. She could feel the ground beneath giving way, crumbling a little bit at a time, but she didn't know what to say or do so she prayed again—for wisdom, for Robbie and Lauren, for Spence, for the investigation—a kitchen-sink prayer for the many things that pressed down upon her spirit. When she finished, she still had no words, so she stood silently, wondering if her brother had memorized the details of every opening or whether like her, he wasn't really seeing anything. When she gave his arm a squeeze and lifted her head, he finally spoke.

"I've left her at least five messages today, and that doesn't include the times I've called without leaving one. She won't answer. She won't call back."

"Maybe she needs some space. That's part of why you came here, right?"

"Yeah," Robbie said hesitantly. "I just need to talk to the girls, you know? I didn't get a chance to say goodbye before I left, and I don't want them to think . . . I have no idea what she's telling them."

"Maybe you should go home."

"Home," he echoed. "You think we still have a home, a chance at a home?" He shook his head. "I don't know anymore."

"You won't if you don't fight for it," Kate said. "Take whatever time you need before you make any decisions. I'm not kicking you out."

Her phone rang, and she grabbed at it. As she answered, she motioned to Robbie that she was stepping outside, and he waved her on.

"Hi, detective, this is Chief Clay Teton of the Larsen Police Department. I understand you're trying to track down Marion Lukas, just like that journalist was trying to do." His voice was deep and flat, its rhythm methodical.

"Yes, Darshan Spence is missing, and I'm trying to figure out if his disappearance is connected to his research on Lukas. Is there any more you can tell me than what's in your database?"

"Not much, I'm afraid. I've only been chief here for five years. Don't let the voice fool you; as I told your writer-friend, I'm a good bit younger than your Mr. Lukas so I never knew him. I can tell you he's been out of the area for a long time. Seems like he left shortly after his last arrest."

"There was no picture in the file."

Teton sighed. "That doesn't surprise me much. You'd think twenty years ago things would have been a bit more orderly, but Former Chief Wharton, my predecessor, struggled to move beyond the Andy Griffith approach. I don't mean to speak ill. Back in his day, the department had only three staff, and we've added only one more since then, and that's just so the officers don't have to take all the phone calls. It's been quite the job dragging us into the new millennium, let alone the current decade. A lot of records from that period are less than complete for one reason or another."

"I suppose the former chief is long gone by now?"

"Oh, not exactly. He's living out his retirement in a pretty smart cabin on Harper's Ridge. I drive out to check on him once a month, more if he hasn't been into town recently. He may be able to tell you more about this Lukas fellow. He's older than the trees but about as sharp as they come at that age. Got more sense than one of my patrolmen. Let me get you his number."

Kate hurried to her sedan and rummaged up something to write with and on before Teton read off the number.

"I really appreciate this," she said.

"I hope you find your man. If I can help in any other way, you give me a call."

Kate checked the time and dialed the former chief's number, hoping it wasn't too late.

THE SOCIAL CIRCLES chat feature identified the sender as J-Tank16.

"Do you know a J-Tank16?" Colin asked Brendan.

"No. At least not that I know of." Brendan nudged Dylan's shoulder. "Answer him."

Hey back.

The three boys chortled and waited to see if the mysterious writer would respond.

What do you do for fun? I saw your avatar. You into gaming?

Heck yeah! I'm a total gamer girl.

Fresh waves of laughter swept the room, and the boys launched into a fifteen-minute chat about which video games Spacey thought were best and the other hobbies she enjoyed. Dylan typed away as Colin and Brendan gave suggestions amid giggles and snorts, a false trinity of teen female psyche. They found the whole enterprise hilarious.

So you went to Keene Prep too?

"Yeah, I put the school on there," Brendan said.

Well, I go there, Dylan answered. *Just transferred.*

J-Tank16 didn't respond. The boys exchanged glances. A misgiving started to sprout in Colin's stomach.

"Huh," Brendan said. "Do you think—"

The dancing dots appeared next to J-Tank16's name.

How old are you?

"How old is she?" Dylan asked.

"Say sixteen," Brendan whispered.

Dylan tapped out the numbers.

No way you're 16! You're way too hot for that. 🙂

Right? Seriously, you are totes sweet. Brendan made a barfing sound. *But for reals, I'll be 17 next month. Everybody says I look and act way older.*

They waited again before the dancing dots reappeared.

If you're really into older guys, we should meet up.

"Whoa." Dylan pushed back from the keyboard.

The three of them stared at the screen, listening to the whistling sound of the last bit of humor being sucked from the room like the cabin pressure in a crashing plane.

AS AWKWARD, ELONGATED, and even painful as the caged sponge bath proved, Spence felt a sense of order, of balance, as well as physical relief at shedding his filthy clothes and cleaning himself. What a state he'd been in that being clean should feel like a luxury, a gift. Lukas had been correct about the heater, and Spence was grateful for the warmth that blasted from its glowing coils. The water, probably hot when run, had gone tepid while he slept, and its temperature combined with the chilly air would have made the experience far less charitable had it not been for the heater. Discomfort that Spence told himself he could have dealt with easily enough under normal circumstances but a discomfort he was thankful to forego given the many others he already dealt with. He wished he could wash his hair, even thought about taking the bar of soap to it, but as his fingers gingerly probed the wound on the back of his head, the thought of raking through the dried blood caked against his scalp with a chemical substance easily dissuaded him.

Dressing afterward came no less awkwardly and felt even more surreal. While Spence recognized the garments as his own, they had been chosen by someone else. He wouldn't have put together this combination himself, surely not for the comfort of caged life as the chinos and thin dress shirt had been plucked from his work wardrobe. He felt as if Lukas were dressing him, perhaps even more so than if the clothes had not been his own. But Lukas had forgotten little—just his glasses (he wondered if they'd survived the attack) and a belt, which those pants would require under normal circumstance. Spence even spied a pair of polished wingtips sitting outside the cage, shoes that he wore only with a suit.

One other thing was missing, his grandfather's ring. Lukas hadn't observed Spence that carefully to know to grab that. Apart from activities like yardwork at Kate's or helping his dad with some home improvement, Spence always wore it when he left the house. From a distance, it looked like a gold nugget clasped to his finger. A close inspection of the ring's large face showed an ornate elephant's head with the trunk curved back under the Hindi word for family, परिवार. The ring was solid, and he felt the absence of its weight when he didn't wear it.

"This ring will come to you when I die," his grandfather said in an accent much stronger than Spence's mother's, the words coming out from underneath his brilliant mustache, a steely white mark in the middle of his brown face. Spence had been ten years old. The visit had seemed momentous since it was the last time his grandparents would come from India. In truth, Spence and his siblings would see them far more often because they were moving to the States the next year.

"Do not let your Uncle Rajesh take it." His grandfather waved a sturdy finger at him. "I have told him it is to come to you." He took Spence's hand and held it up. "It belonged to my father and his father before him, and next it will belong to you. One day you will be big enough to wear it. Hopefully before it's time for you to do so, eh?" He gave the smaller hand a little shake and winked at Spence, who would be seventeen before he slipped that ring on for the first time, winding thread around the back of the band to keep it in place.

"Why does Nana want me to have his ring instead of Uncle Rajesh?" Spence asked after his grandparents had left. His mother sat at the dining room table, folding the freshly

laundered cloth napkins that she would stow in the drawer beneath the glass hutch filled with good china. She smoothed out a wrinkle, leaving her hands at the fabric's scalloped edge, her mouth pursed in a tiny frown.

"Your grandfather loves you very much, and it's an important inheritance he's giving you, a legacy. Did he tell you what the symbols on the ring mean?"

"Parivaar," Spence pronounced the word slowly. "Family."

His mother nodded. "Yes. I think Nana wants you to have the ring because he believes you will remember how important family is. Your uncle . . . he has other priorities. For him, family is not so important, not as important as maybe it should be." She reached out across the table. "Do you understand?"

He had. He did.

If he never made it home, at least the ring would be with, stay with family. It should go to Sanjay, he thought, though with his hands, he'd be lucky to fit it on a pinky. On second thought, Spence couldn't imagine Sanjay would grasp its significance, its value any more than Uncle Rajesh would have. Would it end up in a pawn shop or sold on eBay the next time Sanjay was in between jobs? He hoped not. Maybe Spence's disappearance and the inheritance of the ring would serve as a wake-up call to his little brother. Spence hoped. Out of ashes.

Lukas stepped into the garage and eyed Spence carefully. Spence returned the favor, wondering what he'd been up to. He had a bottle in either hand, one looked like the flavored water and the other looked like alcohol as far as Spence could tell without his glasses.

"Do you feel better now?"

"Some, yes. Thank you."

Lukas sank heavily onto the dining chair. He dialed the heat back, silencing the hum, and then propped his feet up against the crate. Every movement he made seemed to cost him great energy.

"You haven't eaten anything."

"I'm not hungry." Spence couldn't tell whether his fever had abated, but he felt nauseated.

"You should eat. And drink. I brought you a bottle of water." Before Spence could respond, Lukas added, "For when you've finished the shots."

"That's a lot," Spence said with a nod to the bottles. "And my stomach's uneasy. I wouldn't want to vomit on the clean clothes. I'm guessing you only picked up one set."

Lukas pointed. "You've got a bucket now."

"Did you build this pen?" A sidestep.

"I'm not really a builder. The previous owner had dogs."

How flattering.

"What happens now?"

Lukas frowned, still looking at the food in the corner.

"A drinking game," he finally said. "You said you didn't drink alcohol, so I'm guessing you've never played any drinking games."

"It would stand to reason."

"We'll keep it simple then; most don't get too complex anyway."

"Also would stand to reason."

"You ask a question, then take a drink. Then I'll answer."

Spence motioned to the bottle in Lukas's hand. "Did you bring your own set of questions?"

Lukas tutted at him and pointed at the row of tiny bottles. "That's a question."

Spence stiffly collected the bottles and the sandwich and scooted back into the corner that was regrettably beginning to feel like home. He wanted to keep as much space between himself and the stink coming from the filthy clothes piled next to the bucket.

He looked at the assortment of nips, mostly whiskey and vodka. "You keep these from your last airplane ride?"

"That's another question."

Crap, he was bad at this. He cut himself some slack for the head injury. He also thought about refusing. What would Lukas do, come in the cage to force him? It seemed unlikely since that would give him a chance to escape. Although in his current condition, he doubted whether he could fight past the wiry little man. Maybe adrenalin would do it. Maybe he would experience a preternatural surge of adrenalin, although the way he currently felt, he couldn't imagine it.

The cage rattled as Lukas tapped the top of it twice. "Time to drink up."

"Those weren't real questions. I don't think we should count them."

"Rules are rules. And you strike me as a man who values… or maybe *honors* rules." Lukas became smug in his evaluation. "Do I have that right?"

Spence gave him a mirthless smile. "That's a question."

"Touché."

Lukas unscrewed the cap of his bottle and held it aloft. Spence did likewise with one of his. A dark and insincere toast. While Lukas swigged from his own bottle, Spence took the tiniest sip he could, but Lukas was neither distracted nor fooled. He frowned at Spence's bottle.

"You can do better than that."

Spence took another small draught and grimaced as the trickle of whiskey snaked a tiny burning trail down his raw throat.

"Wow." Lukas shook his head. "You really are a booze virgin." He held up two fingers. "You owe me another."

Another sip. Spence shook the remaining liquid in the bottle. At this rate, he could eke three drinks out of a bottle.

"Yes," he said. "As you astutely gathered, I tend to follow the rules. If the rules aren't working, the answer is to change them, not break them. Rules help us delineate between right and wrong—"

Lukas threw his head back and groaned.

"Morality aside, they provide society with order—"

"Maybe you need to learn to embrace chaos."

"I'm pretty sure I'm on the receiving end of chaos right now, so you'll forgive me if I fail to romanticize it."

Lukas jutted out his jaw. With a click, the heater hummed again as its coils began to glow.

"No," Lukas said. "The minis are not from my last flight. They were part of a gift basket from my editor."

"Nathanael Carver?" Spence asked in disbelief.

"No, the new one, and that's another question."

Disgusted with himself, Spence finished the bottle and set it down. It seemed like such a small amount of liquid, but his stomach already rumbled and his head buzzed slightly, reawakening rather than dulling its ache.

"I'd advise you to eat some of that sandwich. It'll slow down the effect. You're not a small guy, but clearly, you're not used to this."

Begrudgingly, Spence grabbed the sandwich and stuffed a bite into his mouth.

"I'm sure it has nothing to do with being smashed over the head," he said around a mouthful of peanut butter.

They sat, listening to the heater hum, as he chewed.

"So no more questions?" Lukas asked and took a drink without prompting.

Spence swallowed his bite of sandwich, wishing for a bottle of water, even one laced with sleep aid.

"Why, Mr. Lukas, if I didn't know any better, I'd think you were trying to get me drunk. I do hope you're not intending to take advantage of me."

His voice sounded a little slow in his own ears. Maybe it was too late to dilute the alcohol he'd drunk already, but he took another bite.

"That's less than funny. You don't earn any points for facetiousness."

Having found that limiting his movement limited his pain, Spence gave the smallest of shrugs. "Probably just as well, I've never been particularly funny. I don't believe that this is all because of money."

"Maybe you don't realize how much money I'm talking about."

"I don't doubt it was a factor. In your mind. At the time. However, misguided that may have been." Spence couldn't be sure, but he thought he sounded less sleepy than before. "But I think it was more about what people would think."

"I believe I admitted as much."

"Yes, but I don't think you were being honest about the motivation."

Lukas huffed. "Are you coming to a question? Because I have yet to hear one." He took an agitated pull on his bottle.

"You've doubtlessly heard that Atwood quote about women being afraid that men will kill them, while men are afraid . . ."

"Women will laugh at them. Nice inversion there. You think I was afraid of women laughing at me?" His scorn underlined his impatience instead of masking it.

Spence motioned to Lukas's bottle. Maybe he was getting the hang of this, tipsy or not. Lukas drank.

"Not women in particular, but I think you were more afraid of being a laughingstock than being a fraud. Eirik Boudreau, a big fat joke. Or maybe just a small, skinny one." Spence realized his words and their underlying emotions were running away from him and endeavored to bring his filter back up.

Lukas leaned forward and glowered at him. "I still don't hear a question."

Spence couldn't resist echoing Lukas. "Do I have that right?"

"You're not wrong."

Spence drank in the guardedness on Lukas's face as he unscrewed the resistant cap of a fresh bottle. He took a sip, letting a little dart of fire down his throat. He licked away the dryness of his lips.

"That's not all though. There's something else."

Lukas straightened up on the chair. Even with his slight stature, in their current geography he towered over Spence.

"Something you didn't put in your article." Lukas pushed the crate away with his feet, hefted himself up, and walked aimlessly into the open space between the pen and the steps. He kept his face turned away as he continued. "Considering everything you did include, that surprised me. I read it through twice, making sure I hadn't missed something, but it wasn't there amidst all the wreckage you collected. And then I thought, maybe our Mr. Spence isn't a sensationalist after all. He didn't put it in because it has nothing to do with the story. What a stand-up guy."

"Which detail is that?"

Lukas turned to him and made a drinking motion. Spence complied.

"Stop the charade, Darshan." Beneath his thin sweater, Lukas's chest rose and fell quickly. "Unless it's possible you really don't know. I—" He chuckled bitterly and ambled back to the chair, on which he sank like a stone down a well. Its feet shuddered backward on the concrete floor. "Maybe I gave you too much credit as a researcher."

"You didn't answer my question," Spence said without a hint of curiosity, his tone as level as the alcohol and who-knew-what-else in his system would allow.

Lukas looked down at Spence, the chipped-ice eyes behind the glasses weighing him.

"I'm talking about the rape."

Chapter Seventeen

ormer Police Chief Wharton was awake and expecting the call Kate made from the privacy of her car.

"Clay told me you'd be calling. Said I might be able to help you out with a missing-persons case?" His voice carried a bit of gravel lightened by the breathiness of advanced age.

"I'm certainly hoping so, sir. What can you tell me about Marion Lukas? It looks like you brought him in a few times on minor charges."

"Marion Lukas," Wharton repeated. "Is he the one missing?"

"No, we're actually looking for a local journalist named Darshan Spence. Did he contact you?"

"Can't say that he did. I figure I'd remember that name."

"We think he may have been working on a story related to Lukas, but we haven't been able to turn up anything on him in our area. We're also looking for a possible connection between Lukas and a writer named Eirik Boudreau. That's what led us to your part of the country."

"I can't say I ever heard of the Boudreau fella either, but I remember Lukey." Wharton's voice fell away. "I do at that."

Kate lay her head against the driver's headrest and waited.

"It's like you said. I brought him in a few times . . . probably more times than it says. Definitely more times than it says. But it was always for something foolish, something juvenile. At least at first. Vandalism, trespassing. Then it was public intoxication and drugs of course. But Lukey—that's what he went by here—he never hurt anybody or anything like that. There's not a lot out here for the kids to do, you know, small towns in the middle of nowhere and if they don't take to the outdoors or have parents that keep a close eye on them . . . you can guess how it goes."

"I can. Did Lukas not have anyone watching out for him? Is that why you didn't always process him?"

"That's a complicated question. He did at one point, I think, but I know he got hisself into a place where he didn't or at least where he felt he didn't. He, um, he lived with his mom and stepdad in Moose Hollow, a few towns over. They were religious folks, pretty strict or what a young fella feels is strict."

"I can relate to that, believe it or not."

Wharton chuckled. "Well, good. In our line, it's always good when we can relate to the people we're dealing with. Keeps them human, keeps us human. Anyway, they got to butting heads like teenagers and parents do, and he wanted to move in with his dad and stepmom. I don't know whose idea that was, but I know he was glad to get outta there, and that's when he came to Larsen."

Kate wanted to hurry the old man along, but she held her tongue and, as he talked, she jotted notes on a small pad of paper lit by the rectangular button light above the windshield.

"But you know how it goes, that grass on the other side is never as green as you're thinking it's gonna be. After things soured, by that time he'd gotten into enough trouble the first set of parents wouldn't have him back. Maybe if it'd been sooner, that would've work out. I even talked to them, but they had little ones and they were scared what would happen to them with the drugs and such."

"Sounds like you took a real interest in him."

Kate listened to the whistle of Wharton's breathing on the other side of the line.

"Well, like I said, it's not uncommon for the youngsters to get theirselves in scrapes out here, and if I could keep them out of the system so they didn't have a black mark following them, I'd do my best to get them turned around right." Wharton exhaled a discomfited rush of air. "But I did feel responsible for Lukey somewhat. I cut him extra slack where I could, you know, calling the parents instead of running him in. I didn't write up every incident, but as I say, it was always pretty minor stuff. Even when he did spend time at the jail, it was only ever overnight at the station. He never made the trip to county. More about letting him cool off or sober up, so he wasn't a danger to hisself. Unfortunately, he didn't ever level out, not when he was here, but he left pretty much as soon as he could."

"Do you remember when that was?"

"Not rightly. I mean it'd have to be twenty-five years ago or more."

"Do you know where he went?"

"I do not. For everything bubbling up inside him, Lukey was a smart kid. I talked to his teachers a couple times, and of course, he gave them trouble too, but they recognized he had potential. I always hoped that wherever he moved on to, it was someplace he could . . . succeed, I guess."

"He ever come back to your area?"

"Not that I heard tell of."

"You said you felt responsible for him. Is that why you kept his picture out of his file?"

"Oh, no, we just didn't bother to mugshot the piddly stuff in those days. We're not exactly New York City. Heck, we ain't even Laramie. We knew what the locals looked like, so it seemed overkill for minor offenses. I'm sure they snap everybody who comes through the station nowadays, but we were more relaxed back then."

Kate wrinkled her nose but kept her tone neutral. "Any idea where I could obtain a photo?"

"Hm, I bet you could get one from the high school. They have a display in the library of all the graduating classes, or at least they used to. If they kept up with it, they'd have his picture. Or maybe in a yearbook. It was a few years after that before he left. The school will be all locked up for the weekend, but Clay—Chief Teton—could probably get it for you faster than waiting on the school to open."

Kate thanked him and clicked off the overhead light, thinking to end the conversation there, but Wharton had danced around something in Lukas's background and while she didn't know whether it would or could be relevant, she hated to risk not exploring it.

"Before I go, do you mind if I ask, why you felt responsible for Marion Lukas?"

A heavy sigh came through the phone. She waited, her own breath fogging the window and dimming the light that angled into the car from the parking lot lamps.

"His stepmother had a son of her own from a previous relationship, a little older and good bit bigger than Lukey. His name was Braden Findley. He didn't live with them all the time, one of those arrangements where they bounce back and forth."

When Wharton paused, Kate prompted him. "The stepbrothers not get along?"

"I think that was the situation from day one. The older one kinda bullying and resenting the younger one. Although I don't think anyone would have said Lukey was a peach to begin with. But then something happened between them. You have to remember it was a different time back then and things like that didn't happen here, or so we thought, I guess. Nowadays, it's not hard to imagine; you hear a good deal worse on a daily basis if you watch the news, but back then—sure, there were a couple of kiddy diddlers or perverts in the area that we kept our eyes on—but boys their age, stepbrothers at that, that type of thing, and Lukey had already gotten himself a reputation as a liar, so..." Wharton took a breath. "The parents brought him in, but they didn't put much stock in his story and so neither did I. Plus, it was so long after the fact there was no evidence. But I... I should've followed it up more. Because it happened again. That time he told us right away, and there was no denying it on anyone's side."

"Do you know what happened to Braden Findley?"

"He ended up in prison for a spell, as you might expect. But last I heard he ran a used-car dealership in Green River."

Kate thanked Wharton for his help and hung up, leaving him alone with the regrets that she had so mercilessly unearthed.

"SAM SOMETHING!" Brendan said, but before Dylan's hands could touch down on the keyboard, Colin snatched the laptop closed.

"What are you doing?" Brendan exclaimed. "This is getting really good."

"No, it's getting really bad. I think," Colin said. "I don't know." He looked to Dylan. "What do you think?"

"Uhhh . . ." Dylan's mouth hung slack beneath wide eyes. He snapped to and waved his hands at Colin and Brendan. "Just calm down a minute. For all we know, he's not that much older than she is—"

"We are," Brendan said.

"Or *that*," Dylan said. "Whatever. He could just be fronting."

"Or he could be a total perv, a real-live pedophile," Colin countered.

"Even if he is, he's obviously not looking for little middle-school boys, is he? So I think you're pretty safe." Dylan pried the laptop back open. "Besides he doesn't know who or where we are." He put his hand on Colin's arm, and his tone dropped. "Don't freak about it."

"Yeah," Brendan said. "Let's just see what happens."

Sorry about that, Dylan typed. *My momster burst in here without even knocking. She's the worst.*

No reply.

You still there?

But apparently he wasn't.

"Ugh!" Brendan threw himself backward onto his unmade bed. "Just when it was getting intense."

Colin dipped his head, letting a swathe of brown hair fall in a curtain over his eyes. He felt like he should apologize for being a killjoy but also felt like if he did, that might make him seem like an even bigger loser. Guilt won out.

"Sorry," he mumbled.

Dylan punched him lightly in the arm. "It's no big." He swiveled toward Brendan, who still sprawled face-up on his bed. "Right?"

"Yeah, whatever. It's fine," he said with zero conviction. Then he sprang from the bed. "Hey! He could still write back. He might not be gone for good."

Dylan shrugged. "That's true. Maybe when he gets a bit thirstier."

"Yeah," Colin said, trying to play it cool, but the thought made his stomach knot. They all regarded the screen as if speaking the possibility might cause it to happen instantaneously, but a watched inbox doesn't ping. As they each began to grow restless, Colin cleared his throat. "If he does—"

"I know, I know. Wait for you." Brendan draped a conspiratorial arm over Dylan's shoulders. "Just to warn you: Colin's very possessive of Spacey. You might have to fight him for her love."

They both laughed, and even Colin smiled.

A knock at the bedroom door hushed the laughter. Brendan's dad stuck his head inside.

"Wigley boys, your presence has been requested at your own domicile."

"What's a domicile?" Colin asked.

"House, home, dwelling place—your mother wants you there, inside it, in short fashion. Shall I give you transport?"

"Nah, thanks, Mr. Tyrell," Dylan said as he stood. "I'll see the little one gets home okay." He took a swipe at Colin's head that Colin nearly evaded.

"See that you do, young man. I want no blood on these baby-soft hands." Mr. Tyrell held up his long fingers and then tapped one of them against his watch. "Out the door in ten, capiche?"

"Capiche."

Brendan groaned about how weird his dad was as the Wigleys pulled their shoes and coats back on. If something more was going to happen with J-Tank16, it wasn't going to be tonight.

PERHAPS IT WAS his imagination, but Spence felt as though the fuzziness that had crept into his mind immediately evaporated, or more accurately that it distilled itself into a sharp pain behind his eyes.

"What?"

Lukas stared at him with eyes that threatened to devour him. Lukas sat so still, seemingly calm except for the rapid rise and fall of his chest. He licked his lips twice.

"You didn't find that out. Not that it matters. Once you published who I was—used to be—it would have come out somehow. Some vulture would have dragged that carcass into the road for everyone to see as they drove by."

"You raped someone?"

Lukas cocked his head and studied Spence so intensely that it took all his self-restraint not to squirm under the fevered look in his captor's eyes.

"No," Lukas said, as if stating the obvious. "I was raped." He almost choked on the latter words. He removed his glasses and redirected the fierceness of his gaze to the middle distance, putting Spence only marginally more at ease. "When I was young, a teenager." He rested his head in one hand, the thin fingers cradling a scalp left mostly bare by recession. "I figured you would have found police records or something."

"They would have been sealed, certainly if you were a minor."

Lukas looked up, but his eyes were blank now. Had that not occurred to him?

"People talk," he said. He bolted off the chair and launched into a pattern of tight pacing between the steps and pen. "They do. Or will." He stopped abruptly and fixed his eyes on Spence again. "You owe me a few drinks."

Spence gave no argument and sipped out the rest of the bottle. The heater clicked and died, enveloping the garage in a most uncomfortable silence. Neither of them moved, preserving the stillness, but Spence wasn't sure how long his clear-headedness would persist and felt there were things, rather obvious things, that needed to be said.

"People wouldn't think less of you for that."

"Right."

"People are more understanding, more compassionate than you give them credit for."

"You must not be on Twitter."

"I think we've come a long way in how our society views rape victims."

"Sure, if you're a woman. Coming forward makes you brave; you're not a victim, you're a survivor. There's no rallying of the sisterhood to denounce your rapist if you're a man. And what *woman* is going to want a man who couldn't take care of himself, and what man is going to respect you?"

"But you weren't a man, you were a kid. And even if you had been, that wouldn't matter. There's always someone bigger, stronger, more manipulative." Spence cut off his argument, wary of the irony he'd drifted into. "It's not seen as a single-gender issue anymore."

"Not outside of prison and priest jokes, it isn't."

"I can understand the fear—"

"*I'm* not afraid," Lukas shouted. "Don't you get it?"

Lukas's heaving breaths filled the space between them.

"No, I don't," Spence said calmly as his fingertips slipped around the cap of the last shot bottle. "You had a story, one of your own, one that could have even helped other people, *something true,* and instead you published a lie. You passed off some tawdry romanticization of rebellious youth, a fiction, as your life. Why? Why sell a lie for the truth when you had something real to share?"

"Because it was *my* story, and *my* choice whether to tell it! And it's not the story, not the truth that I want told." As Lukas shouted, foamy spittle flicked from his lips. "I've erased that life, that history. That's not who I am!"

But it was, and Spence could see that all too clearly as the man standing over him came into focus. Small, yes, but in a different way than he had judged before. Small like a frightened and wounded animal backed into a corner, and Spence knew how dangerous such a creature could be. He finally loosened the lid of his bottle and drained it because he had no desire to stay sober any longer. Because he also knew he wasn't getting out of this garage alive.

Chapter Eighteen

Kate stumbled, first as she climbed the wide stone steps leading to the station's entrance and then again as she approached Potter's desk. Even against the disquiet of the Friday evening crowd, Potter and Robbie heard her the second time and turned soon enough to catch her righting herself.

"You look like the final definition of *rough*," her partner said.

"What are the earlier definitions?" she asked.

"None of them smooth. When did you last sleep?"

She sank into the chair next to his desk. "What day is it?"

"We're veering headlong into Saturday."

"If you don't count falling asleep in my car while waiting for the chief in Wyoming to answer his phone, then Wednesday."

"You didn't sleep at all last night?" Robbie asked.

Kate shook her head the bare minimum. "I swear I was fine until about fifteen minutes ago."

"You only thought you were fine," Potter said. "Perhaps you should let your brother take you home so you can sleep a few hours."

"Spence is still out there."

"You've hit the wall, Katie," her brother said. "Probably about fifteen minutes ago. If you don't sleep, you'll be no good to him or anyone else."

Kate stood and felt as if she were doing so in slow motion. She only hoped it didn't appear that way to everyone else. "I just need some more coffee."

"If you don't rest, you're not going to be able to blame your next collision on Boudreau or McIver," Potter said.

"McIver?"

"The new guy. The one they've started calling Britboy," Potter supplied.

"Ugh, him," Kate said.

"Is he the guy who thought you were a man?" Robbie asked.

Tired or not, Kate gave him a look intended to freeze his blood, while Potter supplied him with a curt nod.

"Sorry," Robbie said out the side of his mouth.

"Well, I'm awake now," Kate announced at full volume.

"But you are not alert," Potter said. "I'll keep scouring the Web; if you found out anything from Wyoming that could help with the search, tell me now before you pass out. Then go get some shut-eye."

"Chief Teton is going to scan a picture of Lukas from the local high school. But it'll take him a few hours to get it."

"There you go," Robbie said.

"I want to be here when it comes in!"

"Do you guys have a bunk room?" Robbie asked Potter.

Potter shook his head. "There's a couch in the break room, but on a Friday night? Good luck with getting enough quiet to sleep. Our soundproofing isn't that good."

A ragged shriek flew in from booking, followed by some procedural bellowing.

"That may not be a problem." Robbie looked at Kate. "I'm betting she could sleep through Armageddon."

Kate groaned. "Stop mother-henning me! I'll grab a quick nap in the car." She pointed a threatening finger at Potter. "I want to know the minute the photo comes through."

She stalked away with her brother on her heels.

"You realize you're coming off punch-drunk, right?"

She didn't answer. Even stepping out into the cold night air had no restorative effect. At the car, Robbie pulled open the passenger side door for her.

"I'll sit in the driver's seat," she said.

"No, I will."

"Why?"

"Because a cop sleeping in her car alone in the station parking lot is just asking to be shot, and if you weren't so tired, I wouldn't have to explain that to you."

Sighing, Kate slid clumsily into the seat and yanked the door closed away from Robbie. She let her head fall back and stared blankly through the windshield as Robbie settled himself in the adjacent seat.

She knew she was starting to behave badly, even petulantly, and while she hated it, she just felt so rotten that she couldn't contain it.

"There's got to be something else we can do while we wait on the photo," she mumbled.

"What was that?"

She repeated herself with greater distinction and a little extra attitude.

"You can rest so that you're ready for when the photo comes in."

She turned to look at him. The lines around his own puffy eyes seemed pronounced.

"Looking rough yourself."

"I imagine."

"I'm sorry." Kate faced forward. When she shut her eyes, the car rocked forward suddenly. Her eyes shot back open, and she clutched at the car door.

"What—" Through the windshield, she saw her little house, a lamp in the living room glowing behind the drawn curtains.

"You were out before I even turned the car on," Robbie said.

"Seriously?" She pinched the bridge of her nose in an effort to alleviate the ache in her head.

"You forget that I'm the master of driving sleeping children. I draw the line at carrying you inside though."

"I concede. Just don't let me sleep longer than two hours." Robbie didn't respond. "Three," she bargained.

"I'll wake you when your partner calls and says he has the photo. Now get in the house."

"Maybe we should be looking for other leads. Maybe we're doing the same thing I accused Kirkley and Kotono of doing."

"You can sleep on that and maybe something will come to you. Now . . ." Robbie reached across her to push the car door open. "Get—in—the house."

"WAKE UP!"

It was the jostling of his shoulder rather than his brother's hushed voice that dragged Colin into consciousness. The only light in his room emitted dimly from the red numbers on his alarm clock, and Dylan stood mostly in the way of that.

"What time is it?"

"I don't know, but listen. The guy answered!"

"What guy answered what?" Colin pulled himself up to lean against the headboard.

"The guy from the computer!"

Dylan didn't sound sleepy at all. He parked himself on the side of Colin's bed, letting Colin see the clock. It was 3:27.

"Why are you even awake?"

"I woke up and had to pee, so I thought while I was up, I'd check Spacey's account."

The story sounded thin to Colin, but he wasn't nearly awake enough to poke holes in it, so he stayed with the one aspect that didn't compute.

"In the middle of the night?"

"Bruh, get over it. He *answered* already."

Colin scrunched his eyes together and then rubbed the sleep out of them.

"What'd he say?" Colin asked around a yawn.

"Something about how lame his parents were, so he totally understood where she was coming from."

"What?"

Dylan gave an exasperated groan. "Remember, I put the part about the mom coming in, and that's why we—she—didn't answer right away."

"Yeah, right. Yeah." Colin felt like he finally had a handle on the situation. "Is that all he said?"

"He asked if we liked to party." Excitement ran through Dylan's voice.

"Do we?" Colin asked.

"Oh yeah, Spacey loves to party. You can tell."

"You answered him?"

Dylan squirmed, sending a tremor through the mattress. "Well, not yet. I thought . . . you would want to come answer with me. Like we did before."

Colin thought about it. He didn't want to get caught by their parents, but Dylan had obviously weighed that risk and found it worth taking. Plus getting in trouble together was always less awful than getting in trouble by yourself. Blame was always spreadable. And wasn't this a sign his plan had been a success? Maybe too much of a success.

"You coming?" Dylan prompted with a poke at Colin's leg.

Colin shook his head as he peeled the covers back.

"Brendan's gonna be ticked we did this without him."

SPENCE HAD SEEN the full progression only a few times, but he knew that his brother on the path of inebriation generally made stops at manic jollity and recalcitrance before arriving at black-out central. His friend, or colleague, Lily always said that alcohol just made her sleepy, which was why she preferred to pair it with Red Bull. Spence guessed that he fell into the latter group, although who knew what other substances lingered in his system dragging him into lethargy.

This time when he woke in the darkness, he felt warm inside and out, his body relaxed and gelatinous, but his head ached like it had been riven in two and hastily Scotch-taped back together. It took him several minutes to wade through the pain to any mental clarity, and when he shifted his weight, his stomach burbled in an ominous manner.

He saw no sign of Lukas, but since the head-banging music wasn't playing, his captor couldn't be far. Spence had fallen asleep shortly after Lukas had blown out of the room in agitation. Not shortly enough. He'd had enough time to cogitate on the deep-seated nature of Lukas's fear. Spence couldn't move it, certainly not from within this cage. And certainly not with how quickly his thoughts began to slosh about. They were sloshing still, only now they caused immense pain as they bumped against the inside of his skull. He remembered thinking he was going to die. That thought cut through the mental stew and the pain. The pain, it left behind, but he now had an unfriendly point on which to focus.

Don't give up! spoke a voice inside his head, but it sounded shrill, desperate. Despite his circumstances, Spence didn't feel desperate. For the first time in days, he felt calm—sad and in great pain—but completely calm.

How do you want to go out? That was the internal voice he listened to.

In that moment, Darshan Spence opted to pray. Not for himself but for the people he loved. His mind, sluggish as it was, landed first on Sanjay. He prayed—with what fervency his condition allowed—that his brother would come to his senses, come to faith, and Spence asked that maybe this, maybe Sanjay's losing his brother in this way could be the pivot point, a wake-up call. Spence didn't expect to find the meaning of everything that happened in his life—certainly not in his current situation—but this possibility, however slim it might be, comforted him. He even tried to picture it, his brother sitting alongside his parents at church, joining a family meal, maybe even making a family of his own to come home to at the end of a workday. A completely plausible reality, if only the heart would shift. Spence thought of his sisters and prayed for their families, glad they would be there to take care of their parents if Sanjay never came around. Sometimes his thoughts muddled, such as when he confused Gauri's children with Tabby's, but whenever that happened, he just ploughed onward, trusting the original Word to interpret his feeble communication.

He fell back asleep before he progressed to his friends, but the lapse was momentary and one he didn't even realize himself. In fact, he spent the better part of an hour floating between consciousness and the care that reknits unraveled souls. He didn't presume to know what was best for his friends, but he had inklings of their desires and weaknesses, and he brought those to

God's attention. How Heidi wanted a family of her own, how Danny relied on others to motivate him, how Kate . . .

"Katherine." He said her name out loud, the utterance thick and quiet in the tomblike garage. He asked for her safety and protection. He knew she faced dangers not only from criminals on the street but also from within the ranks of her profession itself and from those that would demonize her for political currency. But he also prayed for the young woman whom he laughed with over dinner, on whose porch he sat in the sweltering heat, who drank coffee with him in the wee hours of the morning. The woman who often stood in her own way and perhaps had stood in his.

Lily flitted through his mind, but he couldn't pray for her. He wished he could, but he couldn't. He told God that and trusted in him to sort her out.

The air had cooled and the concrete beneath remained perpetually cold, although in the corner in which he'd propped himself up, the proximity of the heater kept it from being icy. Now the machine buzzed awake again, sending out its waves of parching heat and orange illumination. As the heater reached peak output, Spence could see his dirty clothes had been removed from the other end of the cage. He could guess the purpose of the empty plastic bottle that stood next to the bucket. A fresh hand towel hung over the bucket's side, and Spence hoped that indicated clean water inside. Clean enough to drink? Doubt twisted his knotted stomach further. No paper plate with sandwich sat in the opposite corner, just another group of shot bottles. Why did Lukas keep pushing alcohol at him, to make him more manageable?

He couldn't imagine that more liquor would sit well on his roiled-up stomach, but the idea that a drink might lubricate his throat as well as knock him firmly back into sleep tempted him.

Look at you, he thought, one night of drinking and you're already self-medicating.

Had it just been one night? No, Lukas had given him some before, when he first came into the garage. But when was that? Yesterday, the day before that? He couldn't be sure.

He closed his eyes and thought about the ramification of downing one of those little bottles, but then he heard one of the voices from earlier.

How do you want to go out?

Spence opened his eyes, and they latched onto the opening of the cage. In the full intensity of the heater's light, he could make out the padlock that hung from the closure. He'd not had the opportunity to examine the door in the light with his hands free. And while he still didn't expect to live through this ordeal, it seemed irresponsible not to investigate.

Chapter Nineteen

Kate woke violently, her body jerking away from some dream danger that fled from memory as soon as she reached consciousness, panting slightly in the dark of her bedroom, unsure of the time, why she was fully dressed, or why she could hear the shower running. There was something more important though, floating on the edge of her brain, something she desperately needed to do or remember.

Spence.

Every bit of the last few days flooded in like a broken sewer main, washing out her panic only to replace it with a fetid unease.

She swung her legs over the side of the bed. Her stockinged feet bumped against her boots, which she didn't remember removing. She couldn't even recall entering the bedroom. She groped along the bedstand for her phone and discovered it was 6:18 in the morning. No messages.

She went to the living room to check the voicemail on the land line and found nothing there either. Her cats, St. Joan and Louis, entwined themselves around her legs, reminding her they needed attention too, mainly of the alimentary kind. She picked up Joan and kneaded her short black coat as she walked to the kitchen with Louis padding after. The shower stopped as she poured out food into the cats' plastic bowls and refilled their water dish. She stepped out into the living room as Robbie exited the bathroom wrapped in a towel. The water drops on his temples and shoulders glinted in the hall light until he shivered, causing them to run.

"I left you some hot water."

"You let me sleep too long." Her voice came out packed with gravel.

"Potter would've called if your photo had come in. Clean up and we'll head back in."

A quick shower, a quick change, and Kate felt nothing resembling good as new, but she did feel a little sharper and less grubby. The poppy dribble of the coffeemaker and its accompanying sharp aroma met her before she reached the kitchen. Robbie, dressed in the clothes he'd worn the day before, sat at the table. His phone lay screen down, but he stared at it blankly, batting it back and forth with his thumb and middle finger.

"Did you sleep any?" Kate asked. "You sure don't look it."

"Finally heard back from Lauren."

Kate waited until she finished pouring mugs for Robbie and herself before responding.

"I'm guessing from your tone that it wasn't a promising response."

Robbie took a mug from Kate but just set it on the table alongside his phone.

"All she said was that the girls are fine and she doesn't want to talk. She's freezing me out. I don't know what to do with that."

Kate wanted to comment on the maturity of her sister-in-law, but instead she said, "Maybe you just have to give her more time."

"I'm just afraid that giving her time or space or *whatever* could look like giving up. And that . . . it could end up being that."

"That sounds valid. Balance isn't easy, and usually not at the beginning of any endeavor."

"How can I fix what's wrong if I don't know what it is?"

Kate sipped her coffee, much stronger than when she brewed it. She picked up the canister of sugar sitting on the table and shook in a cascade of crystals.

"I'm sure it's not going to be this simple, but you mentioned she had a problem with you being on the force. If that really is the issue, would you quit—switch jobs?"

Kate could see in Robbie's pause, his intent stare at the steam rising off his coffee, that he'd considered the question himself.

"Could you just pick up and quit the force?" he asked.

"I said *simple*; I didn't say *easy*."

"It's all I know how to do, Kate. It's all I've ever done."

"But it is not all you are." She reached out and tapped his hand. "Being a cop is not your identity. If it is, then that's a problem. You're more than that."

"It's a pretty big part," Robbie grumbled.

"It shouldn't be the most important, not even second place," Kate said. When Robbie didn't respond, she asked, "Is it more important than your marriage, than your family?"

"Of course not," Robbie said, but his reply was beaten and rote.

"I'm not sure you're convinced of that, Robbie. Maybe in your head, but I'm not sure about your heart." Kate set her mug down. "As officers of the law, we take an oath, but that oath is for the duration of the job. You made vows to Lauren and to God, and those were for life."

Robbie met her gaze. "What would I do?"

"I don't know. But you two could figure it out together. Isn't that supposed to be the idea?"

Kate took another sip. She had no clue what she herself would do if she were to leave the force. From behind her coffee mug, she watched her brother struggle, thankful she didn't have to face such a decision, thankful for the first time for the lonely late nights she sometimes faced.

COLIN AND DYLAN huddled in front of the computer, a bulky desktop tucked away in the far corner of the living room. They left the lights off in case their parents should wake and see the glow from beneath their bedroom door down the hall. Their first message to J-Tank16 didn't elicit an immediate response. Colin pointed at the timestamp on the previous message.

"He sent this like two hours ago. Maybe he's asleep like a normal person."

"Give it a minute," Dylan said.

"It's been five."

"Then give it five more. C'mon."

From the back of the couch, Colin plucked one of their grandmother's afghans, its vibrant diamond pattern reading black and white in the minimal screen light. He wrapped it around his shoulders. They stared at the screen for another five minutes. Something in the house settled, causing Colin to shoot worried eyes over his shoulder. He wished the desk didn't place them with their backs to the room's entrance.

"Who would be awake now?" Colin asked.

"Duh, it's Friday night. Lots of adults, especially ones that like to party, are still awake. They stay out all night and then eat breakfast at a diner and go home."

"Right, but if he's out partying why would he bother messaging some teenage girl back?"

Dylan pouted at Colin's logic. "Because he's a pervert, that's why." After another minute, he conceded. "Fine." His hand went to the mouse, just as the dancing dots appeared. "I told you!" He elbowed Colin, probably a little harder than he intended.

"Shh! You'll wake up Mom and Dad."

J-Tank16 seemed pleased that Spacey was a self-professed party girl but also insisted that he liked to keep things "chill."

Oh, me too, Dylan typed.

Mostly just buds and Buds, right?

"What the heck does that mean?" Colin whispered.

"He's talking about weed . . . and beer, I think."

I like wine coolers better, but if I'm smoking, a beer is cool.

"Wine coolers?" Colin asked.

"Trust me, girls are all about wine coolers. They're pretty and fruity."

"You're a freshman. How would you know?"

"I may not be at all the parties, but I hear things. That's all I'm saying."

The messaging wound its way from partying through various subjects on which Dylan and Colin provided Spacey-appropriate answers based on Dylan's first-hand experience and the data Colin had mined from Sissy's social accounts with a dash of adolescent male thrown in because—really—they couldn't help it. At times when they talked about a shared interest, the creepiness almost faded from the conversation, and it seemed like they were just talking to a new friend. Then Colin would remember his cousin Tommy's warning about online strangers.

J-Tank16 probably didn't like *Fullmetal Alchemist* at all. He was probably a forty-five-year-old man pretending to like *Fullmetal Alchemist*, so that they—Spacey—would like him and think he was cool. He probably read things like . . . the *Wall Street Journal*.

"Grooming," he whispered in Dylan's ear.

"What?"

"This is called grooming, where he pretends to like the things we do so we'll relate to him."

"I know what grooming is. I've seen *SVU*."

In the kitchen, the coffeemaker clicked loudly and began its noisy percolation, causing both boys to jump. The sharp smell of Dad's dark roast wafted in.

Colin looked at the computer's clock. They'd been messaging their mysterious stranger for over two hours.

"Look what time it is!" He nudged his brother's shoulder with a fist wrapped in afghan.

It's been real cool chatting, J-Tank16 said.

"Hey guys, you're up early." Their dad, impervious to the cold, stood at the living room entrance in his boxers and a v-neck undershirt, his eyes half open and his hair sticking up in several sleep-produced cowlicks. He yawned cavernously and then asked, "Whatcha doing?"

J-Tank16 had a question of his own: *Are you free later today?*

"Yeah, we just decided to get up early," Colin said as Dylan typed a hasty goodbye.

Dad looked suspicious but not overly interested. "C'mon, no computer until after lunch unless it's for school."

"I'm helping Colin with a social studies project," Dylan equivocated. He shut the computer off. "But it's extracurricular."

Dad didn't seem sure how to interpret that, but he opted to focus on the "helping" part. "Well, that's nice of you."

"Can we go over to Brendan's later?" Colin followed his father into the kitchen.

"Sure, as long as his folks don't mind. Don't forget you two have leaves to rake today."

Dylan's groan carried from the living room.

"Bedrooms cleaned, leaves raked, then you can hang out with your friends or play your computer games."

Colin looked over his shoulder to his brother standing in the doorway, who gave him a nod. Their dad might have been more restrictive in his instructions for the day if he'd any idea the game they were playing.

SPENCE WORKED his way across the cage, each scoot rattling the pressure cooker that was his skull. When he got close to the corner, he paused, the fingers of one hand laced into the chain link above to keep him from pitching over. He pressed the palm of his other hand against his head and waited for the throbbing to subside or at least abate. When he opened his eyes, the first thing he spied was the nips.

"It couldn't make it any worse," he mumbled.

He picked up a random bottle and swigged the biting liquid. Hair of the dog—that was a thing, right? Of course, for all he knew his headache could be the result of a slow brain bleed. He finished off the bottle and turned his attention back to the pen's opening while he waited for his medicine to kick in.

The door took up a good amount of one of the pen's shorter sides, maybe two by three feet, leaving only a few inches above and below the door. He tried to gauge the width of it with his own shoulders. Of course, it had to be big enough for him to fit through. He wondered how Lukas managed that on his own, especially given that the smaller man had likely been intoxicated at the time. Perhaps that came after, and perhaps he was much stronger than he looked.

Had it been comical? He imagined Lukas, the amateur kidnapper, maybe tipsy, engaged in the farcical task of Shove the Journalist Through the Little Door. While he didn't find it strictly humorous, he hoped his imagination was accurate because the more foolish Lukas felt or seemed, the more it comforted him. The idea also sparked a memory, a very old one that usually made him chuckle. The best he could muster at present was a shadow of a smile. It had been the summer before he'd gone to college.

"Get me out!"

Spence and Tabby had come running when they heard Sanjay's bellowing from the other side of the playground. His chubby little legs and posterior, showing a bit of plumber's crack, hung several feet off the ground outside a green plastic porthole of the jungle gym, one that apparently wouldn't admit his girth.

"Get me out, Darsh!"

Finding the problem to be benign, Spence and his sister caught a case of giggles.

"What's wrong, buddy?" Spence asked. He approached his little brother, but Sanjay's legs kicked outward as he squirmed, causing Spence to jump back out of range.

"I'm stuck!"

"I see that. Stop kicking." Spence hefted his brother's shorts up by their belt loops and then wrapped his arms around his waist. "I think you're getting too big for this jungle gym."

"I'm only seven!"

"I didn't say too old; I said too big," Spence said and gave a tug.

Sanjay yowled but didn't budge.

Tabby's laughter grew in volume, making it harder for Spence to keep from laughing.

"Is that Tabby?" Sanjay asked. "Tabby, stop laughing. It's not funny!"

"Stop it," Spence mouthed to his sister. Aloud he told her to grab hold of Sanjay's feet. He encircled his brother's waist

again. "When I say 'go,' I want you to suck in your tummy as much as you can, okay?"

"Okay."

"Go!"

It didn't work. They tried pulling from the other side with no better outcome. Spence handed his car keys to Tabby.

"Go get my phone out of the car and call Dad."

While Tabby ran to alert a full-fledge adult, Spence poked, prodded, and pried at his brother's stomach to see if he could inch him out with Sanjay protesting at each attempt.

"I hate to break it to you, but getting out of this thing is probably going to hurt a little. How did you get your shirt pulled up out of the hole?"

"It just did! Can people see me, Darsh?"

"Yeah, buddy." He patted him on the behind. "But don't worry about that. We'll get you out."

Though he tried, in the end, Spence hadn't been able to do it himself, but he'd stayed with his brother, comforting him until their father arrived with a tub of petroleum jelly. Getting out of some fixes just required a father.

Spence reached through the chain link to grasp the padlock with his fingertips. He couldn't get too firm of a hold, but he tugged on the lock on the off chance Lukas hadn't turned the dial and it would spring open. It didn't. He tried again and once again, as hard as he could with the awkward angle, but the lock stayed closed and his fingers slid off.

He felt around the door's corners opposite the hinges to see if he could bend back the chain link. The edges weren't reinforced, but Spence couldn't force them far, and they sprang back immediately when he released them. He wouldn't be able to effect a big enough opening to facilitate an escape effort anyway.

He scooched back from the door and eased himself down until he lay flat on the concrete floor. The movement made his head swim for a few seconds. Then it took extraordinary effort to raise his legs, but he kicked with both feet at the latch that held the padlock. Each kick produced a spike in his head and a lance in his ribs as well as a cringey screech of metallic friction and the resounding spring back of the chain link. The sturdiness of shoes would have helped. His socks snagged on the metal, and by the third attempt he'd torn holes in the bottom of them.

He righted himself and examined the latch as best he could. No damage. He just didn't have the strength to force it. He was too weak. He was stuck.

The heater's hum died, and his meager light faded.

Chapter Twenty

Kate and Robbie arrived at the station before the picture of Lukas did. Potter still sat at his desk, his eyes extra puffy and tired.

"I told you I'd let you know when it came."

"I wasn't going to sleep any more. Have you found anything new?"

He shook his head, his eyes downcast. "I switched from trying to find Lukas to backtracking through Boudreau's life for a connection, but that's difficult as well. Eirik Boudreau is all over his legal documents, so it's definitely not a pen name, but the only locations I find records for him are here and in New York, not the other places he's lived."

"You checking court records for name changes?"

"Yeah, but I haven't found anything. Knowing where to look would sure help."

"So we have Lukas in Wyoming but not Boudreau."

"Correct."

"And in Illinois we have Boudreau but not Lukas."

"And New York."

"What about California?" Robbie asked. "Didn't you say Boudreau lived there before New York?"

Potter shrugged. "So far I haven't found a record of either of them there."

The three looked at each other in silence for a moment.

"Could Lukas be Boudreau?" Kate asked.

Potter considered it. "Their pasts don't line up. The only thing we have connecting them is the state of Wyoming and a circumstantial Post-It note."

"And juvenile delinquency and substance abuse," Kate pointed out.

"Which the chief said were super common for teens in his area," Robbie said.

"They just don't match up," Potter reiterated. "The landmark experiences don't align, at least not from Lukas to Boudreau. Knowing what I do from the book, I could call Wharton and see if there's some alignment from Boudreau to Lukas."

Potter didn't sound hopeful, but Kate figured it was worth a shot. She gave him the contact information.

"Let's hope he's an early riser," Potter said, phone in hand.

"Have you heard anything from Kirkley or Kotono?"

"I know they still have someone in the conference room reviewing security footage. I'm not sure what else."

Knowing how territorial the other two detectives were, Kate knocked on the conference room door before entering, but inside she found only McIver, his copper hair shining under the fluorescent lighting. Compared to everyone else she'd interacted with this morning, he appeared fresh and alert, though a landfill of food wrappers and coffee-stained paper cups covered the table where he sat, giving evidence of a lengthy session scanning footage on the computer that sat amidst the debris. Although perhaps not all the trash was his, at least Kate hoped not.

"Detective Baxter!"

McIver jumped up from his seat, but Kate motioned him back down. She circled around the table to watch over his shoulder. Directly in front of him lay a small pad of paper, the top page nearly filled with notes written in a sharp hand of all capitals.

"Found anything?"

With a press of a button, McIver resumed the video play.

"Not yet. There aren't any roadway cameras in the area, but we got security footage from three different shops relatively near Darshan Spence's house. Each a different direction from the residence. It's impossible to cover all the bases, but these are the main ways into the neighborhood, so we're looking for vehicles that show both on Wednesday night and Friday evening." McIver pointed at the monitor. "This is from a liquor shop on Elston Street."

The quality of the footage didn't inspire Kate. It came from an outside camera aimed at the front door but which captured the passing traffic in the background. They could ascertain vehicle color and body type, but they sure wouldn't be able to pull a plate number.

"Look, about yesterday, I didn't mean to offend you."

Kate waved off his apology. She was far too tired and anxious to hold a grudge.

"Forget about it. I have much larger concerns at the moment."

"Darshan Spence is a friend of yours, right?"

"Yes, a very good friend."

"I'm sorry. I imagine you must be gutted." McIver paused the footage again. "So you know, I'm not the only one who's reviewing the video. Some other officers are giving it a go as well in Interview 2, but Detective Kotono asked for another set of eyes."

"Thank you," Kate said, now trying to figure a way out of this conversation. "Keep it up. Have you seen Detective Kirkley or Kotono recently?"

"Kotono was in here about an hour ago looking over the notes the other officers had made, then Kirkley poked his head in and told him he'd found something. He seemed excited. I think they went to the break room."

Kate thanked McIver again and set out for the pair of detectives, hoping they'd unearthed something more promising than the security footage.

COLIN WAS RIGHT about Brendan.

"It's not fair! You made me promise to wait for you guys, and then you guys didn't wait for me. Not cool, man."

"He answered in the middle of the night," Dylan said. "What were we gonna do, call you to come over?"

"You still could have waited."

"Get over it."

Brendan glowered at Dylan until Colin asked, "Do you want to know what he said or not?"

"I already know. I'm the one who set up the account, remember? I read the whole freaking thing this morning." Brendan strode away from them and perched on the edge of his bed with a martyrish pout.

"Look, we're sorry."

Dylan rolled his eyes.

"I'm sorry," Colin amended with a scowl at his brother. "It was a spur of the moment thing."

"You chatted for *two* hours," Brendan objected, though his tone had mellowed a half-note.

"Yeah, two hours that you were asleep," Dylan said, "so we couldn't have included you even if we wanted to—" Colin shot his brother a work-with-me look. "—which of course we wanted to. Anyway, we're including you now. We came over as soon as our parents would let us."

Reluctantly mollified, Brendan inched his way over to the desk and opened his laptop. Spacey's account was already up on the screen.

"We had to stop because our dad came in," Colin said.

"I figured based on how it ended."

J-Tank16 had replied to Dylan's last message.

I'll be waiting. ☺

"Ew," Colin said.

Hey big boy. U around? Brendan typed.

"Big boy?" Dylan said. He gave Brendan a light shove. "Move over and let me drive."

"What? Trust me, he'll like that," Brendan said but got out of Dylan's way nonetheless.

The reply dots were already bouncing up and down.

Hey you, just woke up. But already been thinking about you.

Colin made a retching noise.

"Told you," Brendan crowed.

Whether it was Brendan's kick-off or J-Tank16's underfed libido, the chatting maintained a much coyer tone this time around, one Dylan struggled with compared to their two previous conversations. Strangely and somewhat inexplicably from Colin's viewpoint, Brendan's input kept the flirtation humming, but not without some cringing and balking on the Wigleys' part.

"I'm not typing that," Dylan said for the third time, though he had caved on the two previous protests.

"Puh-lease," Brendan said, tapping in to take the seat in front of the computer. "Now I know why you don't have a girlfriend."

"Like you do," Dylan shot back, but he still gave the seat to Brendan. "You don't know anything about real girls."

"Maybe he doesn't either. Maybe that's why this is working. After all, if it's some old dude on the Internet trying to pick up teenage girls, he's probably not bringing his A-game with ladies his own age."

"He could have a point," Colin said.

"Well, just don't misspell any of the easy words, okay?" Dylan said.

Brendan shook his head. "Like Spacey belongs in National Honor Society."

"We don't want him to think she's a total idiot."

Brendan arched an eyebrow. "Or do we?"

"*No,*" Dylan said and then immediately turned to Colin. "Right?"

"It's just got to match," Colin said. "It's got to seem like the same person as before."

With Brendan at the helm, the USS *Spacey* sailed more recklessly into the waves of juvenile passion, but Dylan made the rulings on what was too much or too far and Colin kept an eye on continuity. The panel approach slowed their reply times, but if J-Tank16 minded or suspected anything, he didn't let on. It wasn't long before he brought the conversation back around to an in-person encounter.

So when are we gonna meet up? You're not gonna leave me hanging, are you?

Would I do that to you? lol

I sure hope not. XX

U said ur older, but like how old? Ur not like a grandpa or something gross like that?

LMAO. No! Definitely not a grandpa, but I could definitely be your daddy if you like.

All three boys made gagging noises.

J-Tank16 continued, *Old enough to buy some party supplies. In fact, I already picked you up some wine coolers. Strawberry kiwi, your favorite, right?*

Brendan looked at Colin, who nodded.

Awwww, SO sweet of u!

How about tonight?

"Wait!" Colin said. "What are we doing?"

"We're gonna see who this guy really is!" Brendan said. Excitement shone in his eyes, and it was clearly mirrored in Dylan's. Colin just felt queasy.

"I don't know—"

But Brendan had already sent a big thumbs-up.

Sounds awesome, Brendan typed. *Where do u—*

"No," Dylan interrupted. "Don't let him pick where. We should. Tell him we'll meet him at Inoca Park, at the picnic tables near the tennis courts."

"What time?" Brendan asked as he machine-gunned the info to J-Tank16.

"Not too late but after dark," Dylan said. "Maybe six-thirty?"

Brendan punched the final key extra hard on the last message.

6:30 – don't be late!

She knows what she wants. Love it. See you then.

The three boys looked at each other with varying degrees of amazement.

"What the heck are we doing!" Colin shouted.

"DO YOU HAVE something to say to me?" Katherine asked.

"About what?" Spence regarded her from across the Steak 'n Shake booth, where they sat, their legs stretched out on their respective benches. Many a late night found them here drinking decaf, comparing notes on their days. The savory scent of frying burgers hung in the air, and Spence knew from experience it would follow him home, but he liked how bright the lights were inside against the darkness outside. He could see every detail of her tired face, the wisps of dark blonde hair that had escaped her ponytail to trail on either side of her face. She shrugged.

"I thought there might be something."

"Nope." There was nothing, nothing he wanted to say. He swirled the quarter inch of darkness remaining in his coffee cup. He could tell her how she needed to ditch that outdated tan trench coat, how it made her look like a cosplayer at a Sam Spade convention. She even wore the collar flipped up tonight against the chill and damp. But, no, he wouldn't tell her that because it might hurt her feelings, because her attachment to the coat was both fond and long-lived, and because even though it was a sad fashion choice—or maybe *because* it was—he actually found it endearing.

He had the feeling she was fishing for something far more substantial. He studied her profile as she looked out over the restaurant. He opened his mouth but shut it again before any words could tumble out. She leaned toward him, her eyes still focused elsewhere, and said, "Look at that guy."

Spence followed her gaze to a small man who sat with his back to them, shoulders hunched. Even from the back, he thought he recognized the man. He looked at the windows, turned reflective by the bright light against the dark, but for some reason he couldn't find the man's face. But he knew who the man was and also realized that he was dreaming. This never happened, he told himself. The man rose from his seat. Spence quickly turned back to Katherine.

"Hey, I do want to tell you something—"

"Oh, yeah?" She barely seemed to listen, more interested in perusing the menu. "Do you want to split a milkshake?"

Spence could feel the man walking toward their booth, and his heartbeat quickened but the words felt leaden in his mouth. He couldn't force them out fast enough.

"No, I need to tell you . . ." He struggled with each word, could feel the man walking around behind him, drawing ever closer. The words piled up in his throat.

He felt a hand clamp down on his shoulder and jerked awake on the garage floor. He could still feel the man's grip, but no one was there. He'd been trying to kick out the door to the cage, and he'd fallen asleep. He tasted acid in his mouth. He curled his fingers into the chain link and, grunting, pulled himself into a sitting position. He leaned against the cage. The very core of him felt as if it had been dug out of week-old garbage and stuffed inside.

You tried, said the voice in his head. *What else could you do?*

Oh, shut up, he thought.

The door to the house swung open, and Lukas stood there, surrounded by diffuse natural light. Daytime again. He held Spence's laptop in his arms.

"You're awake. You were asleep when I checked earlier." He sounded hostlike, as if he were popping around to see if Spence needed more towels, as if the last time they'd spoken he hadn't been raving.

Lukas descended the steps with a careful eye on his feet, and Spence felt an echo of what he'd felt in the dream as the man approached. The dining chair had disappeared at some point, and Lukas sat heavily on the crate, puffing out a sigh that had its own proof rating. He avoided Spence's gaze, keeping his eyes focused on the computer he held.

"Do you have something to say to me?" Spence asked.

Lukas frowned, his jaw going crooked for a moment.

"Is . . . is there anyone to whom you'd like to say good-bye?" he finally asked. When Spence didn't answer, he continued. "Because I'm writing a note for you."

"I thought you weren't a killer," Spence said.

"Eirik Boudreau isn't, but I guess Marion Lukas has to be." Lukas met his eyes. "Maybe you shouldn't have dug him up."

Chapter Twenty-one

Kate caught Kirkley and Kotono as they were exiting the breakroom, shrugging themselves into their overcoats. A foreboding look flashed across Kotono's face when he saw her.

"McIver told me that you'd found something?" she said.

"Who's McIver?" Kotono asked.

"Britboy," Kirkley supplied. He tilted his well-coiffed head at Kate. "You may not like it."

"Don't make me wait all day to find out."

"The prints you got from the bedroom all came back as matches for Darshan Spence."

"Not entirely a surprise," Kate said, swallowing her disappointment. "So not even Sanjay," she pointed out.

"No, but there's more," Kotono said. "We got a hit for Darshan Spence's debit card. A liquor store at Fairby Plaza. Late last night."

"It has to be the kidnapper," Kate said, a surge of adrenalin rushing the words out. "Spence doesn't drink. I told you that."

The other two detectives exchanged a dark glance before Kotono continued. "The debit card wasn't used to purchase anything in the store. Someone used it at the ATM inside the store. They emptied his checking account. The clerk recalled 'a tall Middle Eastern–looking dude' making a cash purchase around the same time. Seems like that could described either Darshan or Sanjay. We're going there now to see if they can make a photo ID."

Kate wanted to object, explain why it couldn't be Spence, but she knew it would be fruitless, counterproductive even. She stepped back to let her colleagues leave. "Please let me know what you find out."

They nodded sharply and were gone. The sudden surge of energy had passed leaving Kate all the more drained. She reached out a shaky hand and pressed it against the wall, firm and flat against her palm, cool to the touch.

"Kate!" Potter called from the end of the hallway. "The picture's come in."

A fresh wave of adrenalin coursed through her, smaller and less efficacious than the first as if her body refused to be fooled into hope so soon again, and she had to force her legs to move. When she reached the end of the hall, Potter handed her a printout.

"Look like anybody you know?"

The page came from the Juniors section of a yearbook, and circled on the lower left side was Marion Lukas. She took the sheet and held it close to her face to study the portrait, wishing it were larger and in color. She drank in Lukas's nearly gaunt features split by a forced grin, the ears that stuck out below the fair spiked hair.

"Not particularly," she said. "What about you?"

"I was hoping you'd recognize him right off. I'm running the picture through the database; maybe we'll get a hit."

Kate squinted at the photo again. The eyes looked familiar, but it was as if they had been plopped down in the middle of the wrong features. She thought perhaps, based on what Wharton had told her, she might see a well of pain within those eyes, but she didn't. They just looked back blankly at her, if anything they conveyed the same impatience as the artificial smile below them.

"The photo's over twenty years old," Potter said. "We should get an artist to come in and do an age progression."

"Two steps ahead of you, Potter." Kate motioned to a stocky, spectacled man seated on the other side of the CID office. He had a thick pencil tucked behind one ear and a messenger bag on his lap, but he was absorbed in whatever was happening on his phone. Kate gave a sharp whistle, and he looked up. She waved him over. "I called Dalton on the drive in and asked him to come in as soon as he could."

Potter gave her a half smile. "Then let's put him to work."

"CHILL OUT," Dylan said. He pushed Colin down to sit on Brendan's bed.

"You just told this guy that we're going to meet him!"

"Actually," Brendan said, "we told him Spacey was going to meet him. Do you think he thinks Spacey is her real name?"

Neither brother answered him.

"What do you think you're going to do?" Colin said, looking pointedly at his brother, who still crouched at his eye level.

"We'll catch him." Dylan stated it with an eye roll that went all the way to the ceiling, as if it were obvious, but the bravado didn't fool Colin. "It's like that show *To Catch a Predator*."

"Seriously? Me, you, and Brendan are gonna catch a pedophile?"

Brendan bolted for the door. "Keep your voice down, man!" He cracked the door and scanned the hallway for his parents.

Dylan said, "Look, we'll go see who it is, and if he actually shows up, and it's actually an adult, we'll call the police, and they'll come get him. We don't even have to get anywhere near him."

"Yeah." Brendan bounded back across his room to an in-wall shelving unit stuffed with toys, models, games, books, and a few odd articles of clothing. He knelt on the floor and dug something out from a bottom cubby. "I've got binoculars!" He held the small plastic set aloft. "We can set up on the other side of the parking lot or something. He won't even see us."

They both looked at Colin as if they were puppies and he held their favorite ball, and since their assurances were slowly assuaging his incredulity, he tossed it.

"Okay, fine."

Dylan brought his hands together with a loud clap while Brendan fist-pumped. It was like Colin had delivered an early Christmas.

"Do you have a camera?" Dylan asked Brendan.

"On my phone."

"Make sure you bring it. I think our dad has a pair of binoculars too."

Colin slid off Brendan's bed. "I'm going to go home for a bit."

"Why?" Dylan asked.

"I'll look for Dad's binoculars," Colin said. That and something else, but he didn't mention the other thing.

"I DON'T WANT to do this, but I just don't see any other way," Lukas said without meeting Spence's eyes.

"Now who's being cliché?" Spence let his head loll back against the cage wall. "I can't say that I'm shocked. You have a history."

"I've never killed anyone."

"I meant of being cliché. But the murder's hardly a shock either."

"Look, I'm giving you the chance to say some goodbyes. Do you want it?"

"Because it's the least you could do, right?" All Spence could think to do was stall, to keep Lukas talking. "I think the least you could do is not kill me. I think that is the *very least* you could do."

Perhaps he'd pushed it because Lukas had no trouble meeting his gaze now, and those pale eyes conveyed no emotion, a window into an expansive void. If Lukas was compartmentalizing, he was tucking away the parts of himself that Spence needed forefront.

"I think you know how you ended up where you are, and *I'm* not the one to blame. If you'd stayed out of my life, then we wouldn't be here." Lukas gave a small lunge toward the pen. "*You're* the one who's put us in this untenable situation."

Spence wanted to point out some holes in Lukas's logic, but he opted to poke holes in the suicide plot instead.

"You think anyone who knows me is going to believe that I committed suicide? It's very off brand, Marion."

Lukas settled back on his crate. "Oh, trust me. People are suckers for a tragic tale, the bigger the shock, the more they'll accept it. They'll talk about how they never saw it coming, how incredibly sad it is, how well you hid the signs. But it'll be more believable when they find out about your recent problems with alcohol and money."

"Pfft. That's going to be a harder sell than you think."

"I can be pretty convincing, as the *New York Times* Best Sellers list will attest. Your friends may be surprised, but you're a fairly private guy, right?"

Spence frowned.

"Exactly, and how well do we ever really know anyone? Everyone has their secrets; I know that better than most. Besides, they'll find alcohol in your bloodstream, won't they? Just like they found a broken bottle of wine at your house." Lukas looked too pleased with himself. "And then you cleaned out your bank accounts last night, trying to pay off your debts, to some shady off-the-books people I might add."

"That's quite the narrative you've crafted. Sounds like a chapter out of your book."

"It won't sound like it. I think I really captured your voice. I'm a quick study when it comes to tone, and having access to all your emails and articles definitely helped."

Spence licked his lips, but the action didn't do much to moisten them. "You sound very proud of yourself."

Lukas jerked back, and the smugness slipped from his narrow face. When he answered, his tone was defensive. "I'm not, but obviously I have to protect myself. I have to do what's best for me."

"Obviously," Spence said, wondering for the first time whether Lukas might succeed in covering his tracks. Spence had underestimated his desperation, his determination; perhaps he'd underestimated his cleverness and his capability as well. After all, his original charade had gone this long without discovery by anyone else, or at least anyone willing to expose it. But when Spence looked at the man's face, a conviction rose in him: Lukas was smart, but Katherine was smarter. "Can I have a few minutes to think about what to say?"

Lukas studied him with a clinical expression. "No," he said slowly. "I don't think so. I think if you have anything to say, you better say it now. It's time to speak from the heart." When Spence didn't answer immediately, Lukas rose from the crate. "Unless you don't care to."

"No, I want to." The magnitude of what he was doing weighed on him. As a wordsmith, he felt how important it was to express what might be his final thoughts to those closest to him and how inadequate his efforts would be without the opportunity to weigh those words. But having dangled this carrot in front of him, Lukas exacted a cost before he'd receive Spence's dictation.

"Before we start, I want you to drink another one of those bottles."

"That might make it kind of hard to focus."

"I'm confident you'll do fine, and don't worry—I can clean up the prose if you go off the rails."

Spence fervidly wished that Lukas were drunker. He fumbled through thoughts of love and gratitude toward his family, trying to arrange them quickly, especially since he knew the additional alcohol would hit his system soon. "Sanjay, I'm sorry, sorry I wasn't a better brother to you, that I didn't know how to help you. And I pray you find your way home. I want you to have Nana's ring; it's on my dresser."

Lukas's fingers clattered on the keyboard a little longer, and Spence suspected his captor of tweaking his comments to fit the suicide story he'd concocted.

"To my friends, I wish I could say goodbye in person. Thank you for holding me up, for sharing your strength, your time, and your love with me. And, Kate . . . I want you to have my surfboard. And don't forget: When you find a penny, pick it up."

Lukas paused. "What's that supposed to mean?"

"You've never heard that saying? Find a penny, pick it up; all day long, you'll have good luck."

Lukas gave a beleaguered sigh. "Of course I've heard it, but what does it mean in context?"

Spence leaned his head back and shut his eyes, trying to concentrate past the residual pain in his head now swirling with the sedation of alcohol. "It's an inside joke. I'm always picking up loose change when I find it on the street. She gives me a hard time about it, says it's dirty and not worth the trouble."

Spence kept his eyes closed, not for concentration's sake but afraid that Lukas would read something in them, and he held his breath. When he heard the tapping on the keyboard resume, he prayed Lukas wasn't taking liberties with this last message. The sound stopped, and Spence slitted his eyes just enough to watch the man outside the cage.

"It's done," Lukas said.

He closed the laptop and stood, but he dithered a moment before he made his way up the steps to the door, where he paused again. He looked as if he would say something more, but he abandoned the impulse, going inside and shutting the door.

Spence sat again in the darkness, solaced that if he was going down, he'd done what he could to take Lukas with him.

Chapter Twenty-two

Kate had worked with Dalton on other cases, but she'd never requested an age progression before. Her illusion that she could simply hand a photo over and say, "Age him twenty years," quickly dissipated.

"Um, I'm gonna need more than this," Dalton said, although to his credit, he was already scrutinizing the photo as he unshouldered his canvas messenger bag onto the table of a cramped empty room where he could work in quiet.

"Such as?"

"Photos of his parents would be excellent."

Kate shot a look half-way between hope and panic at Potter, who stood in the doorway.

"I'm on it." He dashed back toward his desk.

"And it'd also help if you could tell me everything you can about this guy. Where's he from, what's he like, what's he do for a living? Anything you can tell me."

Kate spued out what little she knew about the young Marion Lukas. "We don't know anything about him after high school, or shortly after, at least. He kind of disappeared."

"So you want the photo to help find him," Dalton said as he took a sketch pad from his bag.

"I figured it couldn't hurt."

"I'll do my best."

"How long will it take?"

Dalton looked at her with trepidation, and she followed his eyes to her fidgeting hands, which she quieted.

"I'll work as quick as I can. But you know this isn't a science, right? We're forensic artists, not forensic scientists. I can only extrapolate based on available information. But teenager to adult is going to be more accurate than child to adult. I just want you to have realistic expectations."

Kate nodded, perhaps a little too rapidly, and then left him alone.

"How long does it take to do an age progression?" she asked Potter when he returned to their desks after delivering some DMV photos of Lukas's parents to Dalton.

"I have no idea. I've never needed one. It's too bad the department doesn't have software for that."

"Good luck getting that on the budget, besides Dalton is a pro. I'd trust him over a computer." Kate glanced at the entrance of the office as she wandered between her desk and Potter's. "Maybe Kirkley and Kotono will be back by the time he's done."

"Do you think it might be Spence, who was at the store?" Robbie asked. Kate's desk chair clinked as he leaned forward, elbows on the desk.

Kate shook her head. "But I'm afraid it might be Sanjay, and I'm afraid how that might look."

"You think he'd take Spence's money?"

Kate stopped pacing and perched on the arm of the padded chair next to Potter's desk.

"He's 'borrowed' money from family before. It's one reason his parents wouldn't let him move back in. And he did just lose his job. Maybe he found Spence's debit card." She groaned. "I hope he wasn't that stupid."

Her phone rang, and she answered quickly, not bothering to check the caller.

"Have you seen Spence's Social Circles account?" Danny asked without preamble.

"Not recently." Kate moved quickly to her desk, shooing her brother from her seat with her free hand. "Did someone post something?"

"It's a suicide note."

Kate's hand froze on the mouse.

"It has to be fake," Danny insisted. "It has all this stuff in it about owing money to people—like gambling debts—and how he started drinking recently. It doesn't make any sense. Right? If he were going to drink with anyone, it would be me."

"Let me look." Kate quickly punched up the site and found Spence's account. Reading the note made her sick, and she was only half aware of Danny rambling in the background, Robbie reading over her shoulder.

"I've been keeping tabs on his accounts, like you said, and this popped up about an hour ago. I would've seen it earlier, but I'm on shift and I'm not supposed to be on my phone. I've been checking whenever I can anyway. It's not from him, right?"

"It's fake," she assured him, though she reserved such judgment for herself. The note was cogent, concise, and carefully phrased, and except for the content, sounded like Spence to her. But the details of the message didn't reconcile with what she knew to be true. But how many times had she sat opposite the families of murder victims and opened a window into their loved one's life that they'd somehow missed? And some details did ring true.

"I knew it!" Danny said. "Look at the end, where he talks to you. It doesn't make any sense."

Kate's eyes dropped to the bottom of the post.

And, Kate, I want you to have my surfboard. And don't forget: When you find a penny, pick it up.

"He never calls me Kate."

"Right! Except maybe when he's angry at you, and I think that's just because 'Katherine' is harder to yell. And he doesn't sound angry here. And the surfboard thing? That's so random."

"He surfs when he visits his cousins in California," Kate said.

"Yeah, but he doesn't have his own board. Who in Illinois owns a surfboard?"

"The end does seem disjointed, like this thing with the penny."

"Well, that actually does sound like Spence," Danny said reluctantly. "That thing you and he do sometimes."

"What are you talking about?"

"C'mon. You guys feed each other half a saying, half a song line, whatever, and the other one finishes it. Usually, you're the one who starts it. It's kind of annoying."

"*Comme çi, comme ça,*" Kate said under her breath.

"Yeah, like that one."

"Danny, I've got to go." She hung up. She needed to think.

"You don't think the note is real?" Robbie asked.

"I think it's a message, which means he was still alive when it was written. But I also think it means we're almost out of time. 'All day long, you'll have good luck.' There's something in the note that will help us." She scrutinized the end of the note. "Surfboard. Surfboard! Wasn't there a surfboard keychain on Spence's desk?"

"Yeah, but there weren't any keys on it."

"I don't care. We need to 'pick it up.'"

Robbie's bewilderment read plainly on his face, and Kate wished she'd been talking to Potter. She spun her chair to look across the walkway to her partner. He was already on his feet, struggling into his overcoat.

"Give me his key. I'll get it."

But before Kate could pass him the key, Dalton hurried over with a sketch in hand.

"I hope this helps." He handed the paper to Kate.

The nose was a little different and the facial hair was missing, but . . .

Potter rushed over behind her. "That looks a lot like Eirik Boudreau."

"It *is* Eirik Boudreau," she said.

"But their stories don't match up," Potter said.

Kate leaned back in her chair so she could look Potter in the face.

"Their stories don't match up," she repeated.

"No," Potter insisted, and then his head jerked back. "Their stories don't match up!"

"Stop repeating each other!" Robbie commanded, though no one listened.

"That's the point," Kate said. She scrambled to her feet and shoved her keys at Robbie. "Get the keychain."

"But what's . . ." Robbie sputtered, but Kate and Potter were already running for the door.

COLIN FOUND HIS father's binoculars easily enough, though he required the assistance of a folding chair to retrieve them from the top of the hall closet, where they were stowed inside their worn leather case, tucked between the wall and a stack of tightly folded Thanksgiving placemats that his mother would doubtlessly be retrieving soon.

"What you need those for?" his father asked, and Brendan started, nearly losing his balance on the chair. "Careful there, chief."

"We're gonna spy on people in the park." Colin figured that was true enough.

His father chuckled and gingerly took the binocular case out of Colin's hands.

"Well, be careful with these. They belonged to your grand-father," Dad said as Colin clambered down from the chair unencumbered. His father handed the binoculars back to him, and he felt their heft, physically and historically more substantial than the pair Brendan owned. His father arched an eyebrow at him. "And don't let anybody in the park catch you."

"Spycraft 101, Dad."

"Have fun. Be good. Oh, and Mrs. Thompson dropped off your dog-sitting money." Dad pulled a small white envelope out of the hip pocket of his jeans and handed it to him.

In his room, Colin laid the binoculars carefully on his bed and stowed his new earnings in the drawer of his bedstand. From underneath a stack of papers and cards in the same drawer, he took a small silver key. The binoculars weren't the primary reason he'd come home. He had something more important to retrieve from his bookcase across the room. From in between his Hardy Boys and his Series of Unfortunate Events, he removed a chrome-framed pencil box bearing a huge dragon eye on the front. Colin balanced the box on the ledge of shelf left by the books, unlocked it with the key, and flipped open the latch. The box didn't hold pencils or any school supplies but rather odds and ends that Colin wanted to hold onto, or at least had wanted to at one point. A lot of it was junk now, like the purplish blue rock that was still kind of cool but that he didn't even remember picking up. Other items, such as the foreign currency that his uncle brought back from his travels as an airline pilot, still held significance. Most of the paper items were tucked into a mesh pocket sewn into the lid. He pulled out the packet and sifted through it until he found, between an old valentine and a concert ticket, a white business card. The corners were blunted and the front had a smudge, but its text was still perfectly legible. He held up the card and studied the name on it: Detective Kate Baxter.

LUKAS REENTERED the garage carrying another bottle of water. When he offered it to Spence through the cage, Spence took a gulp but pulled back when he tasted the alcohol mixed with it. Lukas tilted the bottle further, and some of the liquid splashed onto Spence and against the concrete floor.

Spence coughed and hacked before he could say, "I don't want that."

"If I were you, I would." Lukas nodded to the full mini bottles still in the cage. "In fact, I'd get as drunk as I could as quickly as I could."

"I'm sure that would help sell your story."

Lukas worked his jaw for a bit. "That's not untrue, but it also might make this a little easier, for you." He managed to meet Spence's eyes if only for a moment. "Believe it or not, I'm trying to be kind. Like I said, I'm not a monster."

Spence's head was pounding anew and not just because he actually believed Lukas or believed that Lukas believed himself, a distinction that Spence drew even through his pain and the haze of his earlier consumption. He held out his hand. Lukas screwed the cap on the partially filled bottle and crammed it through the chain link.

Spence took another drink. Maybe the alcohol (and who-knew-what-else) mixed in the water would help alleviate his ever-present headache. He wondered how painful "it" would be, whatever method of dispatch Lukas had contrived. Involuntarily, he gulped again from the bottle.

Lukas moved toward the door.

"Where are you going?"

Lukas paused on the steps, the rubber-capped heels of his leather driving shoes hanging in the air. "I have a few last details to tend to. I'll be back shortly." He climbed another step and paused. "Do you want anything to eat?"

Spence's stomach knotted, and he shook his head. The movement hurt less than he expected, and he told himself the alcohol must be working this time. Lukas put his hand on the doorknob, but Spence stopped him.

"Does she know? What you're doing."

"No, not exactly." He shut the door.

Spence had tried so hard to force Lily from his thoughts, but he'd found it impossible not to replay some of their conversations in light of what he now knew. When had he said too much? When had she traded on their friendship to get close (or closer) to Lukas? Had she given signs that he'd missed. He thought of their last conversation.

"You have got to stop reading these books just because some celebrity puts them on their book-club list!" Spence teased. He and Lily sat at a cramped table in the Tribune's break room, their lunches spread out between them. "You're not getting the best of contemporary literature; you're getting self-indulgent memoirs and novels that cater to the political flavor of the month."

"That is not . . ." Lily threw up her hands in defense and then froze. "Completely true."

Spence guffawed, drawing a dirty look from Marty, who sat in the corner eating a stinky tuna sandwich.

"Take, for instance," Lily persevered, "Collings' The Music You Cannot Hear. *That was on everybody's list."*

"Eh, it was good, but—"

"But what!" Lily's dark and lovely eyes widened spectacularly behind her glasses.

"It was good! It was just a hundred pages too long. Collings is a poet, and every sentence has to be a beautiful poem.

So he takes forever to say anything or get anywhere. I find him a bit exhausting. And the gratuitous rape scene at the end? It was like he was afraid of getting too close to a happy ending."

Lily shook her head, her long, straight hair shimmering in the fluorescent lighting as it swayed. "You are such a critic. That book is heart-wrenchingly beautiful."

Spence sipped his canned iced tea. "I am indeed hard to please."

"So what are you reading right now?"

"Nothing remarkable. It's not out yet, but I'm really excited about Elena Hidalgo's new book."

Lily made a scornful face over a spoonful of yogurt. "She's not even a novelist. Like this is her first one, you really think it's going to be good?"

"She's a good writer, and it sounds intriguing."

She tapped his shin with her foot, and it sent a little charge up his leg. "You should write a book."

He made a face at her. "What?"

"Lots of novelists start out as journalists, and you're a good writer. If Hidalgo can go from writing nonfiction to novels, so could you."

"I am not creative."

"I bet you could be," she said. A smile perched on her lips. "Or maybe you could be the next Malcolm Gladwell. Who says it has to be fiction?" She gathered her empty containers, and as she passed by him on her way to the trash can, she nudged his arm with her hip. "You should think about it."

He had. It seemed like a wholesome thing to daydream about. But there would definitely be no book now. His mind jumped to his mother's green chutney, and he swallowed the absence in his throat. He did not want to start thinking about all the things he'd never do again, all the things he'd never do at all. That seemed more painful than thinking about the method of his demise.

It would have to look like a suicide, reasonably like a suicide. Spence still hoped Lukas couldn't pull it off. Suicides were harder to fake than people thought. They had to be, right? He took another drink, leaving less than an inch of liquid in the bottom of the bottle. Whatever it was tasted wretched, even watered down.

The blasted music started up again.

"No," he shouted, but Lukas had already left because Spence heard an engine growl itself awake on the other side of the garage door. "Maybe it'll be worth dying to never hear this stupid album again!" He drained the last of the bottle. "This is not music to die to, although it does make you want to kill yourself." He paused. "Not really. Didn't mean that. I may be a little drunk." He wondered if Sanjay talked to himself when he was drunk . . . and alone. It seemed like Sanjay was usually drunk in company. "That would be better, I think. Alone . . . alone's not good."

His stomach gurgled, and he groaned. He looked at the nips standing in the corner, one filled with amber liquid and the others clear.

"Good idea . . ."

Bad idea, he heard Katherine finish.

He crawled over and picked up a vodka shot, not intending to drink it necessarily, but he procured it for insurance. It might be a good idea after all, despite the burbling in his stomach. He stuffed another bottle in his pocket, planning to crawl back to his corner, but then he decided that he was fine where he was. Moving, after all, continued to be imminently painful.

He found himself unscrewing the lid of the bottle in his hand. He frowned, then shrugged. Maybe it would keep his mind off what was to come.

Dear God, what's to come. There was acceptance, and then there was acceptance. His head fell back against the cage, and he stared at the ceiling through the gridwork of the chain link. At least this time Lukas had left the lights on. Not much of a view though. Dingy beige slatted vinyl. The lines between the slats wavered in his vision.

He closed his eyes. He didn't want to think about the last thing he'd see; he didn't want to think about the most likely method Lukas would use to end his life; he didn't want to think, period. Without opening his eyes, he removed the lid and sipped from the bottle.

Were there thoughts Sanjay avoided when he drank? He made it all seem very recreational, but still. Maybe something painful crouched underneath. Maybe he regretted turning down that football scholarship. Maybe he felt trapped in the life he'd made. Maybe . . . maybe Spence should've dug into that, though he was no therapist.

"You just can't not think, can you?" His words came out lethargic but not slurred. "I think there was more alcohol in that water than water." That didn't stop him from taking another sip of his newly opened bottle.

He didn't hear the car pull up, but he heard the door open, a small miracle since the music still played. Lukas hadn't been gone long at all this time. Spence turned his head, and it swung relaxed and lazy on a neck devoid of its former stiffness. Lukas came down the steps holding a red plastic gas can, the sight of which sent an electric shock through Spence's system. He involuntarily spun and scrambled to the far side of the pen, oblivious to the pain his hasty movements caused.

"You're not going to burn me alive, are you?" His voice had lost its grogginess.

"No." Lukas set the jug down, and the liquid inside sloshed with a bong. "That would be hard to sell as a suicide. Unless you were making yourself a political martyr."

He had a point.

"Not very American," Spence mumbled. It didn't escape him that he once again sounded half-asleep.

"I see you took my advice about the drink."

"It was something to do." Spence took a shaky breath. "Would you turn the music off?"

"I don't think you're drunk enough for me to turn it off."

Spence took another drink. "How about now?"

"I think I'd better let it play."

"Please do not let this be the last thing I hear."

Lukas considered his plea. "I suppose I could change it out. Any requests?"

"I want to hear something beautiful."

"Something beautiful," Lukas echoed. He left the room. Spence couldn't keep from staring at the red plastic jug. It crouched on the concrete like a snarling animal ready to spring at him. He finished the nip and hurled it in the corner.

The music stopped, and he sighed. After a few moments of blessed respite, the strains of different music poured into the garage. He didn't recognize it, but it contrasted starkly with the previous cacophony with its lush strings, rippling piano, and soaring mezzo vocalise. It bore an epic, cinematic feel, the kind of music he listened to while drafting an article. Even at this high decibel, it remained unoppressive, beautiful.

Lukas reappeared in the doorway. "This better?"

Spence nodded. He watched leadenly as Lukas, with gloved hands, stuffed a roll of duct tape, a blanket from the trunk of Spence's car, and a hose into a duffel bag. Lukas stowed the bag and the gas cannister in the back seat of Spence's car. Then he stood in front of Spence, but he said nothing. He'd changed his clothes at some point. Spence almost asked if he was going out, but he knew Lukas was, knew Lukas would leave, that he had lined up some diversion to keep his mind off what would happen here. Because brain fogged or not, Spence knew what was coming.

"I'll be back in a bit," Lukas finally said.

"Leaving so soon?"

"I have somewhere to be."

"Me too," Spence whispered.

Lukas opened the driver's door and leaned into the car. The engine came to life and emitted a steady thrum. He shut the door and quickly strode to the steps, not looking in Spence's direction as he passed. The door to the house closed, and exhaust began to fill the enclosed space.

Spence made an attempt at prayer, though in his condition it struck him as a tad ironic. Drunk dialing God. But the prayer was simple enough that he felt confident in getting it right.

Into your hands, I commend my spirit.

Chapter Twenty-three

Kate and Potter sped across Fulton Springs with lights and siren helping to clear their path. Their backup, a patrol car crewed by Officers Nash and Sanchez, pulled in behind them from Garlington Road to follow in their wake. Kate felt as though every neuron in her body fired on double time. She gripped the steering wheel so tightly that her knuckles ached.

When they reached Boudreau's community, her hand shook as she punched in the emergency security code at the gate, so much that she feared she'd have to waste precious seconds reentering it. The indifferent gate opened with agonizing slowness, but once past it, Kate and Potter made a three-turn blur to Boudreau's house. They sprinted from the car to the porch, where Kate pounded on the heavy front door.

"Fulton Springs Police Department! Open up!"

Potter motioned to Nash and his partner, and they followed his signal, Sanchez making her way around the house to the right, Nash to the left, their service weapons drawn.

Loud music, oddly orchestral, filtered out of the house, but Kate heard nothing else. No answer to her knock, no shout for help. Trying to make herself heard over the music, Kate pounded on the door and called again. She peeked through the door's security window but saw no figures, no movement.

The radio in Potter's hand crackled. "We got called out here a couple nights ago for loud music," Sanchez said in her lilting voice. "Nobody answered then either, and then they called us off because the owner was down at the station. Very different music though."

"Kate!"

Kate backed off the porch to see Potter with his ear pressed to the garage door.

"I can hear an engine running in there."

She locked eyes with him and felt the *click* as they thought the same thing.

She looked back at the front door. Its polished hardwood gleamed even in the waning afternoon light. "We need in there now."

Potter radioed. "Sanchez, Nash, can you breach the back entrance easily?"

Nash's response of "Give us five seconds" was followed by the immediate sound of breaking glass.

"I'll stay; you go," Potter said.

Kate sprinted around the house and dashed past Sanchez and Nash in the process of clearing each room in succession. She reached the door in the hall ahead of them, threw it open, and immediately spied Spence, crumpled on the floor in the center of a large cage, his head resting on his arm as if he'd been lulled to sleep by the hypnotic thrum of the car a few feet away. She gathered a big breath, pulled the front of her shirt over her nose, and plunged into the room.

She ran straight to the cage, only to find the latch secured with a padlock. A paucity of tools hung on the wall, but the sight of a button above them next to the door arrested her. Sanchez appeared in the doorway.

"Button!" Kate said, pointing.

Sanchez buried her face in her elbow and smacked the button with her free hand, and the garage door clanked and rolled upward. She backed out of the room, radioing for an ambulance.

Kate grabbed a hammer from the wall as Potter ducked beneath the still-rising garage door. He dove into the driver's side of the Civic and turned off the ignition. Kate popped open the padlock with one swing of the hammer. She fumbled the lock out of the latch and yanked the door open. She crawled halfway into the cage to reach her friend. Her lungs burned, and she took one shallow breath of exhaust-filled air. Clutching the shoulders of his shirt, she heaved him toward the opening. Despite his greater size, he slid easily across the floor.

Lifting him over the lip of the opening proved more difficult, but Sanchez appeared kneeling on Kate's right, Potter at her left. She cradled Spence's head, too aware of the matted blood below the crown, as black as the hair itself, while Potter and Sanchez pulled him through, popping buttons from his shirtfront and opening tears in its fragile fabric as the garment snagged on the chain link opening. Once clear of the cage, they carried him outside, where the air was clean, and laid him face up in the yard. His shirt fell open to reveal massive bruising along one side of his ribs.

"He has a pulse," Potter said. "It's weak but it's also crazy fast."

"I don't think he's breathing," Kate said.

She took in as much oxygen as she could and breathed into Spence's motionless body. She heard Sanchez say that EMS was en route, but her voice sounded far away. After that, Kate's mind shut off, and all she did was breathe.

AS COLIN, DYLAN, and Brendan biked to Inoca Park, Brendan maintained a steady stream of speculative chatter on what would transpire once they actually arrived. Dylan would respond, but Colin pedaled in silence, though he was thinking about the same thing. The streetlights blinked on in the late-afternoon twilight. Someone along the route was burning leaves, and the rich scent of their smoke carried in the air. The boys had nearly two hours to wait for J-Tank16, but they'd packed sandwiches and thermoses in their backpacks and Dylan had insisted that they should get "into position" early. In truth, they simply couldn't handle puttering around either of their houses waiting for the rendezvous and decided it would be better at the park.

They locked up their bicycles at an empty rack near the entrance. Colin read the sign posted overhead.

"You know the park closes in twenty minutes," he said. "What if he doesn't show because the park is closed?"

"It's not like there's a gate or anything. He'd be less likely to show if we were meeting when the park was open," Dylan said. "He's meeting an underage girl after all."

"What if we get kicked out before he gets here?"

"We won't get kicked out. Stop worrying."

"Besides," Brendan added, "they never patrol over here after dark."

"And how do you know that?" Colin asked.

"Jayden."

"And he's a reliable source?"

"He spends a lot of time here, I bet." Brendan pantomimed smoking a joint. "What's the big deal? If they find us, all they'll do is send us home. We just get on our bikes and ride around to another entrance. They're not going to put you in jail for playing in the park after dark."

Or they could call our parents, Colin thought, but that possibility didn't seem to occur to the other two.

They walked across the grass, kicking up the dead, crunchy leaves. As they passed the skate ramps, Brendan pushed Colin's shoulder.

"Told you so. Check it out."

Alone beneath the lights, Jayden rode his BMX up and down the ramps, his red hair flaring out beneath his beanie in the draft. He swung his bike onto a platform and stopped. Seeing them, he leaned over the handlebars squinting.

"Is that little Brendan?"

"Bleh," Brendan said.

Jayden pushed off the platform. He popped over the lip of the skate park and skidded to a halt a couple of yards from them. He gave an overly nonchalant up-nod to Dylan.

"Dylan."

"Jayden."

"You on babysitting duty?"

"No."

"You wike playing wiff little kids then?"

"You're out here playing with yourself."

Colin and Brendan snickered. Jayden glowered and swore.

"Look, we've got stuff to do," Dylan continued. "Why don't you run along home and play with yourself there?"

Jayden swore at them again. "I'm meeting somebody here, so go home yourselves, you losers." He stood up balancing on his pedals. "But if you stick around, you might actually learn something, *boys*." He spun his bike around and jetted back to the skate ramps.

"He is such a tool," Dylan said.

"You don't think . . ." Colin said.

"What?"

"The person he's meeting," Colin prompted.

"Nooo," Brendan said.

"Didn't you say maybe it was someone just pretending to be older?" Colin asked Dylan.

"Yeah, but . . . I hate to say it, the guy on the computer seemed cooler than Jayden. Right?"

"Definitely," Brendan said. "But . . . I mean he didn't used to be so bad." He shrugged at Dylan.

"Guess we'll find out," Dylan said.

"It'd be kinda disappointing," Brendan said.

But Colin felt a flood of relief. He leaned toward Colin. "Really? Because this would be the ultimate goof on him."

A grin blossomed on Brendan's face, and he chortled. The Wigley boys shushed him, amid their own chuckling, as they moved farther from the skate park. For their stakeout, they picked a compartment in the jungle gym across the parking lot from the tennis courts.

"He won't be able to spot us here," Brendan said as he wiggled into a tube with his binoculars.

"Will you be able to see him from there?" Dylan asked.

"Yeah, I think I'll be able to see between the bars on this side," Brendan's voice echoed back. The camera on his phone *ker-shicked*. "But I'm not sure about getting any good pics."

"Turn the sound off just in case it carries," Dylan said.

Colin peered over the top of the compartment with their father's binoculars. No trees obscured his view of the two picnic tables sitting across the narrow parking lot. The court lights weren't lit and there was no light directly above the tables, but the poles in the parking lot on either side cast enough illumination for the boys to see the picnic area, though the shadows were deep.

Brendan reverse wriggled his way out of the tube. "I'm hungry."

They divested their backpacks of the snacks and peanut butter sandwiches they'd brought. Colin opened his thermos of cocoa and let the blast of steam warm his face before he drank. As they munched in the darkness, they postulated on who would show and what he'd be like. Brendan had significantly warmed to the idea of it being Jayden and even once sneaked back near the skate park to check whether the older boy had left.

"He's still there, still by himself," Brendan said as he pulled himself up onto their platform. "What time is it?"

It wasn't the first time he'd asked, nor the last, but eventually their waiting ended.

"Guys." Even whispered, Colin's voice echoed in the plastic tube. "He's early. Pervert at twelve o'clock."

Dylan shushed him. "You're echoing."

The Wigley brothers peeked over the edge, Dylan using the binoculars. Colin didn't need them to tell that the figure sitting on the right-hand picnic table was not Jayden.

"He actually showed up," Dylan said, his voice barely making a sound. He passed the binoculars to Colin.

"We need to call the police before he gets away," Colin said, his voice no louder than Dylan's.

Dylan ducked down and tapped Brendan's foot.

"We need your phone."

"It's in my backpack."

Colin sank down beside his brother. As Dylan rustled through Brendan's backpack, Colin plucked the business card, now slightly more rumpled, from his hip pocket. He held his hand out to Dylan.

"Let me call."

THE EMTs allowed Kate to ride in the back of the ambulance. Heaven help them if they had tried to stop her. She thought she saw Spence's eyes flicker open at one point, but it was hard to tell from her vantage point, especially with the EMT's hand holding the oxygen mask tight against Spence's face.

After they came crashing through the emergency room, after she saw the blood drain from Danny's face as he ran up alongside the gurney, after she watched them all disappear through a set of swinging doors, she could do nothing but pace and dig her hands into her hair, pulling it from its ponytail, flinging the band into some hidden corner. At some point, she came to herself and texted Robbie so he knew where she was. She tried not to think about how her hands were shaking. She called Spence's parents, delivered a tremulous but terse report to them, and then texted Heidi before Potter came briskly down the hall to her, his brow uncharacteristically knitted.

"Any word?"

She shook her head. "His parents are on the way. Danny's with him or was."

"We're searching for Boudreau; everyone's on it. We'll find him."

"Good."

Potter studied her carefully. "Do you want me out there looking, or do you want me in here with you?"

"Go. The sooner we find him, the better."

"Okay." Potter nodded but didn't move. "I'll head out as soon as someone else gets here."

"I'll be fine."

"But I'll feel better if I wait." He sat down and patted the chair beside him. Kate reluctantly perched on the edge, one knee bobbing. "We found a kit in the back seat of the car. Hose, duct tape, a full gas can."

Kate's knee stopped. A placid sourness spread in her chest.

"I wonder where he planned to leave the car."

"My guess is someplace we wouldn't have thought to look already, isolated enough so it wasn't found too quickly, but not too much so it would be discovered soon."

"Because he didn't want us to keep looking."

"But we'll keep looking. We will."

Danny came back through the swinging doors, his face grim. Kate jumped at him.

"Is he awake?"

"He was conscious when I left, but he's not . . . here. He's very disoriented."

"Is he going to be okay?"

"We got him into the hyperbaric chamber."

Kate wasn't sure how that answered her question. "What's that do?"

"It'll help flush out the carbon monoxide in his system and replace it with O_2. It's like the oxygen they gave him in the ambulance, just more intensive. We want to clear it out as quick and as much as possible. Hyperbaric treatment helps prevent..."

"Helps what?" Kate prompted.

"It decreases the likelihood of lasting brain or nerve damage." Danny let the thought hang in the air for a moment before he rushed on. "It's a good thing you came here; they don't have one over at St. Elizabeth's. They don't usually like to put people in there with alcohol in their system, but . . . given the circumstances. You know, they've done some studies recently that show alcohol might slow the body's absorption of carbon monoxide, so maybe Spence's first bender actually helped him out. Usually being intoxicated just keeps people from realizing that they're . . ."

He didn't finish, and Kate could see the tears welling up in his dark eyes. She slid her arms around his waist and felt his arms encircle her shoulders, the bristle of his short black hair against the side of her face. She held him tight as he began to shake and she let go of her own tears.

"Just minutes, Kate," Danny whispered in her ear. "A few minutes more, and he'd have been gone."

When they pulled apart, swiping at their red eyes, she saw that Potter had disappeared.

"He'll be out in about an hour," Danny said.

Spence's parents arrived in an avalanche of questions, which Kate all too happily let Danny field, although she knew some would come her way, ones Danny couldn't answer and that she might not be able to either, not yet.

Her phone rang, and she answered it without checking the number.

"Detective Baxter?" It was a kid's voice. "I need your help."

Chapter Twenty-four

Though she had spoken to Colin Wigley only a couple of time before, Kate recalled him with no difficulty. His witness had proven critical in solving a recent case of hers, and his caution and thoughtfulness, given his age, impressed her at the time. But now she wished that Potter hadn't slipped back to the hunt for Eirik Boudreau so that she could pass along this errand to him. Though he hadn't interacted with the boy as much as she had, Potter would still be a known entity. If she should be anywhere, it was here at the hospital for Spence or out with Potter searching for Boudreau. She could pass the call onto some patrol officers, although she hoped as many of them as possible were searching for Boudreau as well. But she did know this kid, kind of, or at least he knew her. And trusted her enough to call.

"Go," Danny said. "I already told you it'll be an hour or more before he's out of his treatment."

Robbie had arrived during her phone conversation. "I'll stand guard," he said, knowing what she was thinking. "Until you get some guys over here."

"I will be *right back*," she said. "Did you find it?"

He held out his hand, and the little plastic surfboard dangled from the key ring encircling his middle finger.

"Just hold onto it for me." She didn't anticipate her trip to Inoca Park being particularly adventuresome, but she didn't want to risk losing it either. "I'll be—"

"Right back. Yes, I know. Go."

As she sped through the darkened streets, the lampposts creating a slow strobe, Kate radioed for a patrol car to meet her. Her lethargy had disappeared, but she knew underneath this new energy, she was exhausted and worse than that, distracted. And exhausted and distracted could both lead to stupid on their own, let alone combined. And all she knew was that Colin and his friends had "caught a predator."

COLIN HAD SNEAKED back to the park entrance to wait for the police while Dylan and Brendan remained at the playground to keep an eye on J-Tank16. A dark sedan pulled up, and the detective got out of the car. Her dishwater blonde hair fell in uneven waves around her face. Perhaps it was the shadows, but the corners of her mouth and eyes seemed to droop, pulling down that otherwise attractive face into a weary expression. Despite the cold, her tan trench coat hung open revealing its insulated lining as the wind pushed against it, the belt dangling forlornly on either side.

"Colin," she said.

"Hey, Detective Baxter, did you come by yourself?"

"It's just one guy, right?"

Colin nodded.

"I think I can take care of that, and if I'm wrong, I've got another police officer on the way. Why don't you explain to me a little more clearly why you think this man is a predator?" Her words formed quick-fading clouds in the cold light of the lampposts.

Colin checked the time on Brendan's phone. "We were supposed to meet him—I mean the girl we made up was supposed to meet him five minutes ago."

"If he's the kind of guy you think he is, I think we can spare a few minutes still. Where are your friends?"

"They're watching to make sure he doesn't leave, from the playground across from the tennis courts." Colin then launched into an abbreviated explanation of how they all came to be here. The brevity of it surprised him, and he showed the detective their conversations on Brendan's phone. A police car, nearly silent, pulled up alongside the detective's car. Colin was a little disappointed the lights weren't even flashing but figured they didn't want to scare the predator away.

The officer who exited the car wasn't tall or particularly big, but perhaps the weight of his heavy jacket hid his muscles. His hat was set back enough on his head that the light glinted brightly off his coppery mustache.

"This is Officer McIver. I want you to hang back with him while I go talk to this guy, okay?"

Colin nodded.

"Don't let the mustache fool you," she said behind her hand. "He's an okay guy."

Colin smiled.

"Colin and his friends have enticed an online acquaintance out to the park for a romantic liaison under the guise that they are an underaged girl."

McIver whistled.

"Why don't you have a chat about how dangerous that was?"

Colin wanted to say that he didn't need that lecture, but she set off immediately on a direct path toward the tennis courts, leaving them behind.

"Hiya. Let's round up your mates, so we've got everyone accounted for, and that way I'll not be far off if Detective Baxter needs me."

Colin gave the cop a sideways look as they circled back toward the playground.

"Are you English?"

"Yep."

Colin thought a British policeman in Fulton Springs was weird but didn't say so. After all, there was an Irish girl in his class at school, and her parents had to work somewhere.

"What's going to happen to this guy?" he asked.

"Unless he has a bloody good excuse for being out here, Detective Baxter's going to arrest him. Then it'll be up to a judge after that, but we'll make sure he doesn't hurt anyone."

They stopped in the shadows of the playground. Colin hissed, and Dylan climbed down silently to meet them. Brendan stayed in his tube watching through his binoculars.

McIver peered at the man on the picnic tables and then glanced at Dylan.

"Hey, mate, gimme those a minute."

Dylan handed the binoculars to him, and McIver raised them quickly to his eyes and swore under his breath.

The detective approached from the other side of a storage shed.

"Hey, get your pal," McIver said. "I think it'd be best if we waited a bit farther off."

"What?" Brendan echoed in his tube. "This is the best part!"

EVERYTHING ABOUT SPENCE hurt, though in the last few days he'd come to accept that as status quo, but the ears—that was new. They felt like he was trapped on an ever-descending airplane. Despite their stuffiness, he could hear the car still running. So why was he waking up? He didn't expect to feel this bad in heaven.

His eyes flickered open to lights brighter than the garage's, lights that glared down on him through a clear casing. He tried to lift his hand to press against it, but he couldn't manage that. He squinted against the brightness. He now recognized the mechanical hum as different from a car's engine, more subdued, or at least that's what his clogged ears told him. A slight woman in blue scrubs appeared above him and disappeared just as quickly. He blinked, and when his eyes reopened, Danny stood over him.

"Hey, buddy, you doing all right in there?"

Spence couldn't be sure he wasn't dreaming again. He looked around. He appeared to be on the set of a sci-fi movie, in some sort of incubation tube.

"Just another twenty minutes," Danny promised in a muffled voice. "Are you understanding me, Spence?"

His head hurt. He was so utterly tired. He let his eyes shut and slipped away again.

Chapter Twenty-five

Rounding the storage shed, Kate gained a clear line of sight to the picnic tables. She stopped. The hand resting on the gun holstered at her hip fell to her side, and she felt a similar sinking sensation in her stomach. She recognized the figure sitting atop the nearest table, even with the hood of his sweatshirt flipped up over his head, a sweatshirt that said J-Tank across the shoulders. How she wished it were someone else.

She didn't bother to conceal her approach, and the crunch of leaves caused Sanjay to swivel his face toward her. He started.

"Katherine, what are you doing here?" The way he glanced around after asking did not escape Kate.

"We found Spence."

"Oh." Sanjay's face went blank. She'd thrown him, and now he didn't know which him he was supposed to be. "Is . . . is he okay?"

"I don't know. He's not in good shape. He's at Fulton Springs Memorial. Your parents tried to call you, but they said you didn't answer."

Sanjay seemed to close in on himself.

Kate brought herself to ask, "What are *you* doing here?" Of course, she knew; just as she had known that he couldn't be capable of what happened to his brother, she knew that he could be capable of this.

Sanjay removed a hand from the hoodie's kangaroo pocket and set it on the table, but as large as his arm was, it wasn't wide enough to completely hide the carton of wine coolers sitting next to him.

"Just meeting up with a friend."

Her eyes still burned from crying at the hospital, and Kate fought against a repeat performance. The new swell of tears came not for Sanjay's sake but because she knew what this would do to Spence, if he lived to find out.

"I know why you're here, Sanjay. I know who you think you're meeting."

Sanjay swallowed and tugged his hood down. He looked so young with that frightened, round face, and wasn't he really?

"What do you mean?"

"She's not coming. You fell for a sting, of sorts." Kate took a long cold breath in. "And I have to arrest you."

"Katherine, no, please!" He scooted off the table, his basketball shorts snagging on the wood, revealing his ashen knees until his worn sneakers thumped onto the grass. "Please don't. They said she was just a few years younger than me. Like four years, that's nothing."

Kate ignored that he was shaving off an additional year or two. "She'd still be a minor, and you're still an adult. You told her you would give her alcohol and drugs."

"Just legal stuff!" Sanjay held out his arms, as if to prove he wasn't hiding anything. "Nothing high schoolers don't use themselves anyway. I mean even you experimented when you were in high school, right?"

"No, I didn't."

Sanjay had chosen a poor sympathy target.

"Crap, of course. You're Darsh's friend." He let himself fall back onto the bench, making the picnic table shudder. He balled his hands into supplicatory fists. "Please don't do this."

Kate's boots scuffed the dead grass as she couldn't find the right way to stand before her friend's brother. She stopped, and all her pent-up emotion came spilling out.

"How could you be *so stupid*?"

"You don't understand."

"What? What don't I understand? What could possibly explain, possibly *justify* this?"

"I know, I know! It's just—Darsh was missing and maybe dead and those detectives were convinced I did it, and I just didn't have *anything*! I lost my job, and I mean–look at me, I'm not exactly winning at life that I'm gonna score with a girl my age, and most of the guys I hang with are around that age anyway—"

"That's an indictment, not a justification, Sanjay."

"I was scared and alone and I don't know—" With great round eyes, he looked up at her, pleading. "I just needed something!"

"*This* is not what you needed!" Kate's arms flew in vicious circles around the scenario. "This was not the answer. You ran to the wrong place, and you . . ." She struggled to keep control over her words. "You knew it."

She sank next to him on the bench, exhausted.

"You know where you should've turned, where you could've turned, and instead you followed your basest desires. And they led you straight here, into worse trouble."

For a few moments, they sat in a silence marked only by a faint buzz from the lampposts.

"Katherine, I promise I—"

"Don't—just shut up. In a second, I'm going to read you your rights."

"Please don't!"

"Sanjay, I have to." She fixed him with pained eyes. "Even if I wanted to let you off—and I don't—I couldn't do that—not in the sight of God and not in the sight of the three kids over there." She flung her arm at the dark recesses of the park. "Kids who know why you're here, who know what you planned to do. What kind of example would that be? I can't do the wrong thing for you, not even for Spence."

With no strength in her, she stood.

"Sanjay Spence, I'm placing you under arrest for solicitation of a minor." The rest of the speech came mechanically, without thought, without emotion.

MCIVER DID HIS best to usher the three boys away but not before they got an eyeful of the showdown between the detective and the hulking predator. Such as it was. To Colin, the encounter—what he saw of it—went down oddly with none of the expected shouting and gun pointing. The guy didn't even try to run. Strangely enough, it reminded him of how his mother had reamed out Dylan when he'd come home with detention on the first week of school. The way the detective's shoulders had slumped, she seemed sad more than anything else, though her voice had carried as McIver marched them away. They didn't even get to see her handcuff the guy.

They did, however, get to ride in the back of the police car. Once McIver had packed them into the back seat, as if they were criminals themselves, they waited while he talked outside on his phone. The detective and the big guy came lumbering toward the park entrance passing through the pockets of light created by the lampposts.

"I told you she got him," Colin said.

McIver jumped back in the car before the pair arrived and threw the car into reverse.

"We don't get to see him up close?" Brendan asked.

"If you got to see him up close, that'd probably mean he could see you up close, right? That sound clever to you?"

"Enh," Brendan said.

McIver drove them to the police station. He didn't run the lights or sirens, despite Brendan's request, at least not until they saw someone blow through a four-way stop. Even then, it was just a pop of noise with the lights because the other driver pulled over immediately, but the boys got to see McIver run the other car's plates and confront the driver.

"Why didn't you give him a ticket?" Dylan asked.

"Because he wasn't an—because he was polite and respectful, and I couldn't be bothered since I'm meant to get you gents to the station. Sometimes a warning is enough, and speaking of warnings . . ."

He launched into what sounded like it was going to be a lecture about the dangers of online catfishing, but at times seemed commendatory for what they'd done, so the whole spiel veered headlong into the territory of mixed messages.

When he finished, Colin asked, "So . . . good job, but don't do it again?"

He could see the cop in the mirror trying to suppress a smile. "Basically, mate, yeah. Just that."

They got to see the inside of the police station. Last time, Detective Baxter had talked to him at the Thompsons' house and once again at home. The police gave them some cocoa while they waited for their parents to arrive. The Tyrells looked more concerned than the Wigleys, but neither set of parents looked pleased to be summoned to collect their offspring at the police station and sit in while they gave their statements.

Before they left, Colin had to use the bathroom. When he came out, trying to dry his hands on the front of his jeans, he heard his father murmur to his mother in the echoey hallway, "So where on the bravery-stupidity spectrum do we think this falls?"

She shot him a wide-eyed look, shook her head, and walked away without a word, enfolding Dylan under her arm on the way out.

"Are we in trouble?" Colin asked.

His dad put a hand on his shoulder and steered him toward the exit. "I don't think so, but your mom and I probably need to talk about it. You might be grounded from the Internet for a bit." He looked down at Colin with a smile. "Two run-ins with the police in three months—what are we gonna do with you?"

"Is a medal out of the question?"

Dad threw his head back and gave a big belly laugh, the kind that made the other people standing in the hallway look at them. He pushed the door open, and they stepped out into the snappish air.

"I don't know about that, but I am thinking maybe they should put you on the payroll. And that maybe somebody needs to keep a closer eye on you."

"OH NO, NO," Robbie said when Kate told him about her trip to the park. He sat sentinel in a straight back chair in the hallway outside the ICU. He ran a hand over his mouth. "That is bad."

"When it rains." Kate leaned against the other wall, facing her brother. "I get sick every time I think about having to tell Spence. It will just . . ."

"Well, you don't have to worry about that for a while at any rate."

"Any update?"

"Danny said he's sleeping. In addition to the carbon monoxide poisoning, he's suffering from exhaustion and dehydration, bruised ribs, and probably a concussion mixed in there too. They gave him a few overdue stitches in the back of his head."

"Is Danny around?"

Robbie motioned to the swinging doors. "He's back there somewhere. Spence's mom is also there, sitting with him. She and his dad are taking shifts. The rest of the family went home for now. They'll only let two people back there at a time, and at night it's just one. Your friend Heidi came by." He picked up a square insulated bag that sat on the floor next to his chair. "She brought sandwiches for whoever was here. Want one?"

Kate shook her head. Eating seemed unthinkable still.

Danny pushed through the swinging doors. Dark moons hung beneath his brown eyes, making his angular face appear gaunt. Robbie held the bag up at him, and Danny moaned as he stuck a hand in.

"Thank you, Heidi," he said before taking an enormous bite of a roast beef sandwich.

"Robbie said he's sleeping."

Danny nodded, but the way he paused beforehand didn't seem promising.

"Is he going to make it, Danny?"

"Yeah, yeah, yeah." Danny shook his head. "It's just . . . it's serious."

"You said something about lasting neurological damage."

"One in three, those are the odds." He rewrapped the largely uneaten sandwich. "Let's not talk about that right now. Let's not dwell on it." He paused as two orderlies wheeled a patient on a gurney in between them. "What about the guy who did this? Have they caught him?"

"Not yet, but he'll have a hard time hiding. He's *famous*." Although as Kate said it, she had to wonder, since Marion Lukas had dropped off the face of the earth once before.

"This might help," Robbie said. He dangled the surfboard keychain. "Sitting here with very little else to do, I figured out why Spence wanted you to find it." He flipped the surfboard up into his grasp, and with his thumb pushed apart an invisible seam until the cap of the flash drive came off. "I won't tell you how long it took me to realize that."

"I'll check it out." Kate took the drive from Robbie and then asked Danny, "Can I see him before I go?"

"Just a quick look."

Despite the end of visiting hours, the room was still awash with sterile lighting and far from quiet. Monitors beeped, ventilators clicked and hissed, and two sets of medical professionals conferred, their voices floating amidst the mechanical noise. And over all of it ran the HVAC system, blasting out air so cold that it felt as if it came directly from outside. Danny waved at the clerk as they passed, but they didn't go much farther into the room.

The curtains around Spence's bed were pulled fully lengthwise, but they remained open at the end, like a shadowbox of the wounded. His blankets lay tucked up against his chest to ward off the arctic chill, but his arms lay atop them. Despite the grayish tone his brown skin had taken on, it stood in stark contrast to the colorless blankets and the white cotton gown he now wore. An IV ran from one arm to a bag filled with clear liquid hanging from a pole overhead. Though transparent, the oxygen mask obscured the lower half of his face. Above it, his eyes were closed. Black locks curled over either side of a white bandage that ran around his head. Dressed in faded pink sweats embroidered with flowers, his mother sat crookedly in the bedside chair, leaning on the inside arm. One hand rested on the bed, not touching Spence, but hovering close as if she were afraid of waking him. Her thumb rubbed the fabric, back and forth, back and forth. Kate didn't try to get her attention, but when she stepped toward the door, Mrs. Spence looked up and waved her other hand. Kate returned the gesture and then hurried from the room.

She hid in her car while she cried. The sight of Spence lying broken there, the knowledge that his brother sat in jail across town, the weight of her own brother's heartache, and maybe some things she couldn't even articulate to herself—it all just piled up on the dam of her reserve, crushing it into rubble, and the waters came. When they stopped, she blotted her eyes with the sleeve of her trench coat, which proved nonabsorbent, dug out her laptop, and plugged in the thumb drive.

Only one file existed outside the folders on the drive. It was named "Boudreau." She read the article, which in detailed fashion dismantled the myth of Eirik Boudreau. Spence had uncovered much more than she had, than she would have known to, but his story only proved the negatives, puncturing Lukas's fraud. It didn't point out the truth that Lukas had omitted, and Kate wondered if Spence knew about that.

She didn't know whether she was overstepping any bounds, but she dragged the file into an email attachment and sent it to Malcolm Jenner. She figured it might be too late for tomorrow's edition, but she didn't want it to wait until Spence could send it himself. Before she closed the thumb drive's window, she spied a folder named "Katherine." She pursed her lips and stared at it a while. Then she ejected the drive. Whatever was inside that folder wasn't hers to read. Not yet.

Her phone buzzed, a text from Potter: *We got him.*

Chapter Twenty-six

From down the hall, Kate watched her brother talk to Danny. She couldn't hear any of their subdued conversation, and while Kate couldn't imagine them having much in common, Danny wasn't one to leave an auditory void unfilled. He could converse with anyone, whether they wanted to or not. Robbie nodded at something Danny said and then gestured to him with an open hand. They both bowed their heads, and Kate realized they were praying. Well, that was one thing they had in common, she thought with chagrin. A fundamental thing indeed.

Robbie had stood by her, even watched over her, these last few days, despite his own personal turmoil. Now he sat there, praying with one of her friends, standing guard over another. Strong, compassionate, devout—that was the man she saw. What kind of man did Lauren see?

Kate approached gently, but Robbie, of course, heard her and his eyes flicked in her direction to ensure the sound signaled no danger. She stood silently by his chair until they finished, when she placed a hand on his shoulder.

"You're relieved, officer. The suspect is in custody."

"They caught Boudreau?"

"Or Lukas or whatever his name is."

He rose and crushed her with a hug.

Danny smiled at them. "Why don't you both go home and get some rest?"

"What about you?" Kate asked, taking in her friend's worn appearance. "Didn't your shift end hours ago?"

"Sho nuff," he said with a wry wink. "But you know I can't get enough of this place."

"I'll be back as soon as I can," she promised.

"I recommend bringing doughnuts."

She chuckled. "I think that can be arranged."

As they walked out, Robbie said, "Danny remembered something about Spence's car while you were out."

"What was that?" she asked as she cinched the belt of her coat closed.

Robbie opened the door and then followed her out.

"He took it to the auto shop last month. Danny remembered because he had to give him a ride to the office. They fixed an exhaust leak."

Kate stopped and turned back to look at her brother, not sure if doing so would make her cry again, but when their eyes met, he smiled.

"Providence, Katie."

They drove home mostly in silence, although at one point Robbie told her to keep her eyes on the road.

"What do you mean? I'm looking at the road."

"You keep looking over at me every five seconds."

"Just making sure you're still there."

When she pulled up in front of the house, she didn't park.

"Aren't you coming in?" Robbie asked.

"No." Her eyes felt greedy as if she couldn't see Robbie hard enough, and her mind felt frighteningly clear. She glanced at the dashboard clock. "I'm the furthest thing from sleepy. I'm going to drive around a bit."

"You're probably going to crash and sooner than you think," he said.

"I slept more than you did this morning," she countered.

He held up his hands in surrender. "Be safe."

"Yes, Dad."

She watched him enter the house and the lights blink on. She looked back at the clock, said a little prayer, and drove straight to Centerfield, Indiana.

"DO YOU KNOW who I am?" Lukas said as the policeman steered him none too gently down the hall by the elbow. "You call the chief of police, and he'll sort this out. It's just a misunderstanding."

"Do you know who I am?" the policeman returned.

"What?" Lukas turned and looked at the cop's face, one that he didn't recognize. His uniform nameplate, which read *McNabb*, didn't spark a memory either. The policeman stood just a little taller than he, but the cop possessed a much more solid build.

"That's what I thought, Mr. Boudreau. You—" Other McNabb clamped his mouth shut and shook his head. He marched Lukas the rest of the way to the holding cell. "I don't think the chief is gonna be interested in taking your calls anytime soon. You see, the guy you kidnapped and tried to kill? He's got friends on this force. Nobody around here's going to do you any favors." He opened the cell and pushed Boudreau inside the doorway, shut the door, and then removed the handcuffs through a waist-high opening. "I'm sorry we don't have any private accommodations available, but you'll have to make due with a few roommates until that can be arranged."

Lukas looked around the large dimly lit cell. Five unsavory-looking fellows hovered around its edge either sleeping or tying to, and the smell of urine and body odor drifted in the air, perhaps a whiff of vomit from the guy passed out on the floor.

"I want to talk to my lawyer."

"I bet you do, and you'll get the chance to as soon as he or she gets here, but as you can see, we're a little backed up at the moment, partially because a lot of us spent the evening looking for you." Other McNabb's voice pitched up in volume. "Maybe you picked the wrong weekend to try to kill Darshan Spence." He stepped back from the cell door and nodded to the cop standing guard. "Don't worry; we'll be back to check on you in fifteen minutes," he said, his voice still unnecessarily loud. He looked into the corner of the cell. "Fifteen minutes."

The two police officers trooped out together.

A voice from behind Lukas asked, "You're the one who kidnapped Darshan Spence?"

Lukas grit his teeth. "Mind your own business."

"Oh, it's my business."

Lukas turned and a saw a man at least triple his size rise from the shadows in the corner. Sanjay Spence stepped forward like a bull entering the ring. He flexed his hands, and the knuckles cracked.

"WHAT ARE YOU doing here?" Danny asked Robbie when he found him hovering in the ICU waiting room. Danny rubbed at his eyes with the heel of his hand. "I thought you and Kate went home to get some sleep."

"I couldn't, sleep that is."

"Yeah, that's going around." Even with speaking in hushed tones so as not to disturb the other waiting-room occupants, Danny sounded exhausted, and his eyelids stood at half-mast.

"Maybe you should go home yourself," Robbie suggested.

"I can usually sleep anywhere, so if I can't here, I won't at home either. Where's Madame Columbo?"

"No idea. She drove off after we got to her place. That's why I came back here. If she wasn't here, I still thought this might be the best place to be right now. I brought this for Mrs. Spence." He held out a flimsy shopping bag filled with snacks, a bottle of vitamin water, a small blanket, a toothbrush, and some fuzzy socks, all of which he'd picked up at a 24-hour convenience store on the drive there.

"Let me see if she's awake," Danny said, and he disappeared behind a set of swinging doors.

When they swung back open, it was Mrs. Spence, not Danny, who came through. She enfolded Robbie in a maternal hug.

"Thank you, Robbie," she said, her voice both rich with its musical accent and strained with emotion. "It's so good of you to think of us. Katherine is blessed indeed to have such a thoughtful brother." She stepped back enough to take his face in her hands, making him feel embarrassed and very small despite the fact he stood a head taller. Her eyes glistened behind her large glasses, but instead of crying, she patted his cheek with a cool, dry hand and pursed her lips in resolve. Then she left.

When Danny didn't return, Robbie quietly claimed one of the padded yet still uncomfortable chairs that lined the walls. The many-layered figure next to him, whom he'd assumed was asleep, shifted in his direction and asked, "Who is she to you?"

"Uh, my sister's friend's mother."

His neighbor was a small woman well-rounded by late middle age and buried in a heavy coat, a scarf, and a pink knit cap somewhat yellowed with age. Her full face, lined with wrinkles and framed in mousy gray curls, scrunched in surprise.

"You're here for . . . your sister's friend?"

"I guess so. I was visiting my sister when it happened. It's kind of a long story. You?"

"My husband. He got T-boned by some stupid drunk driver when he was coming home from work on Thursday." The fresh anger surfaced all too easily. "It wasn't even five o'clock."

"You've been here since Thursday night?"

"Yes. He's had two surgeries, and he has another tomorrow."

"Do you need me to get anything for you? I can go pick you up some food or something."

She turned faded blue eyes on Robbie and shook her head with a disheartened and disheartening smile.

"All I want really is to go home. But I'm scared of what will happen if I do."

Robbie rubbed at a callus on his hand.

"I can understand that."

He placed his hand on the woman's arm, and she reached up with her free hand and gripped it tightly. They sat in silence for a long time. Then they talked some more about her husband, who he was before all this. Robbie listened and listened and at some point realized that perhaps listening was something he'd forgotten to do in his own life. Robbie asked the woman if he could pray with her, and she nodded.

When he stood to leave, she asked, "Will I see you tomorrow?"

"No. No, I think it's time I go home, regardless of what happens."

Chapter Twenty-seven

Kate knocked on the door again, more firmly but still mindful of the late hour. She didn't want to wake her nieces. She heard Lauren behind the door, the pause as she checked the spy hole, the second pause as she absorbed the sight of Kate on her doorstep. Finally, the door opened, enough for Lauren to stand in, but not enough for anything else.

"Kate, what in the world are you doing here?" her sister-in-law asked. Lauren's hair, much the same shade as Kate's though curlier, was pulled atop her head. She tugged a pink waffle-knit robe closed over her pajamas.

"I need to talk to you."

Lauren's face immediately closed, and she squared off in the doorway, arms crossed over her chest. An invitation in didn't seem forthcoming.

"Did Rob send you?"

"No, he did not. He doesn't even know I'm here."

That confused Lauren, and her arms relaxed slightly.

"Well, you can't see the girls; they're asleep."

"I understand that, and as much as I love them, I'm here to see you, as I said."

"I hope you weren't planning to sleep here, because I'm not prepared for company."

Kate felt her eyes narrowing and fought the impulse. She'd sat through too many interrogations for Lauren's distractions and defensiveness not to come across baldly.

"I'll either stay at Mom and Dad's or I'll drive back home. Don't worry about it."

"But it's so late. Why did you come here so late?" Lauren's voice was pitching up to continue, and for a frightening moment it reminded Kate of her mother. Kate cut her off.

"Because I had to Lauren. Because you told Robbie you wanted a divorce and then told him to leave. Because I had to talk to you, and this is the soonest I could do it. And I knew that if I called, you wouldn't answer or you'd tell me not to come, and I figured you might listen if I made a dramatic gesture."

"I don't see what the point is. You're just going to take his side."

"No, I'm not. I'm not here to take a side." Lauren started to interrupt, but Kate held out her hand and plowed forward. "Listen, I know we've never been close and I'm sorry for that, and maybe we never will be, but we are family. I know you don't want to believe me, but I do care about you and I'm here for your good. I want to remind you of some things. And if you don't think I've been telling Robbie the exact same things, then you're not being honest with yourself, because you should know me better than that."

A pair of headlights flashed over them as another car pulled into the drive and parked alongside Kate's sedan. Lauren shielded her eyes.

"Who is that?"

"It's your brother," Kate said. "Kenneth."

"Why's he here?" Lauren sounded as if her night was destined to be filled with one incomprehensible event after another, a fate she was not yet resigned to.

"Because I called him."

A car door snapped closed, and Lauren's eldest brother, the one Kate knew she respected most, strode toward the door, his tall, lanky frame cutting through the headlights until they blinked off. When he stepped onto the stoop, Kate could finally make out the handsome if pinched features behind his wire-framed eyeglasses. Underneath his coat, he still wore a suit and tie, though the latter was pulled loose. He looked tired. Kate imagined they all did. His eyes traveled from Lauren to Kate and back to his sister again. Then wordlessly he wrapped Lauren in a hug. For a moment, they all stood silently in the cold.

"What are *you* doing here?" Lauren asked once her brother had released her and stepped back.

"Did you kick Robbie out?" Kenneth sounded as tired as he looked.

"Not exactly," Lauren hedged. "And I don't appreciate being ganged up on, especially in the middle of the night."

"We're not ganging up on you," Kate said. "I called Kenneth because I thought you might be more willing to listen to him."

"I can't see how it's any of your business." Lauren shot her brother a look far more tentative than her words. "Either of you. Especially when one of you hasn't even been married."

"You and Robbie gave us that responsibility," Kate said.

"What?"

"Kate's talking about your wedding. You remember when you vowed that the two of you would covenant together—sickness, health, richer, poorer, all that? Both of us stood alongside you on that platform in the church as witnesses to that covenant. Do you remember what the pastor said to us, not to you, but to us?"

"Not exactly." Her face still wore a stony expression, but her tone had ceded ground. "It was a very hectic day."

"He told us to hold you accountable for the promises you made that day," Kate said. "To support you in your covenant."

"But you haven't heard my side of things," Lauren said.

"That's why we're here," Kenneth said. "I'm sure I'm the one here who knows the least of what's going on. But we'll listen. Will you listen to us as well? We might be able to help, Lauren."

The set of her mouth didn't relax, nor the tension around her eyes, but Lauren pushed the door open to let them in. They settled into the front living room to talk, to listen, and to rehearse the truth together. Hours later, in the early morning dark, as Kate drove back to Fulton Springs, she reflected on the road her brother and his wife found themselves traveling, and while she could see that it was long and winding, for the life of her, she could not see whether it divided.

POTTER DIDN'T ARRIVE at the police station till later in the morning. He didn't need to be there at all, but weekends home alone left him unsettled, and it wasn't uncommon, if he lacked a full social calendar, for him to come in whether scheduled or not. Picking up an extra case, consulting on someone else's, or just quietly working at his desk, whether on something personal or professional, in the thrum of the station's activity. He had stopped on his way in to pick up the fat Sunday edition of the *Fulton Springs Tribune* and to purchase a couple of pastries at a mom-and-pop's bakery, a shop where he'd solved a robbery his first month in Fulton Springs. He laid the *Tribune* on his desk and next to it set the bag of turnovers, their buttery goodness already forming slick spots on the bag's white paper.

He unfolded the newspaper and read the headlines as he set to work on the first turnover, cherry dusted with powdered sugar. Given their proximity to Chicagoland, it wasn't uncommon for the local papers to get flooded with whatever craziness was going on in "the city," much like its crime flowed down to Fulton Springs, but the *Tribune* did better than most at highlighting more-local news. The rescue of Darshan Spence wasn't the lead article, but it did land below the fold on the front page: "Kidnapped journalist saved by FSPD." The article was scant, an obvious rush job, and Potter expected a much fuller write-up would follow in the Monday edition, especially given the kidnapper. And especially if Spence was up to answering questions by then. He thought about calling Kate, but instead phoned the hospital.

"This is Detective Potter Davis with the Fulton Spring Police Department. I'm checking on the status of a victim that was brought in yesterday, a Darshan Spence."

"Detective Davis, it's been a while."

"That sounds like Sharona."

"It is indeed. It's been a minute since I laid eyes on you."

"You weren't on duty when we brought Spence in."

After some shuffling, the nurse said, "Mr. Spence is still admitted, but you know I can't tell you much more than that."

"Can you tell me if he's up for answering any questions yet?"

"I'd say he is not."

"I see. Is Danny . . ." He reached for the last name of Kate's nurse friend.

"You looking for Nurse Bohannon?"

"Yes, Danny Bohannon."

"He's not available right now either," she said and then continued with exaggerated articulation. "He's with a patient undergoing hyperbaric treatment right now."

"Thanks, Sharona."

Potter thumbed through the newspaper looking for the article that Kate said Spence had written on Boudreau but didn't see it. Perhaps it would run alongside tomorrow's fuller treatment of the case.

"Detective Davis." McIver, standing by his desk, sounded surprised. "I wouldn't think you'd be here after all the late hours, given the arrest and . . . everything."

"I like it here," Potter said. "Apart from the smell. And, correct me if I'm wrong, weren't you here for most of those late hours yourself?"

McIver shrugged a shoulder with a duffle bag slung over it. "I'm not meant to be here. Just came in to use the gym."

"Then I guess I can't interest you in a turnover?" Potter motioned to his own bag.

Grinning, McIver shook his head but continued to linger.

"Something on your mind?"

"The bloke Detective Baxter brought in last night, he's her friend's brother."

Potter waited for the question.

"I was just surprised, maybe because of everything that was going on . . ."

"That she actually arrested him," Potter supplied.

"Must've been pretty hard for her to do. I know some who wouldn't have done."

"You wouldn't be surprised if you knew her, McIver. Detective Baxter tends to see things in black and white, and she doesn't mess around in the shadows. That type of moral code can cost you sometimes. But when it comes to policework, you could do worse than follow her example. We all could."

McIver nodded thoughtfully and went on his way. Potter felt a heaviness he hadn't expected to encounter this morning. He pushed the pastry bag away and wiped his hand clean on a napkin. Looking for distraction, he pulled out the *Tribune*'s Arts & Entertainment supplement. He stopped browsing when he spotted a glowing review of *My Girl Leona* by Eirik Boudreau. He checked the byline again. The fingers of one hand drummed against the desk. He picked up the phone and punched in a number.

"Hey, Kirkley, I think we should bring Lily Engvall in for questioning."

WHEN SPENCE opened his eyes, Kate sat in the hospital chair next to his bed. She wore her trademark trench coat, and the button-down shirt and khakis underneath were hopelessly rumpled.

"Hey, sleepyhead. I was about ready to pry your eyelids open."

"Glad you didn't." His voice sounded thick, and he had to concentrate to get the words out. While tubes ran intrusively up his nose, he was thankful to be rid of the mask, which had made speaking impossible. "You really here?"

"Yeah. Sorry I wasn't here when you woke up the first time. I've been tracking down bad guys and giving marital counseling. And you know only one of those is in my wheelhouse. It's been a very busy weekend." She shifted guiltily in her chair. "It's good to see you out of the ICU."

"I kept seeing people who weren't there sometimes, like you and Danny. I just wanted to make sure."

Her expression became wary, concern written too clearly on her face.

"I'm not crazy," he clarified.

"That is good to know," she said. "Because the jury was split."

"You should really leave the jokes to Danny."

"That's harsh. Your dad's in the cafeteria getting some coffee."

The lights, the sun shining through the window, everything was so bright. He closed his eyes to let them rest, but he didn't want to go back to sleep.

"They keep sticking me in this pressurized tube."

"Yeah, but Danny said you've had your last treatment, unless the doctor changes his mind."

When he opened his eyes again, she was regarding him so intently that he couldn't look away.

"I thought I was going to die, Katherine. I thought he was going to kill me."

She nodded, her eyes brimming and her lips pressed firm against each other.

"But I knew that you'd find me. One way or another."

She scooted to the edge of the chair and leaned forward, elbows on her knees.

"I'm sorry I took so long."

He stretched his hand out along the bed toward her.

"Seems to me like you were just in time."

She put her hand in his. Spence grasped it as tightly as he could and in that moment realized he didn't want to ever let go. They let the minutes pass without words, without the need for them.

Acknowledgements

I offer a great big thank you to the following individuals who helped this novel along: Naomi Snow and Adelé Hensley, who read the early drafts; Emma Nelson and the other folks at Owl Hollow Press, who were willing to give Kate and her crew a second outing; Valli Rassi, Stephanie Rees, and Nicola Baker, who answered questions about diverse subject matters that they know more intimately than I; and Jill Garrison, the best Clinton County publicist a brother could ask for.

Soli Deo Gloria

Photo credit: Craig Oesterling

ORIGINALLY FROM the Midwest, Paul Michael Garrison has spent roughly half his life in Upstate South Carolina. In addition to writing and editing, he has worked in the fields of higher education and website management. He whole-heartedly endorses the Oxford comma.

Paul Michael holds degrees in publishing, theater, and creative writing. His short fiction has appeared in *Windhover* and *Quantum Fairy Tales*, and he frequently performs with the Greenville Shakespeare Company. Whether on stage or in writing, he enjoys the art of becoming someone else.

#LetterstotheEditor
#TheLiesPeoplePublish